Shiv Kumar works as Commercial Tax Officer for the Government of Bihar. He was an engineer with a public sector company for nine years. He has travelled extensively throughout India during the course of his work.

He is passionate about reading and writing. He prefers to delve into subjects concerning socio-political realities of contemporary India. Other genres he is fond of are travel writing, thrillers and crime fiction.

He can be contacted at shiv5180@gmail.com.

OPERATION INDIA ONE

Shiv Kumar

OM

Om Books International

First published in 2015 by

OM
Om Books International

Corporate & Editorial Office
A-12, Sector 64, Noida 201 301
Uttar Pradesh, India
Phone: +91 120 477 4100
Email: editorial@ombooks.com
Website: www.ombooksinternational.com

Sales Office
107, Darya Ganj, New Delhi 110 002, India
Phone: +91 11 4000 9000, 2326 3363, 2326 5303
Fax: +91 11 2327 8091
Email: sales@ombooks.com
Website: www.ombooks.com

ISBN: 978-93-83202-24-9

Printed in India

10 9 8 7 6 5 4 3 2 1

To

My wife Sarika, who is not only my love, but also
my friend, philosopher and guide,

and

My darling daughter Lavanya, the sweetest
thing in my life

Contents

Author's Note

> The worst illiterate is the political illiterate. He hears nothing, sees nothing, and takes no part in political life. He doesn't seem to know that the cost of living, the price of beans, of flour, of rent, of medicines, all depend on political decisions. He even prides himself on his political ignorance, sticks out his chest and says he hates politics. He doesn't know, the imbecile, that from his political non-participation comes the prostitute, the abandoned child, the robber and, worst of all, corrupt officials, the lackeys of exploitative multinational corporations.
>
> —*Bertolt Brecht*

Indian society seems to be at the crossroads today. We might have created history with the successful launch of the *Mangalyaan*—India's first spacecraft to Mars—but we are still grappling with social ills like poverty, unemployment and illiteracy. One of the deadliest insurgencies in the hinterland is the Naxalite movement. In the recent past, many civilians and members of security forces have been killed in a series of attacks. According to official reports, 12,000 people have died in the Naxal violence in the last decade.

Is there any hope?

Well, there always is. One school of thought likes to blame the Indian political system for the rise of rebels against the establishment, but, refuses to be a part of the apparatus themselves. The other segment of people is willing to fight all odds to bring hope among the citizens for a peaceful future. This story salutes such people.

The journey of *Operation India One* began many years ago when I was posted at the construction site of a power plant situated in the Naxal-infested interiors of Jharkhand. *Operation India One* was born out of my journey into the conflict areas and my quest for a resolution to the menacing problem of violence plaguing the Indian society. Should development methods overlook the welfare of the poor? Should development schemes allow displacement of the underprivileged? Did I find a convincing answer? I am afraid, I did not. However, the one song that I kept coming back to while writing this book was Kishore Kumar's 'Ruk Jana Nahin Tu Kahin Haar Ke' from the movie *Imtihaan* (1974). Probably that is the reason I couldn't help but quote a few lines in this book.

The journey continues, and the search is still on. *Operation India One* is only a brief stopover.

Prologue

25 March 2010

It was well past midnight. The office building wore a deserted look. A few flickering lights could be seen in the vicinity. The howling winds, growling through the empty corridors, were the only noisemakers till a white car came to a screeching halt outside the building. Two guards ran up to open the doors and greeted the occupant with a crisp salute. Clutching a bundle of papers, the dignitary hurried into the building, without returning the guards' salute. Black Cat commandos were guarding a black luxury sedan whose engraved nameplate read— Ministry of Home Affairs.

The man in a tearing hurry got into the elevator and went straight to his office. 'You are late, Subhash,' Home Minister Prabhat Advani, addressed him.

'Sorry, sir,' replied Subhash Joshi, who was the Joint Director of the Intelligence Bureau (IB). He was puzzled to have been called at the Home Minister's office at that hour. The home minister shifted his glance towards a young woman sitting in front of him. 'You would know her. This is Kavita Sethi.'

'Of course. She was leading the People's Resistance Movement (PRM) in Bihar against the Naxalite outfit, MAF (Maoist Action Front).'

Kavita nodded in affirmation.

The home minister continued, 'Yes, we thought we could use that organisation to destroy the MAF in Bihar. Unfortunately, the move wasn't a wise one. The PRM has failed miserably and has been declared illegal by the Supreme Court. Do you know what happened in Bihar, yesterday?'

'Yes, sir. Gopal Krishnan, the District Magistrate of Jehenabad, was killed in an MAF attack while returning to the district headquarters from Bhagatpur,' said Joshi.

'What is the IB doing? Why don't we have any intervention from the intelligence there?'

'I had updated you about the situation on the ground. This group operates from their camps located in the dense forests of Bhagatpur. The difficult terrain makes it impenetrable for our security forces. Moreover, the security forces do not have a good reputation among the locals there, which in turn affects the possibility of our accessibility to credible intelligence.'

'But something needs to be done. They are expanding.'

'That is true. The MAF has emerged as a formidable force in the area around Bhagatpur. It has spread its tentacles to Jehenabad, Aurangabad, Gaya and is now slowly moving towards Jharkhand. In their vision document, they have spoken about their plan to take the Dandakaranya region in Chhattisgarh and the Khammam district in Andhra Pradesh under their territorial authority. They aim to create, what they call, the Red Corridor.'

'Do you know why you have been called here?' asked Prabhat.

'No, sir,' they replied in unison.

'After yesterday's attack on the district magistrate, the prime minister called me up to discuss the status of our operations in curbing the MAF menace. I want to start an operation to finish them once and for all. But I want it to be a clandestine operation. Both of you are associated with operations against the MAF; I would like to hear your views.'

'Sir, after PRM's failure, I think it is important to regain the confidence of the people. Honestly, the PRM employed oppressive and repressive strategies against the people of Bhagatpur. The language of force does not always work and I have seen that myself. The relief camps at Bhagatpur are filled with refugees who are enraged after being at the receiving end of such violent operations and hunts. The inhabitants are seething with rage,' Kavita explained. 'So, are you suggesting we change the track and completely shun counter-attacks on the naxalites?'

'No, but we need to change the face of these counter-attacks. We need a more *humane* face. That is why I had sent you a proposal to raise an all-women commando force—Razia Regiment (RR). I had talked to the women at the camps. They seemed visibly excited,' Kavita responded. 'I had seen your file. It is a radical move and definitely worth a shot. I have put this proposal in the cabinet, and I hope for its approval. We will not recruit them as SPOs (Special Police Officers) as we had done in the past with PRM, but, as permanent police employees. Also, we will provide a paramilitary status to this force. This will take time.'

'We need to be cautious with our moves. The PRM debacle has had an adverse impact on the morale of the police force,' Kavita argued.

'What is your plan, Subhash?'

'I wish to plant a mole in the MAF.'

'Is that a plausible idea?'

'Yes, sir, for the past few months, I have put my best man, Sudhakar, in this project. He has readied the plan for this.'

'Once the cabinet gives its approval, the Razia Regiment will get a clearance from me. You keep me updated about the success of the mole.

The MAF has become a threat to national security. Its operations have given a boost to all the other Naxalite groups in India. This soon-to-be launched operation shall not only compensate for all the earlier deficiencies our governing systems have been blamed for, but also restore faith in democracy. We should become *one* strong force to eliminate our common enemy. Subhash, I trust you and I want you to take the overall charge of this mission.'

'Yes sir,' Subhash said.

'Any more questions?' he asked.

'Sir, what will be the name of this mission?'

'*Operation India One*.'

'Sir, when are we expected to get the operational clearance?' Subhash enquired.

'Subhash, what do you think this midnight meeting is for?'

They looked perplexed.

'Last year, we started a joint operation along with the state police and paramilitary forces against the Maoists. The media perceived this operation as an all-out attack on naxal forces and termed it—*Operation Green Hunt* although, the intention was not that. This alerted the Naxalite groups, and they responded with much ferocity. In February, a massive attack on the security forces in West Bengal killed 25 personnel. Subhash, you have reported that there is a possibility of more such attacks. We cannot function if we suffer many casualties. Therefore, I need this operation to be clandestine. No one should have inkling about this operation. The RR formation shall be a part of *Operation India One,* but under the cloak of a routine executive decision. Similarly, very few people should know about your intention of planting a mole in the MAF. For all practical purposes, assume this meeting never happened and that *Operation India One* does not exist. I think I am clear.'

'Yes sir,' they said as Prabhat Advani stormed out.

Part I
Genesis of a Mission

1

26 December 2012, 3 A.M.

The fog engulfed the entire area in heavy mist. ACP (Assistant Commissioner of Police) Gautam Dhaliwal's house in Moti Bagh, New Delhi, seemed to reflect its owner's steadfast personality; holding its own against the invading mist. In a quiet corner of his room on the second floor, Gautam lay asleep after a hard day's work. Suddenly, his phone alarm began to ring. He reached for it with fumbling hands and pressed the snooze button hoping to delay the agony of waking up early, if only by a few minutes.

Unaffected, the stubborn instrument beeped again with greater intensity. He then realised that it was not the alarm but a phone call.

Rubbing his eyes, he switched on the table lamp right next to his bed and looked at the wall clock.

Who the hell could be calling at 3 in the morning? His office number flashed on the screen. He answered the call reluctantly.

'Hello.'

'This is sub-inspector, Mohan Singh. We have information from a hotel in Paharganj about a suspicious character...'

'What suspicious character? Who had called?' asked Gautam, anxiously.

'It was the manager of Hotel Diamond, which is situated right outside the New Delhi railway station. He has informed us of a man staying in Room 103. He came to the hotel two days ago and registered as Nikhil, a tourist from Patna.'

'And? What is so suspicious about him? Thousands of tourists come to Delhi every day,' said Gautam impatiently, about to curse his subordinate for disturbing his hard-earned sleep.

'Sir, even though he has registered as a tourist, he seldom moves out of the hotel. Several foreigners come to meet him, even at odd hours. Today, the manager noticed one person who faintly resembled the notorious MAF terrorist whose sketch was released by the Railway Protection Force a few months ago. He is on the list of suspects for last year's blast on the railway tracks near Patna.'

'Fetch all the details from the hotel's manager about this man. I will meet you in office,' said Gautam before disconnecting the call. The ACP in him had woken up.

'You need a break, Gautam,' his reflection in the mirror seemed to be pleading him. After several weeks of chasing leads to any potential disruption of next month's Republic Day celebrations, he deserved a few days off. But, the business at hand could not be neglected. Without wasting time, he immediately called his driver via the intercom.

'Veer,' he shouted loudly, causing the man at the other end to rise up with a jolt even in his half-asleep state. 'Yes, sir.'

'Get the car ready. We are leaving for the police station.'

Grabbing whatever clothes he could lay his hands on, Gautam rushed to the bathroom for a quick shower. He emerged after 10 minutes in a T-shirt, a crumpled pair of pants and a faded blue pullover. Walking towards the wall-hanging calendar, he took a pen and struck off the note he had written for 26 December 2012, which read—*Spend the day with mother.* Wondering what on earth had possessed him to join the police force, he left the room, jogging down to where Veer was waiting in his car. Despite the thick fog, it only took half-an-hour to reach the Parliament Street Police Station.

Mohan Singh greeted Gautam with a salute.

'Sir, here is the residential address of the suspect.' There was urgency in his voice and his red eyes indicated that he had not slept the night. He handed Gautam a piece of paper on which was scribbled in dark blue ink—Nikhil Yadav, 140 B, Kankar Bagh, Patna-1.

Pulling out a diary from his drawer, Gautam flipped through its pages and made a note of a contact number. When he dialled it, the voice on the other side answered—'Superintendent of Police, Patna'.

'This is ACP Dhaliwal from the Delhi Police. We have someone's address that could give us connecting links to a possible terrorist attack. We need all the information we can find on the suspect immediately. Here is his address.'

The Patna SP (Superintendent of Police) assured he would get back with the details soon. Gautam put down the phone and lit a cigarette.

'Sir, would you like to have tea?' Mohan asked.

'Sure. What is more comforting than a hot cup of tea on a cold winter night?' It was 4°C according to the temperature sensor in the room. The weather forecast had declared this to be one of the coldest winters Delhi had ever seen.

'I'll arrange.' Mohan walked out.

I hope the address we have is correct, he thought to himself. *I'll be able to put this man under surveillance only if we have substantial evidence against him.*

The last time the police had made an allegation based on flimsy grounds, the department got the short end of the stick. The businessman whose premises they raided turned out to be quite influential and dragged the matter to court, and the media blew the case out of proportion. We cannot afford yet another disaster.

Mohan brought in the tea.

'Are you alone on duty tonight?' Gautam asked him.

'One constable was with me, but I sent him home as he was ill. Aslam will join us in a few minutes. You take rest, sir. I will wait outside.' He left the room.

Gautam sipped his tea and lit another cigarette. Reaching out for a magazine from the pile stacked by the sofa, he pulled one out. The cover story was titled, India's Unsung Heroes. The edition had been dedicated to people who were largely invisible in mainstream media but had nevertheless pledged their lives to the service of others. One article in particular caught his eye.

> Nisha Kushwaha is the founder of the NGO, Nai Soch-Nai Subah. A graduate in Geography from Delhi University, Nisha decided against going on the conventional career route. Instead, she chose to live in the Naxalite-infested area of Bhagatpur in Bihar to

fulfil her father's dream and educate the people there. Her father, Sunil Kushwaha, a police officer-turned-social reformer was killed by the MAF terrorists for raising a voice against them. Nisha has witnessed how dangerous it is to use violence for bringing about social change from close quarters. Her teachings have served as an eye-opener for several misguided members of MAF, who subsequently abandoned their extremist ways.

Nisha has received several threats, but, that has not deterred her from her mission. Remarkably, she bears no ill-will towards militant organisations, even the one responsible for her father's death. She believes that their outrage, though not justifiable, is understandable given the kind of oppression they have been subjected to.

Nisha has been awarded the Ramon Magsaysay award for her social work but "Master*niji*," as the people of Bhagatpur affectionately call her, shuns the spotlight and prefers concentrating on improving society. Schools for children and adults, set up by Nisha, in Bhagatpur have consistently maintained high standards of efficiency. Our editorial team salutes her for her exceptional contribution.

So, this is where Nisha has ended up after college. It's strange to read about her like this. I wonder if she knew I had feelings for her, Gautam's musings were interrupted by a phone call. He answered.

'This is the Superintendent of Police, Patna. We enquired about the address you had given us. It is fake. We are scanning our systems to find an appropriate match.'

'Okay, thanks for your help.'

He called his subordinate to his office. 'The address is fake, Mohan. There is something fishy out there,' Gautam said. He looked towards the door as another man walked in. 'Oh good, Aslam is here'.

'Sub-inspector Aslam Khan reporting, sir.'

'Mohan and Aslam, gather some men and get ready. We are going to raid Hotel Diamond now. Let us find out the real identity of this man.'

2

26 December 2012, 5 A.M.

Two police jeeps screeched to a halt at the hotel's entrance. A white SUV had left the premises right before their arrival. Gautam stepped out and saw a group of people helping a man get into a car. It turned out to be the hotel manager who was bleeding profusely. He had been shot and was unable to utter a single word, but, his index finger pointed desperately in the direction of the SUV.

'Mohan, make sure he gets to the hospital. Armaan, thoroughly search Room 103. Aslam, come with me. We will follow the car.'

Gautam alerted the control room and Aslam drove them around in pursuit of the vehicle. After only a kilometre's drive, however, they realised they had lost sight of it. Suddenly, they got a message on Gautam's wireless—'The SUV is on the Ring Road and appears to be approaching Ashram'.

'Block the road at Ashram and get in more officers,' ordered Gautam, gesturing at Aslam to head in that direction. 'We'll get him now.'

At Ashram Chowk, barricades were quickly put in place and the few policemen available at that time hurriedly positioned themselves behind their vehicles. They did not have to wait very long. As expected, the SUV driver attempted to charge through with no intention of stopping. As soon as he did, the policemen opened fire.

The men inside the SUV retaliated and started firing a burst of bullets from an AK-47, much to the policemen's surprise. Caught off guard, they gave the SUV a head start. Subsequently, it sped on to the Delhi-Noida-Direct Flyway, crashed through the toll gates and took the Sector 16-A exit route. After entering Noida, it raced towards the Greater Noida Expressway.

'PCR 1 to headquarters, the suspect vehicle has an AK-47. Send backup. They are moving towards the Greater Noida Expressway. One of our constables has been shot,' the officer in charge informed the control room. The message was also relayed to the Noida police headquarters. 'Additional police forces and ambulances are on their way. Greater Noida police are approaching from the opposite side.'

With so many police jeeps in pursuit, Gautam's own car turned out to be the first to spot the SUV because of the route he had taken.

'The SUV is in sight, sir,' yelled Aslam.

Gautam fired at the vehicle but it dodged the storm of bullets and raced further.

'It must be running at 180 kmph. Its owner has an AK-47; he almost killed the hotel manager. There is a terrorist in there...' Suddenly, the brakes were applied with an unexpected jerk that he was thrown forward in his seat.

Despite the foggy condition, he could see the flashing red beacons of the Greater Noida police vehicles and hear their shrill sirens. Confronted with a new horde of police cars, the driver of the SUV swerved sharply to the right in a final attempt to escape, and in doing so lost control and the vehicle crashed into the road divider. Seeing that it was futile to keep ahead of the police in a damaged car, he and another man jumped out of the SUV and fled in different directions.

'Split in two groups and begin the search immediately. They must not get away at any cost,' Gautam ordered his men. Twenty constables, led by one senior policeman each, made their way into the fields. Gautam went near the vehicle which had turned into a mangled heap of metal. His eyes fell on the suitcase lying on the front seat. 'Have the bomb squad check this out,' he commanded an officer.

In the distance, some constables could be seen approaching carrying a body. One of the two men had been found. His head was bleeding profusely.

'Dead or alive?' asked Gautam.

'Breathing.'

'Take him to the hospital. Where is the other one?'

'We are trying to locate him.'

'Did you get anything?' he asked Aslam, who had just returned with his squad of men from the other side of the field.

'Nothing, sir.'

The constables spread out again in all directions but could not apprehend the other person.

Just then, Gautam received a call from Mohan.

'Sir, we have found a Chinese-made pistol, few empty wine bottles and glasses, and photographs of arms and ammunition from Room 103 of Hotel Diamond.'

'Anything else?'

'No, sir. But, there are three glasses here; and as we saw, there were only two people in the SUV.'

'Who was the third person?'

'No idea, sir.'

'How is the manager?'

'He is out of danger but too shocked to say anything. The only thing he has been able to tell us is that the two men who left in the SUV came running from the room and shot him. They were cursing him for alerting the police.'

'Had he seen any third person?'

'I asked. He said one person left about half-an-hour before we raided the hotel. His identity is unknown.'

'Any CCTV footage?'

'The CCTV is not working.'

'How did the hotel manager get suspicious?'

'His staff said that someone had called him up.'

'Who?'

'I enquired. The informer's phone number belongs to one Soumit Banerjee. He is the general manager of a company called Silent Turtle.'

'Silent Turtle? Okay, do one thing. Go and investigate him. How is he involved? If you get something, report to me.'

3

26 December 2012

At 9 a.m. in the morning, Gautam was to report to his senior, DCP Rajesh Kumar. When he was done narrating all that had taken place the previous night, the DCP had a frown on his face.

'You know, Gautam,' he said, 'the Home Ministry has a report from the Intelligence Bureau (IB) which suggests that a communist country plans to supply massive funds to the MAF rebels.'

'MAF. You mean the Naxalite organisation of Bihar?' Gautam asked.

'Yes, the same MAF that had derailed the Patna Rajdhani last year.'

'But what is their connection with what happened yesterday?'

'It's too early to reach a conclusion, but I suspect that there may be a link. You mentioned that one suspect of last year's Rajdhani attack had come to visit the man in the hotel. Also, the two men you chased were armed with AK-47s.'

'Yes, but we have only the manager's word to go with regarding one man resembling the train attack suspect. We still have to verify that,' said Gautam, while glancing through a file the Home Ministry had given them.

'The Home Ministry's report points to a clever ploy by a neighbouring country,' the DCP added. 'The country's government supports certain companies and gets contracts in India using their diplomatic clout. They also offer these companies the raw materials for factories in India at lower costs. In turn, the foreign government strikes a deal with these companies wherein the latter has to provide a fixed sum to terrorists who swear by communist ideologies. With these funds, the terrorist organisations enter the arms market near the borders and procure sophisticated weapons to wreak havoc on our security forces. In this way, our 'friendly' neighbouring countries are destroying us without waging a full-fledged war. Not only do they open up a market for their raw materials and arms but also equip the Left-oriented terrorist organisations like the MAF for waging a war with India. In this era of globalisation, our country is a sitting duck for opportunists hoping to redraw borders without any direct involvement.'

'I assume the country in question is China. But if we have a report from the IB, why does the Home Ministry not take any action?'

'They refrain from blaming any country without concrete evidence. It will create a diplomatic ruckus.'

'What can we do?'

'Let's see if our suspect has any connection with the MAF. If he is a terrorist of that organisation, I am sure he is here to collect funds since Delhi is not on the MAF's radar. Since we found a reference to Silent Turtle—a company that has business interests in China and India—it could be that they are funding these extremists.'

Just then, Gautam received a call from Mohan.

'Sir, the man we arrested last night is out of danger, but, refuses to speak. Even threats do not work on him. I have sent his photograph out for identification.'

'Interrogate him thoroughly. Don't use undue violence. He may be weak and I don't want any accidents to happen. You know the media. Get him proper medical treatment,' said Gautam.

'One more thing, sir. The suitcase you found in the crashed vehicle contained a huge amount of cash.'

'Cash? How much?'

'One crore!'

'We have got something here. Carry on with the investigation.'

After he ended the call, Gautam apprised the DCP of the latest development. 'It seems you have interrupted an arms deal. Let's see what turns up,' the DCP responded.

'Sir, do you know about Silent Turtle?'

'It is a construction company run by Rohit Kumar, a business tycoon based in Malaysia. The company has been in the news recently since it shared its plans to construct a power plant at Bhagatpur in Bihar.'

'Oh, the same place where the massive attack on the Razia Regiment camp took place a few months ago? I remember reading a newspaper report about Kavita Sethi, the brave commandant. A battalion of 50 personnel led by her defended themselves against hundreds of terrorists.'

'Yes, the same place. It is a small hamlet bordering the Gaya district of Bihar. It comes under the Tailorgunj subdivision in Jehenabad district. Don't forget that 20 personnel were killed there too. Kavita, the person behind the Razia Regiment, received the President's medal for her commendable leadership.'

The jarring ring of the antique phone at the DCP's desk interrupted him. Rajesh Kumar took the call and the voice on the other side introduced itself as the Director General of Police, Bihar.

Kumar grew ashen-faced as he listened to what was being narrated. Putting the receiver down, he threw a pensive expression at Gautam.

'The man you have caught is none other than the leader of the MAF, Gireesh Marandi. He has been on the *Most Wanted* list of the Bihar Police for the last five years.'

'I can't believe this. The leader of a dreaded terrorist organisation himself arrives to collect money and is trapped so easily?'

'Yes, it should not have been so easy, but it is our luck. There must have been something extremely important at stake for this man to have come all the way himself and not send any of his men. Listen, Gautam, see to everything else later,' the DCP said. 'First take care of this problem. Get Gireesh Marandi out of the police station and transferred to the central jail. I am going to forward an application for his judicial remand to the magistrate. Form a Special Task Force to guard him as his compatriots are bound to try and set him free. A team from the Bihar Police will interrogate him in a few days. Until then, we must make sure he remains in jail.'

'Okay, sir. I will personally follow this case.' Gautam saluted his senior and left.

4

26 December 2012, 9 P.M.

Meanwhile, in the dead of night, a man was running furiously through a densely forested area. He was heading in the direction of the valley of the Parshuram Hills in Bhagatpur, where the MAF base camp was located. The valley was also called Hanuman Ghati, named after a giant statue, which adorned its starting point. The river Bhagat, descending from the hills in the form of a waterfall, flew right through the middle of the camp, amid numerous caves formed by granite and limestone erosion. Protected by the hills on three sides and the forest on the other, the setting gave the place an aura of invincibility. It had been the nerve centre of the MAF group for the last 10 years. Using this base camp, the group had acquired its reputation as a dreaded organisation with nearly two dozen bombings and almost 50 assassinations to its name. The bombing of the Patna Rajdhani train and the assassination of the Jehenabad DM were two of its most prominent deeds.

Reaching an area that had been cleared of the dry leaves that he had been crushing under his feet all along, the man could now see he was close to his destination. Going straight to the commander of the group upon entering the camp, he stopped to take a breath before raising his hand in salute and said, *'Lal Salaam.'*

The leader, who was dressed in black and had a masked face, reciprocated with the same words. The voice was a woman's.

'Commander, our comrade, our leader, Gireesh, has been caught by the Delhi Police.'

'What are you saying?' she asked in disbelief. *'I had warned him not to go there himself. But the arms dealer, Guhar refused to negotiate with anyone except the head of the organisation. What must they be doing to him?'*

'Commander...'

'How can you be confident about his arrest? He could be in hiding.'

'Turn on the radio.'

The woman signalled someone standing behind her and he immediately moved towards a tree, pulling out from under a heap of dry leaves a large radio set. Carefully tuning the stations, he stopped when the All India Radio news announcer could be heard clearly—'Last night, the Delhi Police arrested the MAF commander, Gireesh Marandi. They refused to disclose his whereabouts but have confirmed that he is under interrogation'.

Silence pervaded the surrounding.

'What shall we do commander?' another group member asked.

'Do not be discouraged. We will find a solution soon. Just give me some time to think. Now, everybody back to your positions. Until I say so, all training and other activities related to the movement will continue as usual. We must not allow this to get our spirits down.'

Left to herself now, she took out a satellite phone and dialled a number.

'Yes, commander,' said the voice at the other side.

'Vikas, how has this happened? You were there.'

'I have no idea. Maybe, they double-crossed us. That night, when we were finalising the deal with Guhar for the arms supply, I got a message from our police source about the impending raid. Someone tipped off the hotel's manager, who in turn alerted the police. As soon as we came to know, we tried to escape but the manager had some men ready to stop us. We were forced to fight our way out and the manager got shot in the melee. As we tried to speed away in our SUV, the police arrived and got on our trail. We managed to race ahead of them until the Expressway but I lost control of the vehicle and they arrested the commander. I was able to flee but the commander did not get lucky.'

'Where are Babu Lal and Samir?'

'They have gone back today.'

'Good. You also remain in hiding. The situation in Delhi is not good. If you get any information about the whereabouts of our leader, inform me immediately. Do find out who informed the hotel manager and how he got a whiff of our plans. Make sure you get rid of the satellite phone you are speaking on. It might be tracked.'

'Okay commander.'

5

28 December 2012, 9 A.M.

Gautam's jeep stopped in front of the Parliament Street police station. Mohan Singh was waiting for him.

'Well, Mohan, what is the news?' Gautam asked.

'Very intriguing, sir. We went to the residence of the general manager of Silent Turtle, Soumit Banerjee, and found him dead. His body was found hanging from the ceiling in his living room.'

'What? Is it murder or suicide? Have you found any clues?'

'Not yet, sir. We searched thoroughly and there was no sign of forced entry or fingerprints. We recovered a CD that he was apparently watching around the time of his death.'

'What is the CD about?'

'It had a year-old interview of Rohit Kumar, the owner of Silent Turtle.'

'Strange. What does the post-mortem report say?'

'He died of suffocation. The doctors also found a huge quantity of alcohol and drugs in his body.'

'So, he was drugged before he was killed? Did you speak to the people in his house?'

'He lives alone with one maid, Urmila, who hails from Bihar. We did a background check but she seems to be clean. She has been living with Soumit for the past 10 years but was not in the house at the time of the incident.'

'Anything else?'

'I checked his cell phone records which showed he had spoken to Rohit that night.'

'What about Rohit's cell phone records?'

'Yes, sir. They show that he was in the vicinity when the calls were made. But...'

'But what? If we have proof he was nearby then we must investigate further.'

'Sir, the problem is that Rohit's house is hardly half-a-kilometre from Soumit's house. Technically, his and Soumit's cell phones are served by the same tower. So, it is difficult to pinpoint whether Rohit was in his own house or at Soumit's residence when the incident took place. Besides that, we have found some tyre marks in the portico of the house. It did not match either Soumit's or Rohit's vehicle. Someone else is involved.'

'There are no signs of forced entry either. That means the killer or killers were known to Soumit.'

'Sir, there is something else which is very strange.'

'What?'

'A few days ago, there was a theft at Soumit's house because of which he had installed a CCTV camera. The CCTV recording was done in a DVR (Digital Video Recorder) installed in his bedroom, which records the footages in CDs.

But, we could not find any recording of that time when this alleged murder happened. Our forensic team is searching for more clues.'

'The recording is gone, maybe taken or destroyed by the killers.'

'Who could be the killers?'

'At present we have three suspects—the maid, the MAF and Rohit. They may have been assisted by someone else as they came in a vehicle not belonging to Soumit or Rohit.'

'But, sir, the motive?'

'That is still not clear. The MAF has a motive as Soumit triggered the chain of events which culminated in the arrest of their leader. Soumit could have alerted the manager of the hotel at Rohit's behest. Had Soumit been arrested by us, he would have spilled the beans on his employer, which gives Rohit a motive too. As far as the maid is concerned, she might have been paid off to be involved.'

'Why did Soumit alert the manager? If he wanted Gireesh to be arrested, he could have called the police.'

'He probably didn't want to be implicated in the arrest. He shifted the responsibility to the manager. But Soumit made one careless mistake—using his own cell phone to call the manager. Perhaps, he was confident the police wouldn't investigate his call records.'

'But why would Soumit want to get Gireesh arrested?'

'That we have to find out.'

'What is the direction we should take for our investigation?'

'Wait for the forensic clues. Can you play me the CD you found in the house? I want to check who Rohit Kumar is.'

Mohan inserted the CD in Gautam's laptop.

'Ladies and gentlemen, we have before us today, the very successful, internationally-renowned businessman, Mr Rohit Kumar. Please welcome him to our show, *Talking Tough,* with a huge round of applause.

'Mr Kumar, you are only in your 30s and have already been ranked the Best Businessman of the Year in the Asia-Pacific region by a leading magazine. How have you managed to achieve such phenomenal success in a short span of time?'

'I am very proud to be here after fulfilling my father's dream. If he were alive, he would have been very happy.'

'Yes, you have always said your father has been a huge influence. It must have shattered you when he committed suicide.'

Rohit was visibly uncomfortable as soon as this subject came up. He shifted in his chair and responded in a soft voice. 'It is a sad reflection on our justice system that a dedicated and courageous army officer, such as my father, was labelled a traitor and forced to end his career. Can you imagine a man who received the gallantry award for his role in the Kargil war was court-martialled because he stood up for what was right?'

'But, according to official reports, he was responsible for the deaths of pilgrims who were held hostage by terrorists at Vaishno Devi...'

'You only know one side of the story. By the time dad's battalion arrived at the shrine, the terrorists had already sneaked through the security cordon and taken their positions. Please note that nobody questioned the members of this cordon or held them accountable for what happened. A crowd of 20,000 devotees was present at the time, making it easy for the terrorists to take 50 of them under captivity. My father wanted to negotiate with the militants to minimise the loss of life but while these negotiations were going on, one of the hostages tried to escape and the militants opened fire. Dad's battalion retaliated with their guns and 50 people were killed in the crossfire. Rather than understanding the situation in its complexity, the committee of officers who conducted the inquiry against him—two of whom were hardliners and hated my father's pacifist stance on many issues—preferred to blame him for the entire mishap. He could not bear the agony.'

'Really sorry to hear that, Mr Kumar. May his soul rest in peace. I am sure he would be very proud of everything you have achieved today. Let us move on to talking about Silent Turtle. Did you think that you would come so far?'

'Foresight, hard work and determination have been my byword. Once I set my goals, I make it a point to achieve them at any cost. These are the strong pillars on which my company is supported.'

'And, there is also news that you are planning to expand your operations in China. Has the Chinese government laid down any conditions for the operation of your company there?'

'No, no, not at all. They are very cooperative.'

'But, there was a report in the Indian media that in return for letting you establish your business there, you have been asked to fund a Leftist group in India?'

Rohit remained silent.

'Mr Kumar?'

'I don't think this question deserves an answer. The media has no right to malign anyone. I used to get affected by such criticism earlier but I have learnt to deal with this rubbish. Those who have propagated this rumour are jealous of my rise. My company is prospering because I value my workers and respect their needs. I make sure work is pleasure, not a burden. In the recent Employee Satisfaction Survey, we have been ranked among the 10 best companies in the Asia-Pacific region, excluding Japan. Everybody knows that,' Rohit replied in an irritated tone.

'Are you planning a big project in India?'

'Yes, we are bidding for a mega power plant in India. We hope we get the contract.'

The CD runtime had ended.

'Mohan, find out everything about Rohit. Find out what he does here, where he goes, which are his favourite places, everything. Let's see if we can get some leads.'

'Yes, sir.'

Gautam decided to inform DCP Rajesh of Soumit's murder in mysterious circumstances.

'Are you trying to suggest there may be some link between Gireesh's presence in Delhi and the Silent Turtle?' the DCP asked.

'I cannot be sure yet, sir. But ever since you told me about certain companies funding extremist groups in India, I've been thinking along those lines.'

'All right Gautam, keep at it. But for now, the Patna police have arrived to take custody of Gireesh. Let them take him. It is dangerous for him to stay here. We do not want any attack by the MAF here to free him. Our hands are already full securing the city for the Republic Day. You can continue your investigations and, if the need arises, go to Patna as well.'

'Right, sir. As you say.'

6

13 January 2013, 7 P.M.

At the MAF camp, the commander was pacing up and down in her cave, tense, hoping to hear some news of Gireesh. The entry of one of her cadres interrupted her solitary meditations.

'*Lal Salaam.*'

'*Lal Salaam,* what is the news?' she asked.

'Commander, they are bringing him on the Patna Rajdhani tomorrow.'

'How many policemen will be accompanying him?'

'As per my information, around 20.'

'Is this news correct?'

'Hundred per cent.'

The commander heaved a sigh of relief and rose from her seat. 'Call all our comrades here. Now.'

Under the bright new moon, about a hundred men had gathered. The serene setting of the moonlit rocky ground and the gurgling of the river Bhagat was punctuated by the thumping of their feet. When they had assumed their positions, silence ensued as their leader stood on a rock jutting out at a slightly higher level and shouted—'Comrades, the time has come to tell this oppressive government they can no longer crush the people's revolution. The MAF is not a terrorist organisation. It is the voice of the people. They think we will accept the arrest of our leader. The time has come to prove them wrong. They are transporting our leader back by train and we will show them that we can free our comrades at our will. Now, listen to me carefully.

'We will divide ourselves into three groups. One group, led by Samir Karketta, will plant explosives on the track that the Rajdhani will cross at the Kulhadia Station, 50 km before the Patna station. The bomb shall go off after the pilot engine goes by and before the actual train passes. As soon as the blast occurs and the train stops, the other group, led by Chakradhar Munda, will attack it, taking care not to hurt any civilian. As per our information, comrade Gireesh is being escorted by 20 policemen; we should not have any problem tackling them. I will lead the third group in disguise at the Patna junction, along with 20 other comrades. If our attack on the train fails, we will storm the train in Patna and free our leader.'

'Long live the revolution,' she shouted passionately, raising her clenched fist up in the air.

'Long live the revolution,' shouted the cadres in unison.

~

The next evening, a team of 20 men from the Bihar Police escorted Gireesh to the train to Patna. At midnight,

Gautam was flipping television channels when he got a call from an unknown number.

'Hello.'

'ACP Dhaliwal?'

'Yes, who is calling?'

'Stop them from taking Gireesh by train. The train will be attacked.'

'Who are you?'

'What I am telling you is absolutely correct. It doesn't matter who I am.'

'It matters. I want to meet you.'

'You will have to come to Bhagatpur to do that.'

The phone was disconnected before he could ask any more questions.

What if it is true? I will have to do something, thought Gautam.

He called at the New Delhi railway station and enquired about the Patna Rajdhani.

'Sir, the train has left on time. It must have crossed Mughal Sarai by now,' the station manager informed him.

'Which station does the train stop at after this?'

'Sir, after Mughal Sarai, the train stops only at Patna. Is there a problem?'

'I am not sure. Thanks.'

Next, Gautam called up Aslam, who was at the police station.

'Aslam here, sir,' Aslam replied.

'Aslam, get to my office and give me the Patna SP's number right now.'

'Any problem, sir?'

'Yes, this is urgent.'

As soon as the SP picked up his phone, Gautam apprised him of the latest.

'What? An attack on the train? It is scheduled to arrive at Patna in six hours. This means they have planned the attack near Kulhadia station. Just look at their audacity—they had done the same thing last year. We cannot risk it this time. I'll give orders to vacate the train and make other arrangements to get Gireesh Marandi here. Thanks for the information.' The Patna SP immediately got down to work.

Gautam, meanwhile, updated DCP Rajesh Kumar.

7

14 January 2013

On Tuesday—the auspicious day of Makar Sankranti—a huge crowd gathered at the Patna railway station at 5 a.m. The numbers would only go up. Most of them had come to pay homage to the Hanuman temple outside the station. Also, there were beggars eager to cash in on the largesse that the privileged sections of society invariably indulged in at this time of the year. To add to the chaos, a series of rickshaws had ended up blocking the traffic.

In the midst of all this, Charulata, disguised as an old woman wrapped up in a blanket, moved towards the entrance of the temple. She looked towards her right, where a beggar with his head covered nodded. As devotees distributed alms to the beggars, one man suddenly approached her, handed over something and left without an utterance. It was a note—'Get out of here, your plan has been detected. The bomb that you planted has probably already been discovered and defused. No train is going to arrive here. There are several plainclothes police officers roaming around waiting to arrest you on the slightest suspicion.' She looked all around, lowered her head inside her blanket and murmured what she had read to the other beggar. Both of them quickly moved away from there, mingling with the crowd outside. They signalled other accomplices to follow suit.

Gautam's anonymous caller had saved the day. Nonetheless, the fact that the train had to be stopped midway and its passengers evacuated were reasons enough for it to become a news story. Quite soon, the news that an MAF plan to bomb the Patna Rajdhani had been hatched for two years in a row flashed on the television screens.

~

At the MAF camp, Charulata was listening to the news in disgust.

'There is a traitor among us. I will soon find out who it is and make such an example out of him that no one will dare to betray us again. Switch off the radio.' She marched to her cave.

Chakradhar and Samir looked at each other and bowed their heads.

~

At his residence, Subhash Joshi, the Joint Director of IB, was watching the news. 'Someone informed Gautam about the raid. So, our informer is alive and trying to contact us. But why Gautam?'

'Sir, there was a notification from the Home Ministry,' said a constable interrupting his silent musings.'What do they want?' he replied.

'The home minister has called for an urgent meeting tomorrow. They want you to be present.'

'So, the news has reached them. Let's see what the home minister has to say,' he thought.

'Dinner is served, sir,' the constable interrupted again.

'Okay, I will have a late dinner. You may go home now,' said Joshi.

8

15 January 2013

Prabhat Advani, the Home Minister, took the news of the train attack very seriously and immediately convened a meeting with members of the ministry and IB officials. Subhash Joshi, also present, was growing increasingly nervous as he waited for the minister to arrive. Even though the attack had been prevented, this had been possible only by chance. The MAF's blatant and fearless attempt to repeat previous year's attack was particularly disconcerting.

The home minister entered the room in his crisp white kurta-pyjama and khadi overcoat. Without wasting any time, he began lambasting all the officers. 'What have you all been doing? They kill the DM, they blast the railway trains going through the territory, they try to free their leaders, and we? We just watch the news on television and trot out routine lines to the press that the situation is under control. It has been so many years and we have achieved minor success in apprehending the terrorists. Why is this so? Can't we do anything?'

'Law and order is a state subject, sir. Beyond a point, we are helpless,' the home secretary mumbled with much hesitance.

'Thanks for reminding me of the Constitution, Mr Bose. But, the problem is that there are people dying and their blood is on my hands. I am the one who is supposed to ensure their security. To say that we don't have adequate support from the State Government in this matter is no excuse. I refuse to believe that nothing can be done about this. It has been seven years and this particular organisation has made us all helpless. Why is it that we have not been able to weed them out?'

'Their leaders are two of the most revered members of the Naxalite movement—Gireesh Marandi, whom we have caught, and Charulata, who is still roaming scot-free. Their exemplary strategic thinking, organisational skills and valour are regarded as benchmarks for other Naxals to follow. They will leave no stone unturned to set their leader free.'

'Mr Bose, are you the Home Secretary of India or spokesperson of the MAF?' Prabhat retorted with contempt.

'Sir, I have an idea,' Subhash Joshi intervened.

'Enough of your ideas, Subhash. It was because of you that I assented to that ludicrous idea of planting a mole in the MAF. The end result—there has been no news of him for the last two years. He didn't give us even one piece of substantial information. Maybe, he too has become one of them.'

'No, sir, I would not be so sure of that. Somebody did inform the police of the impending blast. Maybe, it was him. And you are forgetting, sir, that the only officer he was supposed to report to was killed two years ago. That was when the informer stopped communicating with us,' replied Subhash.

'Two years is not a short time. Surely, he could have found some way of getting back. We both know how often informers change sides in these missions. Do you want to send an officer there now?'

'Yes, sir, but not from the IB. I have someone in mind from the Delhi Police.'

'Do you have someone specific in mind?'

'Sir, ACP Dhaliwal was the one responsible for Gireesh Marandi's arrest in Delhi. DCP Rajesh Kumar has told me that he has already begun investigating why the leader of the MAF himself came to Delhi. And we still are not sure of this, but Silent Turtle, the same company which is setting up a power plant in Bhagatpur, may have some role to play in this matter. The general manager was found dead in his house recently and he turned out to be the one who had tipped off the hotel manager about Marandi. Dhaliwal is competent enough to take charge of this case.'

'But why did the informer suddenly decide to show up and contact the ACP of all people? Couldn't this also be a plan to first earn our trust and then mislead us?'

'Maybe. But, we need to get to the root of it. It could well be that he considered the ACP easily accessible. He has specifically asked Dhaliwal to come to Bhagatpur. Maybe, he is in danger or is looking for a lead. If the ACP can find him, the information that we receive on the MAF and other terrorist groups will be invaluable. Also, the nexus between business organisations and terrorist groups could well be exposed if he manages to gather evidence.'

'All right, go ahead with this. But make sure we get positive results. I will wait for the outcome of this operation before deciding whether more force is the only way to settle the MAF problem.'

In no mood for polite goodbyes, the home minister left the chamber in a huff.

9

16 January 2013, 5 A.M.

'Wake up, son! There is a call from DCP Rajesh.' Gautam got up groggily after hearing his mother's voice.

'Give me the phone.'

'Gautam, come over to my office right now.' It was DCP Rajesh.

Gautam glanced at the clock. It was 7 a.m.

'Now?'

'Come right now in whatever state you are.'

'I'll be right over, sir.'

'Curse this godforsaken job. Nobody bothers about the fact that you have slept at 4 o'clock the last night working on a case. All you have to do is follow orders,' he told himself as he hung up.

'What happened? Why do you look so upset?' his mother asked.

'Nothing, Ma. I have to report to work. Could you please make me a quick breakfast?'

True to his word, Gautam was at the door of the DCP's office at 7:30 a.m. He saw his senior engrossed in a serious conversation with another man.

'Have a seat, Gautam,' said the DCP. 'Meet Mr Subhash Joshi, Joint Director of the IB. He is the one who called for you here today.'

'Congratulations, ACP Dhaliwal,' Subhash Joshi added. 'Your information helped save the police department much embarrassment.'

'Thank you, sir. But I only informed the Patna SP what I had been warned against. Fortunately, the news was correct.'

Turning to the DCP, Gautam asked, 'Sir, any idea where they have kept Gireesh?'

'They are not sharing this information with anyone, not even us. Who knows where the MAF has planted moles. You know, I am of the opinion that we should have eliminated Gireesh.'

'But I still cannot understand why someone would warn me of the attack on the train.'

'I have an explanation,' Subhash Joshi said. 'Three years ago, we started a clandestine operation—*India One* to finish the MAF. As part of *Operation India One*, the IB had planted a mole in the MAF. Unfortunately, contact with the MAF informer was lost two years ago when the officer, Sudhakar, whom he was reporting to was killed. Before dying Sudhakar destroyed all the records of the informer so as to protect his identity. My instinct tells me that he is the one who informed you. He must be aware that you were the one responsible for Gireesh's arrest.'

'Hmm. That is possible.'

'And...' asked the DCP. 'Have you found any more links between Silent Turtle and the case? How is your investigation coming along?'

'We are yet to get concrete evidence. Rohit Kumar is going to have a board meeting on 18th January in Noida. I will pay him a visit. We have not been able to access his Malaysia accounts yet, but one peculiar thing I found was his donation of Rs 1 crore to an NGO named Mahila Shakti in Delhi.'

'Who owns it?'

'A woman named Sulochna Banerjee.'

'Sulochna Banerjee?' exclaimed Subhash.

'You know her?' Gautam asked.

'We have doubts that she is a Hawala operator and involved in transactions with insurgent groups, using her NGO as a front.'

'Has she received any other donations from Rohit in the past?' Rajesh asked.

'No, none from Rohit. But she does receive significant amounts of money from different companies. Over the last few days, we noticed a withdrawal of Rs 10 crore from her organisation's bank account.'

'It may be normal. Many NGOs receive donations from different organisations and they use the funds for various activities,' Rajesh replied.

'Probably, but I have a doubt on account of two things. According to my investigation, Mahila Shakti is not planning anything big right now; however, they do intend to set up a shelter home for women in Bhagatpur. Surprisingly, they have not allotted any fund for that. This is odd considering Rohit had adequately funded the NGO for the purpose. Secondly, my informer has shared news about a deal of 10 crores in the arms market.'

'Do you mean to say the cash you found in the suitcase inside the vehicle that night might belong to her?'

'Maybe. It cannot be a coincidence.'

'Gautam, on the night of the incident, our sleuth intercepted a satellite phone conversation between a person in Bhagatpur and a man in Lakshmi Nagar, Delhi. We noted down a few names—Samir, Babu Lal, Guhar and Vikas. We do not have any information about Babu Lal but Samir is an MAF commander and Guhar is a member of a small-time terrorist organisation in Kashmir which supplies arms all over India. In all probability, this was the third person who visited them that night. Vikas is the terrorist whose sketch was released by RPF (Railway Protection Force). The person who escaped that night was Vikas,' Subhash Joshi said.

'But how does Rohit Kumar fit into Soumit's murder? And it seems we are also dealing with money laundering,' Gautam responded.

'I am glad to hear you are so involved in this case, Gautam, because Mr Subhash Joshi here has recommended to the Home Ministry that you take complete charge of it. Bhagatpur is sitting on an explosive powder keg and you have ignited the fuse by arresting Gireesh Marandi. On the one hand, the MAF claims to fight for the rights of the oppressed and takes a stand against the corporate class invading their land but on the other, they accept money from the same organisations.'

'What is a bigger concern for me is the safety of Gireesh. I don't think the MAF will keep quiet,' Gautam said.

'It is certain they will take bigger steps to get their leader released. The Chief Minister of Bihar, Mr Nilesh Yadav refuses to take any action against the MAF due to personal political motives. The only informer planted by the IB has vanished. So, the Home Ministry wants you to go to Bhagatpur and investigate. I will let Mr Joshi brief you further about the area and the mission,' Rajesh replied.

'Sir, please brief Gautam about the mission. I will take your leave. I have an urgent meeting to attend. Please let me know if I could be of any help,' Rajesh said and left the chamber.

Subhash Joshi began speaking, 'Gautam, Bhagatpur lies about 120 km south of Patna, in Jehenabad district. The majority of the people living there are tribal and Dalits. The Bhagatpur landscape is dotted with granite hills which have made the place a business centre for stone crushing. In fact, the area is responsible for supplying more than 50 per cent of building material to Bihar.'

'How does Silent Turtle come into the picture?' Gautam asked rather impatiently.

'I'm coming to that. The government of Bihar has proposed to build an 800 MW power plant here which it proposes will end the power woes of the state. The contract for this enterprise has been given to Silent Turtle and the land has been acquired from the villagers after paying them compensation. However, the massive eviction and destruction of the forests there have led to great resentment among the local population. Almost 40 villages and vast forest lands are going to be destroyed by this power plant. Needless to say, the compensation does not satisfy the poor. This entire issue is being raked up further by the MAF, which has its base camp there. They are leaving no stone unturned to instigate the people against projects like this. There is a woman called Charulata who is as dangerous as Gireesh. We do not know anything about her.'

'What has the government done to stop them?'

'We'd started *Operation India One* three years back with the aim to finish the MAF. There were two facets of the mission—one was to plant a mole in the organisation which I had told you earlier and the other was to raise an all women commando force to flush them out. You must have heard about the Razia Regiment and their leader Kavita Sethi?'

'RR was part of a mission? *India One*? The first objective of the mission failed as the mole did not report back, but what about RR? Has it been successful?'

'No, that did not perform either. There's no doubt Kavita is a brave officer, but, she did not get support from State Government.'

'What support and why?'

'I am sure you know about the People's Resistance Movement in Bihar. We had raised it as a special police force to root out the MAF in Bihar. The previous government in power had started an all out operation against Maoist forces all over India which was called *Green Hunt*. But the mission failed. Later, PRM was disbanded on the Supreme Court orders. So this time we were going cautiously and we have asked RR to involve the state police in each and every action. Sadly, the State Government has so far refused to assist them.'

'Why?'

'Ah! Politics of our land is like this.'

'I am not getting it,' Gautam was confused.

'The present prime minister has announced his decision to retire from active politics after he completes his term in 2014. Prabhat Advani and Nilesh Yadav were the top contenders for the prime ministerial candidate for the next election. However, INP the biggest Party in the coalition named Prabhat as the next prime ministerial candidate without consulting Nilesh Yadav and his Party members. So, he withdrew support from the coalition and turned bitter against Prabhat. This political rivalry has resulted in Kavita becoming an unwilling causality. Nilesh has given strict instructions to state police force to desist from lending support to the RR. He doesn't wish to use force on poor villagers and gain sympathy votes in the coming election.'

'But MAF is a national menace. It is not confined to an area.'

'Precisely, this is what we try arguing to the chief minister, but he refuses to budge.'

'So, has the RR totally failed in its objective?'

'Not exactly, you need to know more about this area.'

'I am listening,' Gautam replied.

'Have you heard of the RakhtBeej?'

Gautam shook his head.

'In Bihar, RakhtBeej is an organisation that fights for the rights of the landlords. Their motto is to protect the status quo of the upper class supremacy in the caste-ridden society of Bihar. It was started by Raghuvansh Rai and is now being led by his son, Ganesh, in clandestine. Raghuvansh Rai was the son of a wealthy landlord in a small village, Bankapur, in Gaya. He was in the army, but, after being injured during the 1971 war, he retired to his native village and began looking after his father's estate.

During the social unrest, the local armies that had been established to look after Dalit interests attacked Raghuvansh Rai's estate. Raghuvansh pledged to form an upper caste army to fight them. In 1975, he founded the RakhtBeej Sena (RBS) with the support of politicians and bureaucrats. With the help of his military training, he gained notoriety and became a killing machine in the 1980s. When the government launched a police operation to capture him, he acquired shelter in the Bhagatpur forest and started operating from there. Sensing that the military action would not suffice, he decided to shake hands with the government and join politics. He contested the by-election from Bhagatpur in 1980 and became the environment minister. But soon, he was implicated in a multi-crore jungle scam. He was accused of felling trees in the forests of Bhagatpur and illegally auctioning them in collusion with the forest department. Later, he was chased by the CBI.

While in custody, he was gunned down by unknown assailants. His murder case remains unsolved. If rumours are to be believed, his murder was orchestrated by his own son.'

'What? Why would he murder his father?'

'Ganesh Rai was once the student union leader and he wanted to step into mainstream politics. He was estranged from his father, whose image had been tarnished after the scam and the case against him was too strong. Quick to sense his father's inevitable downfall, Ganesh Rai collaborated with college students who belonged to well-connected political families of the state and together they started the SPCCL (Students Power Construction Company Ltd.) by unifying all the businesses of his father under one head. Apart from stone-quarrying and mining, the company also makes full use of its contacts to get government contracts for constructing roads and buildings. Ganesh Rai wanted his father out of the way because he could not risk his father's bad reputation to affect his political career.'

Gautam looked thoughtful as he tried to process all the information coming his way. 'What is the connection of all this with the MAF? Why did they choose Bhagatpur as their base?'

'I am coming to that. I think you are having trouble registering this volume of information. Here, lighten up,' Subhash said and offered him a cigarette.

Gautam lit a cigarette and continued, 'Indeed, this information has made my head spin. It is like a story to me.'

'It is indeed a story but a long one spanning decades. Shall we proceed?'

Gautam nodded.

'During the 1990s, when weaker sections of society in the state started raising their voice against caste oppression, a ray of hope emerged in Bhagatpur as well. James Marandi, a Hindu convert to Christianity decided to stand against Ganesh Rai in the 1995 assembly elections as an independent candidate. Although the odds were against him, he won by a few hundred votes. One night Ganesh Rai and his goons attacked James' house and wiped out his entire family. About 20 people were killed.'

'Yes, in the 90s, Bihar was infamous for caste-related violence. What happened next?'

'Gireesh, James's son, managed to escape and vowed to avenge his father's death. Together with a small band of similarly disgruntled young people he formed the Eklavya Sena. One night, they attacked Ganesh Rai's palatial house, burning it down and butchering all its occupants. The one person they could not kill was Ganesh, who was away in Patna to sign a road contract for SPCCL. His whole family perished in the attack. He later constructed a new mansion inside the village which is heavily guarded at all times.'

'So, Ganesh and Gireesh are fighting a personal war against each other. How is Charulata associated with this group?'

'She came into the picture when the Eklavya Sena had already gained a reputation for being extremely dangerous. At that time, Charulata was heading a communist faction, the Dandakaranya Communist Party (Maoist) in Dandakaranya, Chhattisgarh. She influenced Gireesh to join the Communist Party, and in 2000 they formed an entirely new group—MAF.'

'So, they are leftist.'

'Call them leftist, Marxist, Naxalite or extremist. Their strength grew steadily and the power plant gave them a good excuse. Kavita did achieve some success. Now, the image of the RR is good, but, there are lots of people who would like to see her dead. She is a courageous woman. The intense operation started by the RR drove the MAF to its camps in the forests while she persuaded Ganesh Rai to desist from mounting any raid. An informal ceasefire took place between the MAF and the RBS. The Bhagat River has become a de facto border for these two groups. While the RBS operates from Bhagatpur, the MAF is on the other side. The RR regularly patrols this area to prevent any skirmishes.'

'But, sir, what is my role in all this?' Gautam asked.

Subhash Joshi stood up from his chair and walked towards the window. From now on, you are part of *Operation India One*. Your mission's objectives will be—first, find the informer. Second, look for any clues about this elusive woman, Charulata. Third, investigate how Rohit could be involved in this. And of course, you will continue investigating why Soumit was murdered. Do you need anyone to assist you?'

'I would like to take Mohan with me. As far as the Soumit murder case is concerned, I would like Aslam to continue his investigation and report to me if necessary.'

'Perfect. I will ask Rajesh to arrange for all this. I will give you a file where you will find detailed information about the place. You will also get an idea on how to get inside Bhagatpur. First, study this subject for a few days and then prepare yourself to move into the territory of dispute. Remember, this is a clandestine operation and you are not being sent there officially. I anticipate some good news from such a brave and an intelligent officer like you.'

'I will try my best sir.'

Rajesh handed a blue box file to Gautam and uttered, 'Best of luck officer.'

'Thank you sir,' he saluted and left the office.

10

17 January 2013, 9 A.M.

In the nondescript settlement of Bhagatpur, a woman had just parked her car outside the gate of a building with a signboard that read—'Office and residence of the Special Magistrate, Bhagatpur'.

Land acquisition for the power plant was on at a rapid pace. The State Government had appointed IAS officer, Ajay Mishra, to oversee the entire process and take care of any administrative problems that would accompany it. Just near the site, an erstwhile secondary school building had been converted into his office-cum-residence. It was a spacious 15x15 ft. room fitted with an AC, two phones, a huge table and five chairs. A door at the back of the room led to his bedroom where he stayed with his wife, Rekha Mishra. A smaller adjacent room had been made available for his stenographer, a fax and photocopy machine. Five peons, 10 guards and four vehicles were at his service at all times. There was also a waiting lounge near the fax and photocopy room.

As she went inside towards the reception desk, the woman was greeted by a yawning peon's paan-stained teeth. She told the man that she wanted to meet the magistrate.

'Do you have an appointment?' he asked.

'No, just tell him Nisha Kushwaha wants to meet him,' the woman replied, curtly.

Taken aback by the authority with which she spoke, the peon did as he was told, giving Nisha enough time to take a good look at the place. *They close the only school to accommodate this unnecessarily luxurious office. As if the existing landlords were not enough, the government forced another one on the hapless people of Bhagatpur,* she thought to herself.

Ajay Mishra was going through some files when the peon entered his chamber and announced—'Sir, Nisha Kushwaha wants to meet you.'

'Now what does she want?' he answered angrily. 'Tell her she should come another day.'

The peon went to the waiting lounge. 'Sir is very busy. He has asked you to come another day.'

'Oh really? Tell him that I am also busy on other days. I will wait till he finishes his work.'

The peon looked at her sullenly and went back to Ajay.

'Sir, she is saying that she will wait.'

'Oh! That stubborn woman! Why has she come here? Okay, ask her to come inside.'

The peon reappeared in front of Nisha and said, 'You can go in.'

'He finished his work quite fast, didn't he?' Nisha remarked sarcastically.

She went to Ajay's room and began, 'Hello sir, how are you?'

'Please come to the point. What do you want?'

'Sir, last month you had promised to show up for a public hearing today. The case in question is the eviction of the people because of the power plant.'

'And you believed me,' he said with a wry smile on his face.

'Look Ms Nisha, I will give you an advice. You may be a Magsaysay award winner but politics is a dirty business. If you get too involved, you might burn your fingers.'

'Please do not worry about me, Mr Mishra. I can take care of myself. But, you have to answer why you did not show up for the hearing. It was directed by the High Court and if this matter goes to the court you may well lose your post.'

'Are you threatening me?'

'No, I am trying to remind you of your responsibility.'

'Look, Ms Nisha, calm down. You know how things work. The plant will be constructed whether you like it or not. Why do you want to embroil these poor villagers in a long-drawn legal battle they stand no chance of winning? Let them take the compensation and move to something better.'

'But that is what I am saying. The least you can do is to give them proper compensation.'

'What do you mean? We are paying them according to the government rates.'

'Your rates are 100-years-old. The actual market-rate for the same land today is 10 times higher.'

'Well, I am sorry you feel that way. We are working within the framework of the law. The rules cannot be changed because someone does not agree with them.'

'The courts will see through the design of the government,' said Nisha angrily.

'Maybe, but by then, the plant would have outlived its utility. You know how long-winded the legal processes in this country can be.'

'Forgive me. I had forgotten how well-versed you are with the country's justice system. Your own case has also been lingering in the courts since the last one year.'

'Ms Nisha, please watch yourself. Do not speak of things you know little about.' The enraged man was red in the face. That was his first uncalculated response in the meeting.

'But it is no secret that you have been charged with taking a hefty bribe to hide reports on the corruption of the Vartara Corporation.'

'That is false. There is no evidence against me. And, in any case, I do not need the approval of the MAF agents such as you, hell-bent on destroying the country because of your blinkered worldview.'

'We all know who the agent is here. Do you think the rest of us are fools and do not know that you have been sent in as a government stooge to ensure there is no obstruction in building this plant? And how dare you call me an agent of an organisation that killed my own father?'

'Go spread your malicious propaganda elsewhere. Don't waste my time. This plant will be constructed irrespective of what you do and the compensation will be paid as per government rates.'

'Do you know what the place you are standing in is called?'

'Yes. Vir Birsa Munda Chowk.'

'Do you know who Birsa Munda was?'

'Why are you asking me this?'

'Hundred years ago, the British commissioner of this area, Robert Taylor, made the same mistake you are committing right now. Do you know what the people did to him? They overthrew the government under Birsa Munda's leadership and killed the commissioner. He was hacked to pieces.'

'There it is. Your true violent face. And then you say you do not support terrorist organisations like the MAF. Get out of my office,' shouted Ajay.

'It is because callous and selfish individuals like you rise to power that people are left with no option but to resort to the gun. How can you call them terrorists? Try to live their lives for a day and then we will see how your opinions change.' Nisha shouted back and left the chamber fuming. The peon standing at the door could only look on, bewildered.

11

17 January 2013, 11 A.M.

The moment anyone becomes an officer, they begin thinking they are above the law. Nisha was lost in such thoughts while driving back to her office and residence at the NS2 (Nai Soch-Nai Subah) headquarters, about 5 km away from the plant site at a place called Tower Chowk. The clock tower was the most visible landmark there.

Nisha parked her car and hurried to her office. In a stark contrast to the special magistrate's working premises, the NS2 office was a plainly designed two-storey building with Nisha's office on the first floor. Next to it was the room where she stayed, which had more books than furniture. The ground floor was used as a school where Nisha taught the women of the area.

As she paced up and down, a young woman entered. She seemed to be in her mid-20s and had a well-toned, athletic body and a dusky complexion.

'How are you, Saroj?' asked Nisha.

'I am fine but you don't seem to be so. What happened? Did the officer dismiss your concern about the public hearing?'

'Yes.'

'I told you earlier. I know these officers. They will never pay attention to the poor.'

'There are many other angles to this. It is clear that Ajay Mishra has vested interests and also, he has been sent by the State Government to get the plant constructed at any cost. If he succeeds, his name will be cleared from the Vartara Corporation inquiry. He has many contacts and in addition, his father-in-law is chief secretary of the Jharkhand government. He can afford not to take us seriously.'

'Yes, ma'am. We have heard all this too.'

'How come?'

'Ma'am, we may be illiterate, but we know how power and politics operate.'

'That is very good. I know education will help you understand it further.'

'Ma'am, I don't believe our future will change after studying. But you have made us dream and we will be eternally grateful to you for that.'

'Your future will change and education will play a huge role in it, I guarantee you. Why blame only politicians? It is the people who elect them. For the last 50 years, you have elected someone like Ganesh Rai. Why? It is because we fail to see the ulterior designs behind a smiling face. He visits your area for a few days during the elections and distributes money and liquor so that you give him your vote. How do you expect things to change if this carries on? God will not come down to earth to teach you. The people have to stand together against the crimes that politicians are committing.'

'Now, what will we do against the government's order?'

'I will go to the court.'

'Why do you want to drag us into a court battle? Why don't we go to the MAF? They will set the record straight within days.'

'No,' answered Nisha. 'Violence is never the answer. We will proceed legally.'

'Madam, Gandhigiri died with the death of Gandhi. I still believe the MAF is the only solution, otherwise we will be forced out of our land.'

'Why are you speaking on behalf of the MAF? Not everything they do is perfect. Have you forgotten the attack on the Rajdhani which killed many innocent people? They killed the Jehenabad DM, who was trying to do some positive thing for this place. And what was my father's fault? He just wanted to start a school for all of you. But they, the MAF, do not want anyone in this area to be educated because then they will realise the futility of the gun.'

'But they are also fighting for the motherland. Bhagat Singh fought for the country but was declared a terrorist by the British government.'

'You talk too much. But, remember my words—don't have blind faith on the MAF. One day, they will surely end up destroying themselves. Now, go to the classroom. I have to finish my India lecture.'

'What is the point of talking about a country which doesn't even consider Bhagatpur a part of it?'

'Of course, Bhagatpur is a part of India.'

'No, it's not. India got freedom in 1947. Where is the freedom here? What have we really got in all these decades? No food, no water, no jobs, no roads, no electricity, no proper schools or hospitals. Poverty and indignity have plagued us. When we die, no one cares. They snatch away our land and make us homeless in minutes. When we protest, they label us terrorists and kill us in fake encounters,' lamented Saroj.

'Calm down, Saroj. You are right. But, who is going to change all this? It is you, the people.'

'These are very pleasing words, ma'am. But, we are up against forces much larger than us and mere words are not enough.'

12

18 January 2013, 10 A.M.

The ongoing construction of the Silent Turtle headquarters at 16-A, Noida, bore testimony to the company's resolve to make a grand entry into the Indian power sector. It had clinched the deal for the power plant the previous year, but, work had still not begun. This was the agenda for which the board meeting had been called.

Rohit reached office at 10 a.m. and proceeded towards the boardroom. The directors rose to greet him as he entered. After everyone settled down, he began speaking.

'We have assembled here to unveil the blueprint of the mega power plant we intend to set up in Bhagatpur. Our design team has worked day and night for six months to prepare it. On behalf of all the board directors, I would like to thank the entire team.'

Rohit gestured to his secretary to switch off the lights and turn on the projector.

'This project is the first of its kind in India. The land required by the plant is 1,000 acres and will consist of one unit of 800 MW. Note, that this is the first time an 800 MW unit will be synchronised in India. Bhagatpur lies in a forested area to the south of Patna on the banks of the river Bhagat, bordering Gaya. The water required for the plant will be drawn from the river, which is a tributary of Son. A coal belt lies close to the area—an obvious advantage for us. We have also worked out an arrangement with Aucoal Private Limited, an Australian undertaking which will supply us coal on an annual contract basis in case the quality of coal from our area deteriorates. We can rely on the hilly tracts of Kaimur for the remaining construction material. The overall project cost will be Rs 4,000 crore and the plant will be remotely operated from Patna.'

'But sir, we have heard that the MAF often resorts to violent means to get people like us out of the region,' one of the executives asked. 'And, after the arrest of their leader in Delhi, they have already begun threatening our company officials.'

'That will be no problem for us. I have made arrangements,' replied Rohit immediately, hoping to avoid further discussion on the topic.

'But, how will our personnel adapt to such a remote place? They are not used to working in those conditions. Also, is our workforce even adequate for this task? We have just about 100 engineers and they are already overworked. Designing a blueprint is one thing but its execution is another. Our engineers don't have the requisite practical knowledge; they are all A4-size design engineers,' insisted one of the directors.

'Our HR manager, Nishant Sharma, will throw some light on this,' Rohit responded, momentarily distracted by an unknown number flashing on his cell phone. He cancelled the call.

Nishant stood up. 'Motivation is the key for engineers to work in such difficult locations. We plan to recruit about a 100 more engineers especially for the project. All of them will be experienced so that we do not have to spend much time and money on their training.'

'But why would experienced engineers agree to come on board?' the general manager (finance) interrupted.

'Two things—money and standard of living. At present, the engineers of the best companies in India work at such places on remunerations of approximately Rs 1 lakh. We will double this amount. We will provide them with well-furnished, centrally air-conditioned accommodation with complete security and each of them will be given their own vehicle. After the project is completed, we will send some of them to our projects in China and Malaysia and the rest will be suitably rewarded in cash.'

'Can we afford to be so lavish?' probed the same interrogator.

Rohit jumped in. 'Trust me, it all adds up. If offering all these luxuries saves time, then they are surely worth it. I have worked long enough in the power sector in India to know all the flaws in the system. The biggest problem is an unmotivated workforce and the lack of coordination between its different components—manufacturing, engineering and commissioning. The engineering entity hardly bothers to incorporate new changes in technology and continues working at the same pace. The manufacturing entity follows its own turnover targets and concentrates on higher value items. Less attention is given to what is initially required at the site. Moreover, the site engineers are unmotivated because of the lack of facilities, and the political sensitivities of the area can also be an added hindrance. I have taken care to address all these issues. We have entered into a joint venture with the major power sector companies of the world—GE, Alstom and ABB—and have acquired the latest technology that is not available even in India's top companies. I will lead a group which will coordinate with each of the JV partners and follow the JIT (Just in Time) principle to deliver the needed parts in time. This will ensure the reduction of pilferage at the sites, which is a major hidden cost.'

'But sir, will the JIT model work in Indian conditions? What about the inventory that sister units must maintain?'

'It will work if the assessment is done correctly. At the moment, we have only one project in India. When the volume of jobs increases, we will rethink it. But we have to deliver the first project on time and we are already behind schedule. I have taken care of any disturbances that might arise due to the political situation in the area. The only thing I want from you is dedication. So, are you all with me?'

A chorus replied, 'Yes.'

After everybody had left the meeting, Rohit remained at his seat.

'Sir, a police officer wants to meet you,' announced his secretary.

'Police officer? Send him in,' he replied.

Gautam entered the room. 'Mr Rohit Kumar, I am ACP Gautam from Delhi Police. I need to ask you a few questions.'

'Regarding?'

'Regarding Soumit.'

'He has committed suicide. What more can I say?'

'We aren't sure about the nature of his death, Mr Kumar. The investigation is still on. And I had expected a more compassionate response from someone who just lost one of his chief employees. Surely, there must be something you could tell us to help us understand this case better?'

'It's not like I am not deeply saddened. I knew he was stressed because of work and I had advised him to take rest but he did not listen to me. Had I known about his intention, I would have forcibly sent him on leave.'

'Work pressure? Mr Rohit, we found a huge volume of drugs in his body. Do you think drug abuse was one of the ways he chose to handle work-related stress?'

'What? Drug abuse? I had no idea.'

'We found one of your interview CDs at his residence.'

'Why is that surprising? He was a Silent Turtle employee and one of my favourite officers. We were quite close.'

'How close, Mr Rohit?'

'What do you mean?'

'I don't understand why he would watch your interview just before he died. Were you aware that there was a CCTV camera installed in his house? It must have recorded the events of that night. Our forensic team is looking for data in the DVR of the CCTV.' The tension on Rohit's face did not go unnoticed by Gautam.

'CCTV footage? What are you trying to get at, officer?'

'Oh, nothing. I'm just keeping you updated regarding the investigation. Thank you for your time. Oh, and one more thing. I admire your keen interest in philanthropy and women's empowerment.'

'What do you mean?'

'Don't be so modest, Mr Kumar. Didn't you recently donate Rs 1 crore to Mahila Shakti, the NGO in Delhi?'

'Oh, yes, yes. I take my corporate social responsibility very seriously.'

Gautam smiled and said, 'Of course, but I felt little surprised when Mahila Shakti accountant told me that they have not allotted fund for the woman shelter at Bhagatpur for which you had provided the fund.'

'That's their internal matter. What can I say?'

'Okay, I will take your leave now. Hope to see you soon.'

As soon as Gautam left, Rohit called for his bodyguard, George.

'George, leave for Malaysia tomorrow,' he instructed him.

'But, sir, you are not safe here,' George replied with concern.

'Don't worry about me. You leave. The police are getting unnecessarily involved. In Malaysia, ensure that nobody gets access to my accounts.'

'What is bothering you, sir?'

'George, aren't you one of my most experienced men?'

'I am, sir.' He looked worried.

'Then, how the hell did you miss the CCTV installed in Soumit's house?'

'Did the police find anything?'

'Not yet, but this in itself is bad news.'

'Bad news?'

'The CCTV must have recorded the events of that night. And, if the recordings are not with us or the police, where are they?'

George was speechless on hearing this. Rohit waved his hand at him, telling him to get out of the room. As he left, Rohit's cell phone rang, its screen flashing the same unknown number whose call he had cancelled earlier.

'Hello.'

'Why don't you pick up the phone, you double-crossing bastard?' shouted a woman's voice.

Petrified, Rohit asked, 'Who are you?'

'I am Charulata.'

'I don't think I know you.'

'You will know me very well in a short while. It is because of you that Gireesh has been arrested. We are not going to spare you.'

Rohit froze when he realised who she was. 'Ma'am, there has been some confusion. Neither I nor anybody else in my company was responsible for his arrest. Please believe me.'

'Stop lying. It was your man Soumit who alerted the police.'

'No, ma'am. He had not. And even if he had, he has been punished.'

'It is impossible that you did not know what was going on. Killing one person will not soothe our anger. We want our leader back at any cost otherwise we won't allow the construction of the plant.'

'Look, ma'am, I am offering you the protection money we had offered to the MAF earlier. In fact, we will double it; instead of 20 we'll make it Rs 40 crores. But please do not create obstacles for us.'

'This is no longer about money. You dared to cheat our leader and you will see how our actions speak louder than our words.' She cut the call.

Rohit was immensely nervous now. This was not the way things were meant to unfold. He sat silently for a few minutes before leaving the room.

13

18 January 2013, 11 P.M.

'Ruk Jana Nahin Tu Kahin Haar Ke'—a Bollywood song blared out from the outdated music system of the van. Inside, there were six engineers employed by Silent Turtle who were returning to their residences near the construction site in Bhagatpur. It was 11 p.m. and the van driver was racing to his destination so that he could get enough rest before the next day. He had to report again at 7 a.m. in the morning.

It had rained in the morning and the ground was slippery. The van was no longer on the metalled road and was negotiating a culvert when the driver noticed a cut in the road ahead. He didn't think much of it since such disruption was part and parcel of a construction site. However, as soon as the van passed over it, a deafening explosion threw it several feet above the ground and immediately smashed it to bits. The blast was so powerful that it left a 6 ft. deep crater at the blast site. Some villagers rushed to the spot but all seven occupants were dead in seconds.

The next day, every staff member of the Silent Turtle at Bhagatpur and Noida, from the peon to the chief engineer, went on strike. At around 10.30 a.m., amid the cacophony of loud slogans criticising an unfair management, a white car screeched to a halt at the site's office building. The site-in-charge of the Bhagatpur Mega Thermal Power Project (BMTPP), Rajiv Kumar had arrived. Without any delay, he issued an unconditional apology to his employees, assuring them that he was doing his best to get things under control. He soon realised, however, that such was the anger among the staff that it was only concrete action that would pacify them. He went inside his office and dialled Rohit's number.

'I told you empty words would be of no use, sir. Tempers are too high and rightly so. Who would want to work in a place where one's life is constantly under threat? The district administration had promised to tighten the security; and Special Magistrate Ajay Mishra too had assured me enough. But I think that was all in vain. Our reputation will definitely take a beating because of this. You told us that everything had been settled with the MAF. Now, even they are accusing us of backstabbing them.'

'Don't let their tactics scare you, Rajiv. That is what they want. I have thought of a way to tackle the MAF menace. I know someone who can sort them out. God knows why they claim Soumit had informed the police about their leader's whereabouts in Delhi, but, it is too late to offer explanations now. You stay put and ask your engineers to remain vigilant.'

Rohit's hands trembled as he put the phone down. Worry lines were visible on his forehead. He looked through the glass partition of his chamber. The entire office was empty. Most of the staff had gone to Bhagatpur to show solidarity with the engineers at the site.

'Your car is ready, sir,' Rohit's secretary informed him over the intercom.

Rohit hurriedly left the office to get into his car.

'Where to, sir?'

'Bihar Bhavan.'

~

At Bihar Bhavan, Rohit asked the man at the reception, 'Where is Room 7?'

'Sir, please take the stairs to the left. The room is just near the staircase. Sahib is expecting you.'

'Come in,' said a voice as he knocked on the door.

Two people were sitting on a sofa and talking, one in a white kurta-pyjama and one in a cream-coloured suit with a matching tie.

'I am Ganesh Rai,' declared the man in the kurta-pyjama, gesturing at Rohit to take a seat.

He was a tall, dark man of sturdy build, probably in his late 40s. He sported a shabby, unkempt beard and wore a dark thread round his neck.

'This is Ajay Mishra, Special Magistrate for the BMTPP at Bhagatpur,' Ganesh Rai introduced the other man.

'Sir, I have come to discuss the situation in Bhagatpur.' Rohit decided to go straight to the point.

'I know. Six of your engineers were killed,' said Ganesh Rai.

'But, sir, your government had assured us we would get full safety. The Rs 50 crore we gave your Party was not only to get the contract but also ensure that issues like this do not arise. What answer do I give the workers now? I will be doomed if we cannot get the plant constructed on time.'

'Mr Kumar, what could we have done? We had advised you to take the MAF into confidence. They refused your protection money, so, you got their leader arrested.'

'I had nothing to do with his arrest,' Rohit interrupted.

Ganesh Rai let out a chuckle. 'Do you think I'm a fool? Soumit foolishly used his own cell phone to carry out his sneaky act. Do not think I am unaware of all the details. Our government has helped you in all the ways it could. We gave you the land at half the market price and even deputed Ajay Mishra to look after all administrative problems. But this is a problem *you* have created and must deal with.'

'I know there have been some mistakes. If my motive were to harm Gireesh, I would have asked my men to kill him. I wanted him to get arrested and make it seem like an unfortunate incident. So, instead of directly tipping the police I asked Soumit to get in touch with the manager and plant the seed of suspicion. I was hoping to end this MAF menace once and for all and save my hard-earned money. But my plan misfired. It is a shame that Soumit's carelessness alerted the police. Anyway, he has been paid for his mistake.'

'Try explaining your point to the MAF,' replied Ganesh sarcastically.

'I know this is futile and that is why I have come to you. The MAF has been declared a terrorist organisation and the Central Government has even raised a special commando force to fight them. Why don't you just order them to finish off these terrorists?'

'Are you crazy? The Lok Sabha elections are almost here. Despite what you and I may think, the MAF enjoys significant support among the masses and any severe acts of violence against them would show us in a bad light. As it is, the Opposition Party is ready to rake up such issues and use them against us. For the government to take any stringent step against the MAF, you need to wait until the elections are over and we have won.'

'But sir, the elections are almost a year away. I cannot leave my engineers to die until then. You have to find a solution. Please.'

'Well, there is one antidote to the MAF menace. But, in order to make use of that, you will have to grant me some privileges,' said Ganesh Rai, scratching his beard.

'What?'

'As you may already know, I have a company named SPCCL. Make it a partner in your venture and I will ensure that your interests are safeguarded. You will not have to depend solely on the government. I want you to provide all the manpower contracts to our company and a stake of 20 per cent in your profits,' Ganesh said.

'What?' Rohit blurted out. 'But SPCCL is a petty contractor company. How can I make it a partner in such a big venture? This is my first project in India and I don't want to sully my image. This MAF issue has already given our company a bad name. Our stock values are going down,' he replied.

Seeing Ganesh Rai's face turn red at this insult, Ajay Mishra quickly intervened. 'Mr Kumar, you will only be able to maintain your image when you complete this project. Apart from the funds you have provided the Party, you also had a deal with certain Chinese officials to help fund the MAF and other such groups. You are going to have a hard time convincing them that you were not involved in what has happened. If I am not mistaken, what the hell, I know I am not. Is that not where much of your raw material for this first project in India is coming from? That too at marginal rates? You have put too much at stake to risk any further trouble here. I do not think you have any option but to accept what Mr Ganesh Rai is offering you.'

'I have pleaded with my Chinese points of contact that the entire company should not be put in jeopardy because of Soumit's mistake and they have reluctantly agreed to believe us. But they have made it clear that we are to deal with the MAF ourselves. But Mr Rai, how can you assure me that you are equipped to handle them?'

'I am sure you have heard of the RakhtBeej Sena.' Ganesh Rai was gloating with pride. 'We have been fighting the MAF for years. We had a truce last year because of the Razia Regiment and the damage that was being caused to both groups. But for the kind of money you pay us, I am sure we can rake up old quarrels and at least guarantee that the MAF does no harm to your plant. Moreover, the money I get from you will further strengthen the Sena to fight the MAF. One other thing I can guarantee you, Mr Kumar, is that our police or even the Razia Regiment cannot guarantee your safety. The MAF are too intelligent to decode government plans and motives.

Rohit thought for a moment and said, 'Okay. I agree to your proposal.'

He dialled Rajiv Kumar's number.

'Rajiv, prepare to give all our manpower contracts to SPCCL.'

'What? SPCCL? But they are notorious for poor quality work and delaying projects.'

'Do what I say. I am sitting next to Ganesh Rai right now. It is in the best interests of the plant.'

'But, sir.'

'Who is the boss?' yelled Rohit.

'All right, sir.'

Rohit turned to look at Ganesh. 'Sir, I have kept my end of the bargain. Please keep yours. I will get the papers soon.'

'Thanks a lot, Mr Kumar,' said Ganesh Rai, shaking Rohit's hand. 'Now go and have a good night's sleep. I will see to the rest.'

Rohit thanked his new friends and left the room.

'The MAF has unintentionally provided us a good opportunity, sir,' said Ajay Mishra. 'I am going back to Bhagatpur this evening. The High Court has ruled in our favour and our land acquisition is complete. We will start the construction of the area's boundary wall from tomorrow. Once that is completed, all our problems will end. Please do remember me in all this, sir.'

'How can I forget? It was me who got you posted here. You will get your share. You have to do one more thing. The RBS commander, Munna Yadav, is in jail. Get him released.'

'Sure. It will be done.'

~

One of the criminals from the Bhagatpur district jail was being taken to the court along with two policemen. On the way, they stopped at a roadside dhaba for tea. The policemen alighted from the van they were in and moved towards the restaurant, leaving behind the criminal handcuffed on the back seat. As they went away, the man noticed a key on the seat. He smiled, took the key and put it into the lock of the handcuff and turned it. It clicked and the handcuff opened. He silently got out of the vehicle and moved towards the town.

'Escort one to headquarters—Munna Yadav has deceived us and fled from the police van. He was moving towards town. Put all police forces on alert.'

A call was made from the SP's office to Ajay Mishra. 'Sir, your work is done.'

14

20 January 2013, 10 A.M.

At the Parliament Street police station, Gautam was sitting in his chamber, lost in thoughts. A knock on the door broke into his reverie.

'Come in,' he said.

Mohan Singh entered the room.

'Yes, Mohan, what is the news?'

'There was an attack on Silent Turtle in Bhagatpur. The MAF has killed six engineers.'

'What? But they were providing money to the MAF. Why would they be attacked?'

'I don't know, sir. But it seems quite clear that they were responsible for the attack; they left pamphlets with their slogans and criticisms of the government at the site. That is what they usually do.'

'All this just does not add up. Have you got any more leads?'

'Sir, we put Sulochna and Rohit under surveillance and found something interesting.'

'What?'

'Sulochna is in touch with Wei Yan, the Chinese military attaché in the Chinese embassy in Delhi. This is the same person who is regularly seen with Rohit and reports say it was he who was instrumental in getting contracts for Rohit in China. In China, Silent Turtle has got contracts to manufacture weapons for Chinese troops. The hotel manager identified the person in the photo as Wei Yan, one of the foreigners who had visited Gireesh.'

'What else?' Gautam asked as Mohan opened a brown envelope he was carrying.

'We also probed into some of Rohit's men, one of whose photographs is here.'

'George? He was at Rohit's office when I visited him. What about him?'

'I was examining the history of Rohit. He seemed to be too close to his bodyguard George. When I tried to know more about George, I discovered that he was a member of an arms supplier network in Malaysia before he started working for Rohit. Ten years back Rohit was an average engineering graduate who landed a job at Malaysian Power Tech, a multinational company, thanks to his father who was a high ranking army officer. This company, headed by Subramanyam Swamy, an NRI, was in power plant consultancy business. Based in Malaysia the company had acquired a consultancy contract in Bangalore. Rohit fell in love with Swamy's daughter Sunanda who headed the Bangalore branch. After his father's death, Rohit and Sunanda tied the knot and moved to Malaysia. Unfortunately, the marriage did not last long. Within a year, Sunanda filed for divorce. According to unconfirmed reports, this was the time when Rohit came in touch with George. Call it a coincidence or conspiracy, Swamy and Sunanda died in a car accident. Rohit became the owner of the company. He changed the name to Silent Turtle. There is no doubt that he worked hard towards the growth of the company and moved it to an enviable stature. George has stayed with Rohit ever since.'

'Is George still in the arms-handling business?'

'No, he left the syndicate and works as Rohit's bodyguard. But our informers say he is the one who does the dirty job for Rohit. Guhar is one of George's old contacts and it was through him that Guhar came in contact with Rohit. Rohit knew Guhar is the chief arms supplier to the MAF; and so he influenced Guhar to ask Gireesh to finalise the deal in person. Perhaps, Guhar could not guess Rohit's motive.'

'Why did you not detain George?'

'He left the country before we could. All our attempts to access their Malaysian bank accounts have failed. Our informers tipped us off about a buzz in the arms market regarding Rs 10 crore arms deal for INSAS and AK-47 rifles.'

'Rs 10 crore for ammunition! If the MAF was planning to buy it all then it means they will be receiving ammunition worth Rs 9 crore for their armoury since we have recovered 1 crore. See if our informers can unearth the channel.'

'Guhar belongs to an international arms syndicate which we are not able to penetrate.'

'And this woman, Sulochna?'

'We have nothing against her yet. She started a group of intellectuals—Left-leaning writers, film personalities, etc. who rally for the Maoist cause. If we detain her without proof it is certain there will be a backlash.'

'Any update in the Soumit murder case?'

'The forensic team could not find any recording of the CCTV footage in the DVR. But they did find one interesting thing—a CD was recorded in that DVR around the time of Soumit's death!' They could find some system files which indicated the same but unfortunately could not recover the data which was recorded.

'CD recording? That could have been done by someone who knew about the murder. The killers would have destroyed the DVR. So whoever the killers are, whether it's Rohit or someone else, they did not know about the CCTV. But, the CCTV footage was recorded and a CD was made. It was definitely not done to help the police crack the case but to blackmail.'

'Blackmail?'

'Yes. The maid. Where is the maid? Interrogate her again. She is the only one who knew there was a CCTV in the house.'

'I thought she was clean. She has left for Bihar!'

'I will ask Aslam to carry on this line of investigation. You and I have other important things to take care of.'

'You mean about the MAF?

'Yes. Now things are adding up. Rohit pledged the money to the MAF through Sulochna and the MAF accepted it not because they wished to allow Rohit to build the plant but because this deal was mediated by Chinese groups. I remember the IB report DCP sir had shared with me the other day that contained details about how the Chinese were supplying ammunition to groups like the MAF. Rohit used Guhar to pressurise Gireesh to come here himself and then

Rohit asked Soumit to alert the manager. We got his trail and Rohit, or maybe the MAF, killed him. The MAF came to know about this and attacked the Silent Turtle engineers to take revenge on Rohit.'

'What do we do now, sir?'

'We cannot lay hands on Wei Yan because of diplomatic immunity. We can't arrest Rohit or Sulochna because we do not have proof. But since all this is connected to Bhagatpur, we will proceed to ground zero and investigate. We are going as journalists.'

'Journalists?'

'Yes. Our front will be a newspaper agency, *Janshakti*, whose proprietor is a friend of Subhash Joshi. Start packing your bags. We leave next week.'

'I'm sure we will have a blast, sir.'

'Sure, but not literally, I hope.'

15

29 January 2013, 10 A.M.

Back in Bhagatpur, the boundary wall of the power plant was constructed in a record time of five days. The site was placed under police protection and private security was stationed. However, the MAF had planned another demolition attempt for the second day after its completion. As night approached, the MAF troops arrived in hordes on two boats which helped them cross the river near the village. They moved stealthily towards the gate of the boundary wall, each carrying an automatic rifle.

Two guards positioned at a short distance from the gate noticed some movement and one of them shouted in the dark, 'Whoever that is, stop or I will shoot.'

The movement continued.

'I said stop or I will shoot,' warned the guard again.

No sooner had he finished speaking than suddenly there was a burst of firing and both guards fell down. The guards stationed inside the site took their positions immediately and fired in the direction of the bullets. One of the MAF men threw a bomb at the gate and it was blown to bits, killing more guards and forcing others to back away.

The woman leading the attack now entered the BMTPP site, waving an AK-47 rifle in the air. Her face was masked, leaving only her eyes and nose visible. 'Who is in charge here? Show your face and I promise you, you will be spared. I will not repeat myself,' she said.

With many of their men already killed, the police as well as the private security chief decided it was best they do what was being asked of them. They stepped forward.

'Do you know who I am?'

'You are from the MAF...?' the police chief asked hesitantly.

'Yes. The MAF will always oppose those who make our people suffer. Do you even know who you are protecting? Your bosses think they will drive our people away from their land and we will helplessly stand by and watch. Not anymore.' She pointed her gun towards him.

'Let us go, please. We are only doing our duty.'

'Your duty? You do not even realise it but you are serving the very people who exploit you. But let that be. We are leaving you alive because unlike you we do not believe in unnecessary bloodshed. Now, you can go tell your *masters* that we have struck again and will do whatever it takes to stop the construction of this plant. If they refuse to listen to us, we will destroy whoever gets in our way. Now, tuck your tails between your legs and go hide.'

The terrified men followed her instructions meekly and the woman turned back to go her own way. As she reached the spot where the gate had been before it was blown to smithereens, there was the sound of a gunshot and she fell on her right side. A host of gunshots followed immediately after.

'Commander, are you okay?' asked one of her men, taking cover along with his comrades.

'Yes,' she replied as she fired back blindly with others joining in. A cloud of dust engulfed the whole area.

'Samir, who was that?' she asked the masked man fighting next to her.

'I have no idea. Look.'

Before them, amidst the reckless back-and-forth firing, could be seen 50 men arranging themselves strategically to get a better shot.

'Isn't that Munna Yadav? Why is he breaking our deal and fighting against us?' asked Samir.

'It is Munna Yadav. I heard he escaped from jail a few days ago. We will take care of him later. But for now, we have been outnumbered and must get out of here as soon as possible.'

Signalling to the rest of the group, the MAF members made a quick exit towards the river bank, where they boarded the boats on which they had arrived and sailed back to the other side of the river.

~

The next day, Nisha was reading the front page of the local newspaper which had news of the attack. Saroj sat beside her.

'Did you read this, Saroj? There is only speculation of it here, but my sources in the police tell me that it was indeed the RBS who drove the MAF away from the site after the blast. The district administration dismissed this claim and had the audacity to say that villagers in favour of the plant's construction did the needful. Can you imagine?'

'Yes, madam. There was talk in the village that Munna Yadav escaped from jail. But he and the RBS had signed a pact with the MAF to steer clear of each other's paths and till yesterday both parties were adhering to it. Why this sudden attack?'

'These businessmen, Saroj, can go to all extremes when it comes to earning profits. Apparently, the owner of Silent Turtle, Rohit Kumar, approached Ganesh Rai to ask for protection after the MAF had blasted the plant site. He wants no interruption whatsoever in its construction and struck a deal with Ganesh Rai's company, SPCCL, to give them all the labour contracts for this project along with a 20 per cent stake in the company itself. That is why the RBS chief, Munna Yadav, had escaped, or rather, was allowed to escape, from jail a few days ago.'

'Oh, so that is what this is all about. You really do have a lot of inside information.'

'And inside information it must remain, Saroj. I know you will not break my trust.'

'I will not, ma'am. You have devoted your life to the betterment of our village. It is our duty to stand by you in this cause. Do not worry. Have faith in me.'

'Thank you. But, you must warn the others in your own way that such violent conflicts are only going to be on the rise now and they must be careful. In fact, I think I have a solution to put a stop to this possible bloodshed, at least to some degree.'

'What solution?' Saroj asked.

'I have noted for a long time that the SPCCL openly flouts the pollution level norms set by the Supreme Court for industries in this area, especially given the fact that it falls under the fragile ecological zone. If this can be exposed, Ganesh Rai's business will suffer a big setback and dry his main source of the RBS's income. I've been thinking of filing a PIL in this matter.'

'But can a mere PIL take someone as powerful as Ganesh Rai to task?'

'Much bigger companies have been taken to task this way. Compared to them, Ganesh Rai is small fry. He will obviously try to find a way to wriggle out of the situation, but, that does not mean we should not give it a try. I have no doubt that Ganesh Rai's men will hound us like dogs the moment this news reaches him and we must be prepared for that as well.'

'Your courage is really admirable.'

'Standing up for one's principles always involves a cost, Saroj, and one must be willing to pay it.'

'Very true. I will go and ask our advocate to meet you and file this PIL immediately.'

Saroj was moving out of the room when Nisha noticed she was limping.

'Did you hurt yourself, Saroj?'

'Oh it was just a minor accident, ma'am. I will be all right soon.'

'It does not seem very minor to me. Do go and see a good doctor.'

'Sure. Thank you.'

16

5 February 2013, 10 A.M.

A few days later at his palatial bungalow in the heart of Bhagatpur, Ganesh Rai was enjoying a full body massage when he was interrupted by a lathi-wielding attendant.

'Sorry to disturb you, sir, but Shukla*ji* wants to meet you. He says it is very important.'

'What does that greedy lawyer want now? Send him in.'

Shukla *ji* walked inside holding a file, looking tense.

'What is the matter, Shukla*ji*? Why do you seem so worried?'

Without saying a word, the lawyer put the file before Ganesh Rai.

'What is this?' he asked, irritably.

'A court notice. A PIL has been filed against SPCCL, alleging that we carry out our operations in violation of the Supreme Court pollution norms. The court has asked us to explain.'

'What? Who dares to file a report against me?'

'It is a woman from an NGO. Nisha Kushwaha.'

'That Master*ni*! I should have known. We have had many problems with her in the past,' he said. 'I cannot allow this to happen. If the work gets interrupted, I will lose Silent Turtle's contracts and my 20 per cent share. I must make this woman regret what she has done.'

A few years ago, there had been a similar situation.

'Sir, Sunil Kushwaha has filed a case against you. The SHO (Station House Officer) said that you might get arrested,' one of Ganesh's attendants informed him.

'Tomorrow he is going to inaugurate the BR Ambedkar statue and that will be the last thing he does. The MAF had threatened him a few days ago. Make it look like they have done it.'

'She will also meet her father's fate,' Ganesh muttered to himself.

That evening, while Nisha was in her office, Saroj pushed the door open and ran to her side.

'Ma'am, come quickly, Ganesh Rai's men are trying to destroy the ground floor.'

Nisha got up immediately but was greeted by a six-foot-tall muscular man standing at the door. He was one of many.

'Who is Nisha Kushwaha?' the leader of the goons shouted.

'I am.' Nisha came forward.

'How dare you file a case against Ganesh Rai?' he growled.

'Because he is not following the law and is causing harm to the country and its people. Why is he so worried about it, if he is innocent, there will be no evidence against him,' replied Nisha.

'Oh, really! Come on in, boys.' At their boss' orders, the other goons began ransacking the room, breaking window panes, upturning furniture and throwing files and papers around. Nisha and Saroj could just stand by and watch. The leader spoke again, 'Listen, madam,' he threatened her, looking straight into her eyes. 'This is the first and last time we are warning you. Withdraw your case or we will kill you in the middle of the village and no law will be able to do anything about it.'

He walked out with his men.

17

6 February 2013, 8 A.M.

As their car moved up the slope near Vikramgarh Fort where the Bhagatpur police station was located, it slowed down. Saroj put the vehicle in second gear and began the ascent.

'Ma'am, I still think we should go to the MAF. The police will not be able to do anything.'

'Don't start that again. My mind is extremely agitated. Two negatives may make a positive in mathematics but the same is not true in real life.'

The police station before them was a ramshackle hut and even lacked a concrete boundary wall. The official timings to meet SHO Kanahiya Paswan, posted at the gate of the station, gave the impression that he was a busy man. Nisha had been to the place quite often and her popularity as the village teacher with a heart of gold was not lost even on the constables inside, who greeted her warmly. She reciprocated with equal gratitude and went to the SHO's chamber.

'Master*niji*! How are you? What brings you here?'

Nisha informed him how Ganesh Rai's men had vandalised her office and threatened her. 'Will you be able to identify them?'

'Of course. But the trouble is, sir, these RBS men usually remain underground and can only be seen when they emerge to wreak havoc somewhere.'

Before the SHO could respond, his phone rang. The voice on the other end had shocking news. 'Sir, we are calling from Panchayat Bhavan. There is a corpse hanging from the Banyan tree in front of the office.'

'I will be there right away. Ms Nisha, there has been a murder in the village. We must go there at once. If you do not mind, please come with me.'

The police reached Panchayat Bhavan within 20 minutes. The corpse had an SPCCL gate pass pinned to his pocket with the area manager's number on it. Kanahiya Paswan dialled the number in the hope that he could find a clue but the manager denied any connection with the deceased.'Oh! This is one of the men who wrecked my office! But why has he been killed?' Nisha exclaimed.

The SHO gave Nisha a strange look. 'This is usually how the MAF kills its targets, ma'am. And this was a man of the RBS, you say...'

'What are you trying to insinuate? The same old charge that I have links with the MAF and am behind the killing of this man? If that was so, why would I come to you at all to lodge a complaint on the *same* day the killing took place? Please think before you speak,' said Nisha, bursting with anger.

'I did not mean it that way,' said the SHO. 'But it is evident that the MAF-RBS war has resumed.'

18

14 February 2013, 10 A.M.

It was no surprise that the RBS retaliated to the killing of one of their men with equal brutality. In the week that followed, three innocent villagers were shot to death after a rumour that they were allegedly MAF informers. This brought the situation in Bhagatpur under further scrutiny. Starting from Gireesh Marandi's arrest to the blast at the site of the State Government's pet project and the murder of the Silent Turtle general manager, public interest in the area had gone up by many notches and this was reason enough for a constant stream of print and television media to frequent the area.

Back in Delhi, Prabhat Advani was deeply disturbed with constant questions being raised about the recent lapses in security in Bihar. He arranged for a meeting with Nilesh Yadav to discuss the steps needed to improve the situation. The power ministry had strongly condemned the situation and was of the opinion that the Bhagatpur plant be shifted to another place, Uttar Pradesh being the most sought after alternative.

It was a mark of his arrogance that Chief Minister Nilesh Yadav arrived half-an-hour late on the day of the meeting. He had been around the political scene for more than a decade and in the last Lok Sabha elections, the support of his Party, Bihar Yuva Party (BYP), to the main Ruling Party at the centre, the Indian National Party (INP), had been won after much cajoling. It was an open secret in political circles that both Nilesh and Prabhat were good friends and their parties were the main partners in the United National Alliance (UNA) at the centre. However, the INP, the biggest Party in the coalition, nominated Prabhat for the post of the next prime minister, overlooking the claims of Nilesh Yadav. This created a conflict between them. Last year, Prabhat got embroiled in the CWG scam and that further gave Nilesh enough ammunition to target him.

Nonetheless, the popularity of Nilesh Yadav had also dipped considerably over the past few years and he had been banking on the power plant to move it up a few notches. His dream was in danger, although, he could not reveal it openly before the home minister.

'Nilesh Babu, have you been looking at the newspaper reports?' asked the home minister, waving one of them in his face. It said—

> Bhagatpur slips down to the bottom of lawlessness. The PIL against SPCCL, which is run by one of the chief minister's closest aides, has led to a disastrous effect on the company. All its mining units have been sealed and the High Court has issued a non-bailable warrant against SPCCL owner, Ganesh Rai. But, he has managed to dodge the police stating health reasons.

> Nisha Kushwaha of Nai Soch-Nai Subah (NS2), the NGO that filed the PIL, has claimed that she received almost 40 warning calls demanding her not to testify against Rai.
>
> Meanwhile, there have been regular murders being carried out by the RBS and the MAF. In the last two weeks, the MAF has murdered five of Ganesh Rai's Party workers, since the MLA is supposed to be the secret head of their enemy organisation. In return, the RBS has massacred 10 villagers suspect of being MAF supporters.

The home minister stopped reading.

'Oh, all this is just biased reporting by a newspaper against our Party. I assure you that the situation is not as bad as they have made it sound,' said Nilesh.

The home minister responded politely but firmly, 'The newspapers are not our only sources of information. Many of our trusted Party workers stay in Bhagatpur and what they have told me is no different from these newspaper reports. Without getting into a blame game, I want to put a stop to all that is happening there. Listen, we both recognise the importance of the Bhagatpur power plant for reasons of our own. This project is earmarked for the current five-year-plan but the way the MAF and your...I'm sorry, the RBS are fighting, there are doubts being raised about the plant coming up at all. We already have other states waiting in line to grab the opportunity of constructing this power plant.'

'Your points are valid, Prabhat*ji*. But whoever your sources may be, I vehemently deny that the RBS is back in action. All the violence in that area is the MAF's doing.'

'If they are such a cause for concern and you cannot seem to cope with them, why do you not allow the RR to take action?'

'I cannot allow the kind of direct assault you had created the RR for. I am sorry but the MAF comprises, after all, members of our own society, and this is not the way to deal with them. It is an unfair system that has led them to take up arms and we must be sensitive to the concerns they have raised even though we do not approve of their means. They are not terrorists,' said the hypocritical chief minister, backtracking. He had just proudly regurgitated scraps of one of his previous election speeches, carefully camouflaging the fact that although he hated the MAF, he did not want to get his hands dirty.

'Oh! Now the MAF have become members of our society, even though just a few years ago you were attempting to finish them off using the People's Resistance Movement.'

'That was a mistake. We are paying for it. Your favourite officer, Kavita, was also a party to that.'

'Kavita used to be your favourite officer also. That is all very well, Nilesh Babu. But you won't take any action yourself and neither will you allow the RR to do so. Then, how do you propose to end the problems that the plant is facing?'

'I have thought of something already. A strategically arranged security cordon will surround the site. I also assure you that such things will not take place henceforth.'

'I doubt whether this is going to work. The High Court has ordered Ganesh Rai's arrest for not complying by its directives; the least you can do is ensure that the police take its duty seriously and put him behind bars. The news is out in the national media and the public is laughing at Bihar's mockery of a law-and-order system. And one more thing. You had better make sure Nisha Kushwaha is not bullied anymore. She is a Magsaysay Award winner for God's sake, and a lot of intellectuals and social workers from across the country have come out in her defence. If any harm is done to her, it will erode the respectability of your government immeasurably.'

'I will do my best to see that justice is delivered,' replied the chief minister.

'I hope so.' The home minister shook hands with him, signalling an end to the meeting.

A few minutes after he had left the room, the CM dialled Ganesh Rai's number.

'*Ji Bhaiji,*' said Ganesh Rai as he picked up.

'You fool, your shenanigans have landed us in the soup. Surrender before it gets out of hand.'

'But *Bhaiji*, the elections are coming. I need to be outside to prepare for them.'

'Don't give me that. You know very well how things can be taken care of. That district jailor is a devotee of mine. You will be in jail only in name. Do as I say.'

'Okay *Bhaiji*, as you say. But something will have to be done about this Nisha.'

'Wait for the right time,' said the CM.

Back in his chamber, Prabhat was deliberating with his PA, Shankar Jha.

'Sir, do you think arresting Ganesh Rai and Gireesh Marandi will solve our problems?' asked Shankar.

'Ganesh Rai is very influential in that area. Putting him behind bars will not solve any purpose; he will run his parallel government from inside. The MAF will also try something big to get Gireesh released. But until the election, I don't want to involve myself in that matter because any misstep will be amplified by his Party. If I press him more by involving the CBI or any other agency, he will be viewed as a martyr. Let the court act in its discretion and we will just wait and watch.'

'Sir, shall we shift the power plant to UP?'

'No, I want Bihar to have it. It will be good for the state. I was also thinking…'

'What, sir?'

'In the upcoming election, we do not really have a strong candidate to challenge the Ruling Party in that area. What if we were to ask Nisha Kushwaha to stand for elections on our behalf? She alone has had the guts to challenge Ganesh Rai and I have heard she is very popular there. Get in touch with her to see if she will contest on our behalf.'

'Good idea, sir. I will do that. But talking about the elections, sir, do you think they will have to be held before schedule?'

'Difficult to predict. The way the regional Parties, including Nilesh's, are fighting for their pound of flesh, the government can fall if any maverick Party withdraws their support. And you know how Nilesh is not missing any opportunity to malign my image. Whenever the elections are held, we shall be prepared. Bhagatpur can be the right way to earn brownie points in Bihar where we are practically finished.'

'Okay, sir.'

19

15 February 2013, 7 P.M.

One night in the Bhagatpur forest, while Charulata was overseeing the practice of her cadres and talking to Samir, one of her men approached her. His body language indicated good news.

'Commander, we have received a coded message on our transmitter,' he said, handing her a piece of paper.

'Butterfly has landed in Mumbai, will fly to Delhi tomorrow.' These words brought a smile to her lips.

'Commander, I also have other news.'

'What?'

'Ganesh Rai has surrendered and is in the district jail. A Special Task Force has been formed to guard him at all times.'

'That means he has got police protection. The jail warden is the protégé of the CM and will do anything to please his master. We will deal with him later,' she said, turning to continue her conversation with Samir.

'Samir, what are your men doing? This is not the correct way to fire weapons that do not recoil. Ask them to hold it lightly,' she chided him.

'Commander, these have been made with the latest technology. It will take time to adjust. Don't worry, they will be experts in a few days. When are we receiving the ammunition?' he asked.

'It has landed in Mumbai. Carry on with what you are doing. I am going to my room.'

~

'Nisha!' Sunil opened his eyes slowly and murmured with great difficulty.

'Don't talk, Papa. Lie still. You are injured.'

'Beta, I am not a good father. I have always been away from home and you, thanks to my police duty and of course, NS2.'

'No, Papa. You are the best father in the world. Nothing will happen to you.'

'Will you promise me something?'

'Yes, Papa.'

'Promise me you will always fight for the truth. You will always fight for our people.'

'I will.'

'Narendra, after me, you are Nisha's father,' he said, looking towards his brother Narendra, who stood nearby.

'I will, Sunil. You will be okay.'

Sunil's eyes closed and his grip on Nisha's hand loosened.

'Papa, Papa, speak to me.'

The doctors attending to him took his pulse and shook their heads. They looked at Nisha and murmured, 'Sorry.'

'Papa!'

Nisha woke up with a start. Memories of past events disturbed her. Someone was knocking at her door. She opened the door to find Saroj standing there.

'What happened, madam? Why are you perspiring? Everything all right?'

'Yes! Why have you come so early?'

'Swami*ji* has come. He told me you had called him.'

'Yes. Ask him to sit. I am coming.'

When Nisha met Swami Narendra Nath and touched his feet, he blessed her with a long life.

'You seem to be worried, my child?' he asked.

'You are the only one I can trust when I am troubled.'

'What is bothering you?'

'Yesterday when I was taking a class, Home Minister Prabhat Advani called and offered me a chance to fight the election from his Party. He said he needs a young, dynamic face to lead from here.'

'That is good. You will get more opportunities to work for the betterment of the people.'

'But, I have never thought about contesting elections. Besides, who will look after the NS2?'

'Your friend Saroj is there. I can also help her.'

'But, Mr Prabhat is embroiled in the CWG scam. My soul is troubled in aligning with him.'

'Nisha, you are fighting a greater evil here. For this, you need strength, money and organisation. The INP can provide you all these. Besides, I know Prabhat*ji*. You can trust him, even though his rivals are accusing him of various things. The BYP and their leader Nilesh are his foes. Give him a chance.'

'But the way the agitations against corruption are going on in the country, will it be politically and morally correct to be a candidate of a Party whose boss is embroiled in corruption cases even if not proven?'

'The INP knows that very well. That's why they are offering you a seat. You have a good image while they have resources. Both will make a potent combination against Ganesh Rai.'

'What about the MAF? It is against the elections.'

'I know you do not fear anyone. The MAF will not touch you.'

'They killed Papa.'

'Well, they'll never admit it. Even the police are not able to prove who killed Sunil.'

'Thank you for coming here and talking to me. Will you have lunch here?'

'I have a camp in Jehenabad. I will have to leave. Maybe, some other day. Saroj, can you get me on the bus to Jehenabad?'

'Yes Swami*ji*,' Saroj said.

'God bless you.'

As he left, Nisha made up her mind—she had to begin a new battle in the political field.

20

16 February 2013, 6 P.M.

Gautam was in his bedroom flipping channels when a news report caught his attention. A segment on Bhagatpur was on air.

'Every time the electricity goes off and you are left to toil in the wretched heat, you blame the lopsided government approach towards constructing power plants. You are awed by the exuberance with which the Chinese government executes projects three times the size of this one. But you forget to look at the darker side of the picture. There are scores of people who are forcibly evacuated from their land once it is identified as the probable site of a power plant. You may say this is the 'cost of development' but have you ever wondered how it would feel if you were the victim? It is only the poor who are at the receiving end. Today, we will take you to a place like this, where others are paying the price so that you can watch television and live in your air-conditioned world—Bhagatpur, a quiet and remote place in the underdeveloped society of Bihar. Stay tuned and we will take you into the close quarters shortly.'

Gautam lit a cigarette and waited.

'Welcome back to our story of the week. Our team went to Bhagatpur to unearth the real story behind the upcoming power plant in that area. Here is a report.'

The camera zoomed to dozens of famished faces looking on in despair.

'This is Bhagatpur. It is only 120 km from Patna but the actual difference between here and any other place is almost 200 years. There is not a single metalled road, no schools and no potable drinking water. No primary schools function in this place and the only secondary school has been converted into the special magistrate's office. The only school here is run by the NGO, Nai Soch-Nai Subah.

'This area has now shot to prominence because of the government's decision to construct a power plant to provide electricity to the state. The irony is that Bhagatpur has electricity supply only in name. This project is the first of its kind in India and is being constructed by Silent Turtle, a Malaysia-based MNC headed by Rohit Kumar.

'It should have been a matter of pride for the country but unfortunately, Bhagatpur's inhabitants are paying a heavy price for this development.'

The television then flashed images of police mercilessly beating people and evicting them from their homes and bulldozers demolishing huts. The cameras then zoomed to a woman being taken by some policemen to a waiting van.

'Nisha,' Gautam jumped up from where he sat.

'The person you just saw being arrested is Nisha Kushwaha, the chief of Nai Soch-Nai Subah, who is crusading against the State Government for the distribution of inadequate compensation. Though, the compensation has been declared "just" by the courts, the amount happens to be less than half the market price. This has intensified the tension. Nisha was later released on bail. We have an interview with her for the second half of the show.'

Next, the screen showed a security officer whose face had been blurred to conceal his identity.

'Can you tell us what happened two days ago?' asked the reporter.

'We were guarding the place when there was an attack by the MAF. Our sentry at the entrance was killed. The MAF men entered the site and warned us to leave the place.'

'Who was the leader of the group?'

'She was masked but we presume she was Charulata.'

'Who is Charulata?'

'She is like a ghost who can appear anywhere and do anything.'

'What happened next?'

'We saw some villagers attack them and force them to retreat.'

'Why you are still guarding the area?'

'We are doing our duty.'

The anchor turned to face the camera. 'You may be wondering how the villagers can challenge the might of the MAF, with whom even the government doesn't dare to fight. But, as per our investigation, it was not the villagers but the RakhtBeej Sena, the private militia of Ganesh Rai, who retaliated. Rai's firm, SPCCL, was awarded the labour contract for the plant and he denies the allegations. The RBS and the MAF were fighting against each other last year before a truce was declared, but, it seems Rai has ended the truce and taken the MAF head-on. The latter also has to fight one more enemy here, the Razia Regiment. The all-women commando battalion had been established to fight the MAF but the volatile political conditions of the area have been an impediment. The RR works under the commands of the Central Home Ministry while the law and order of the state comes under the State Home Ministry. The chief minister, who also acts as the Bihar home minister, is one of the most vocal critics of the union home minister. This political rivalry has tied the hands of RR. But the RR chief, Kavita Sethi, has declared that she will finish the MAF one day.

'All attempts to contact Charulata were in vain. However, we did visit the Beaur jail in Patna, where MAF leader Gireesh Marandi is in custody.'

The scene shifted to the jailor's chamber, where a man with stooping shoulders and dishevelled hair was facing the camera.

'When you first thought of forming the MAF, what did you hope to achieve?' asked the reporter.

'Revolution, revolution.'

'What does revolution mean?'

'A total revamp of Indian society and political structure.'

'Don't you believe in democracy?'

'We believe in democracy but in real democracy, not in the fraudulent way it is practised by corrupt politicians. I believe in giving power to the people.'

'Why the armed revolution?'

'The government listens only when we become rebels. Otherwise, they discard us.'

'One last question. Who is Charulata?'

He laughed upon hearing this.

'She is the other part of me, the real leader of the MAF. Ask the people of Bhagatpur; she is the panacea for all the evil.'

He flashed a V-sign for the camera while being led away to his cell.

'That was the MAF leader speaking to us. It looks like Bhagatpur is on the way to becoming another Naxalbari. Only time will tell how much blood the river Bhagat will carry this monsoon. With cameraman Rakesh Jha, this is Rituparna Ghosh for News 365.'

Back at the studio, the newsreader addressed the camera—'Don't go away. We will return shortly with our reporter speaking to Nisha Kushwaha.'

The channel's jingle signalled the next part of the show.

'Welcome back viewers, we have with us Nisha Kushwaha, the leader of Nai Soch-Nai Subah, the NGO that has been striving to educate the people of Bhagatpur.' The camera panned out to show Rituparna standing next to a young lady.

'Nisha, why are you so wary of the media? You have been working in the public domain for so many years, but, this is your first TV interview?'

'I am not shy. I suppose the kind of work I do doesn't attract much interest,' replied Nisha, smiling.

'Do tell the viewers a bit about yourself.'

'I belong to Bhagatpur, but, have lived mostly in Delhi. My father was in the CBI and was frequently transferred to other cities. I lived in Delhi with my grandmother. After her death, which was when I joined college, my father resigned from his job and went back to Bhagatpur to start the NS2.'

'He was in a government job, so why did he resign?'

'I don't know. He had never told me anything. On much prodding, he declared social work was his dream. Perhaps, he was inspired by his elder brother Narendra Nath, who is also doing similar work in that area.'

'How did you get involved there?'

'I was pursuing my graduation course in geography from St. Stephen's college. When my father died, I became determined to carry on his work and address the many problems facing our society. I chose to begin with Bhagatpur.'

'How did your father die?'

'He was killed,' replied Nisha, her eyes moistening.

'He was killed in Bhagatpur. Why are you working for the same people?'

'They killed my father, not his ideology or spirit. I am working to preserve his ideals.'

'Tell us something about your NGO.'

'My father established NS2 as a prominent NGO, working for the improvement of education in Bhagatpur and nearby areas. His mission was to educate the people of Bhagatpur, especially women. After his death, I started a night school for the villagers. The villagers were initially resistant but slowly they understood its importance. My next step was to form a Self-Help Group (SHG) for government schemes. Now, we run the school in two sittings—morning classes for young students and evening classes for the older ones. Women form a substantial number of my pupils.'

'Who helps you there?'

'Saroj, my companion, colleague and pupil. I have a dedicated staff of 10 people. The RR commandant Kavita Sethi also helps out sometimes. She was the one to have my work discussed and featured in the government and the media. We get funds from the government as well as donors.'

'There are rumours that you are helped by the MAF.'

'What rubbish? Why would the MAF protect me?'

'But people say the jailed leader, Gireesh, is your childhood friend.'

'Our respective fathers were friends. I have not met Gireesh for the last 20 years.'

'Why is the MAF shutting down all other schools in the area but allowing yours to run?'

'None of the schools they shut were functioning as centres of education. All of them had either been turned into police barracks or government offices. The teachers don't go to them anymore. Why would they risk their lives if they are getting their salary sitting in their homes? The MAF is not attacking the schools but the police outposts functioning in them. Somewhere in their ideology, the MAF is not averse to development in the area. It is just that it does not trust the government and prefers to employ different methods. It is easy to blame the rebels but does the government even consider why this has happened?'

'Is the MAF in favour of all the work you have planned to do?'

'It has never threatened me but it did warn my father when he first wanted to start a school. Perhaps, it thought he was there to spy. After all, he was a police officer before starting the NS2 and very few people believed he had returned to Bhagatpur for a noble cause.'

'Why were you arrested a few days ago?'

'The power plant has displaced a large number of people in and around Bhagatpur. The local administration started constructing the boundary wall around the plant site which would have cut off the villagers from their land. I went there to protest this and they arrested me for interfering in official work.'

'But the High Court has ruled in favour of the government. Legally speaking, they can construct the boundary wall.'

'Yes, but the complete facts were not shared. I have appealed to the Supreme Court against this. This time, we will go fully prepared and I hope we win.'

'Will you fight the court battle yourself?'

'I have studied Law from Jehenabad Law College. Sometimes, I do handle my court cases.'

'What is the next course of action?'

'I will continue agitating in Bhagatpur against administrative actions to construct the power plant. I will not relent till the time the Supreme Court settles the issue of land acquisition and offers adequate compensation. I request those watching this show to help us in whatever way they can. I hope the media will also highlight the plight of the people of Bhagatpur.'

'Thank you for your time.'

The programme concluded.

It's time to move to Bhagatpur and restart Operation India One, resolved Gautam.

Part II
The Mission

21

17 February 2013, 5 P.M.

As the vehicle neared the New Delhi railway station, the driver addressed the occupants—'Sir, kindly pay here. I will not be allowed to wait inside.'

Mohan took out a note of Rs 500 and handed it to the driver. Gautam slid the window of the taxi and signalled to a coolie who came running behind the vehicle. He gestured to unload their luggage, which comprised two big suitcases and one carrybag.

'On which platform will the Patna Rajdhani arrive?' asked Mohan.

'It's already on Platform 14. It will depart in 15 minutes.'

'How much?'

'Two hundred.'

'That's an exorbitant fee for a short distance!'

'Sir, I will have to cross the overbridge. The luggage is very heavy.' He was a persistent bargainer.

'Okay, okay. We do not have much time. Coach A2,' Gautam intervened.

They went past the overcrowded station towards the train. The porter arranged their luggage underneath their seats, which were at the aisle side, collected his money and left.

'Indian Railways welcome you aboard the Rajdhani Express. The distance of 992 km to Patna will be completed in 12.5 hours. This train will stop at Kanpur, Allahabad and Mugalsarai. Tea will be served shortly while dinner will be served at 8 o'clock. Passengers, whose seats have not been confirmed, kindly disembark the train,' the soft voice of the announcer informed the travellers.

Slowly, the train picked up speed, leaving the city landscape and its unfinished residential buildings behind, cutting through the vast fields on both sides of the tracks. Gautam took the window seat and gazed at nothing in particular. Dark cumulonimbus clouds had gathered at the horizon, an ominous sign of heavy rain. The setting sun produced a silver streak bordering the clouds. Graffiti-laden walls zipped by, coloured with advertisements of quacks claiming to cure infertility. He decided to take a break from such aimless observation and glance through the file provided by Subhash Joshi which had details about the MAF, the RBS and the situation in Bhagatpur.

'Sir, may I ask you a personal question?'

'Yes?'

'Do you know Nisha?'

'Why do you ask that?'

'During my research, I found that Nisha studied at St. Stephen's, like you.'

'Yes Mohan. I knew her. We were good friends. But, she left Delhi abruptly and we haven't been in touch since then.'

Soon, dinner was served. The conversation was kept short and both of them retired for the day thereafter.

In the morning, the train stopped at Patna and a stream of coolies invaded their compartment.

'Sir, do you want a coolie?' one of them nudged Mohan out of his sleep.

'Have we reached Patna?' he asked, rubbing his eyes.

'Yes, sir,' replied the coolie.

'Take all this to the taxi stand,' Mohan said.

At the stand, drivers gathered around them like a swarm of bees. 'Where do you want to go, sir? City, Muzzafurpur?'

'Bhagatpur,' Mohan said.

'Bhagatpur?' The taxi drivers exclaimed in unison.

'I think you want to go to Bhagalpur,' one taxi driver tried to correct him.

'No, I said Bhagatpur,' Mohan said.

One of the taxi drivers came forward. 'Who will want to go to Bhagatpur? It is a dangerous place.'

'We are journalists from Delhi and have come here to write about the BMTPP plant,' Gautam said.

'I hope you both have life insurance,' remarked the driver.

'Why?' Gautam asked in bewilderment.

'Because there is little chance that you will return alive.'

Gautam and Mohan looked at each other.

'How much money will you take?' Gautam asked him.

'My fee is Rs 3,000.'

'Three thousand for 120 km?'

'Three thousand is the final price. Do you want to go or not? None of the other taxis will take you.'

'Where is your vehicle? Carry our luggage over there.'

'You can very well bring your luggage yourself. I am a driver, not a porter,' he said, while leading them to the taxi stand.

'What attitude!' said Mohan, as he and Gautam followed the driver. The vehicle had the word *Texi* written on its rear.

22

18 February 2013, 8 A.M.

'Ready to go?' asked the driver.

'Let us go,' Mohan replied and closed the door of the vehicle.

Gautam looked at his watch.

It's 8 a.m. It will take four to five hours from here, he thought.

After leaving Patna, the taxi took the highway towards Gaya. The vehicle got on a bypass road before Gaya and took the road up Parshuram Hills leading to Bhagatpur. The road was full of potholes and crowded with convoys of trucks loaded with construction material. Most of them had SPCCL written on them.

'This is a road connecting to the highway but why is it so bad?' asked Gautam.

'This road was constructed only last year, but, thousands of heavy vehicles ply here every day. Besides, it was constructed by the SPCCL, which doesn't bother with repairs,' the driver replied.

After a while, the driver decided to talk in English. '*Vhaat weelu* do in Bhagatpur, sahib?'

'Do you know English?' Gautam asked, smiling.

'The *only* graduate from the village. I can talk in English,' he replied, proudly.

'You belong to this place?'

'I'm from Dariapur village. I am a tribal and the first from my village to go to the town,' he added, switching back to Hindi.

'What is your name?'

'Raghu.'

'We are here to write about the MAF and the plant and everything that is happening in this area,' said Gautam.

'They are very dangerous, sahib, look at the poster there,' he said, pointing at one of the posters pasted on the walls of a derelict and burnt house which once used to belong to Raghuvansh Rai.

The poster announced—'We strongly condemn the farcical democratic process that takes place in the country in the name of elections. If anyone is found voting, his hands will be chopped off.' It was signed—Charulata.

'Okay. Now drive.'

'Mohan, what are you staring at?' Gautam asked Mohan.

'I am looking at an advertisement near the poster. That soap claims to be in existence for the last 50 years and can be used for both washing clothes and bathing. I have never heard of such a peculiar thing before.'

'You will find many such things here,' Gautam laughed.

The driver was telling the truth. The MAF is dead against the elections. If Nisha decides to contest, she will have to fight them also, Gautam thought.

The driver switched on the music system.

A loud voice startled them; 'Kha le Tiranga' was the refrain blaring out from the speakers. Gautam and Mohan were perplexed at the lyrics. It was explained in a few seconds, when the driver took out *Tiranga,* a brand of *gutka,* and popped the contents into his mouth.

The vehicle stopped after a while.

'Now what is it?' Mohan asked him, annoyed.

'Sir, some MAF men are at the corner. Don't say anything. Let me do all the talking.'

Mohan Singh moved his hands towards his weapon but Gautam restrained him.

'*Johar*, sahib,' he greeted the men near the vehicle.

'Where are you going?'

'Bhagatpur,' the driver replied.

'Who are these people?' asked one of the armoured men.

'They are journalists.'

'ID, please,' one of the men stretched his hand towards Gautam.

Gautam put his hand in his pocket and produced a card. The man studied the ID and returned it.

The driver took out some money from his pocket and handed it to the man.

'Go,' said the man with the rifle.

When they moved forward, Gautam asked. 'Why did you give him the money?'

'Sir, all the vehicles using this route pay a levy to the MAF.'

'But, how can they roam here freely? What are the police doing?'

'Police, ha! There is no police here. Here there is either the MAF or Ganesh Rai.'

Mohan was fascinated to find a waterfall up in the hills. A small dam was built on the upper slope of Parshuram Hills. A reservoir was formed by the dam.

'Do any tourists come here?' he asked the driver.

'No one is allowed to go near the waterfall. The MAF has their base camp there. PWD (Public Works Department) engineers go there under the cover of Razia Regiment commandos only for maintenance work. Earlier, there was a 5 MW hydro power station operated by the Bihar state electricity board, but, now it has been closed. The reservoir is used only for supplying drinking water to the town.'

'How they have made a mess of such a beautiful place!' Mohan exclaimed.

They were moving further when Gautam noticed a toll plaza in front of them. Some policemen were busy collecting toll from a passing vehicle.

'Sir, we are nearing Tailorgunj; the sub-division under which Bhagatpur lies. They are collecting toll for the bridge over the river Bhagat ahead of us. I am not going to pay. You pretend to be a police officer,' the driver told him.

'Why? When you can give a levy to the MAF why don't you give toll money to the government?'

'The MAF would kill us if we don't pay them. The government will not do anything. You just have to pretend to be a police officer,' explained the driver.

Mohan was getting thoroughly amused at the prospect of pretending to be someone he actually was. Within seconds, a policeman flagged down the vehicle.

'This is a staff vehicle. Can't you see officers sitting inside?'

The guard looked at Gautam and Mohan and tried to ascertain the veracity of the claim.

'Which police station?' he quizzed the driver.

'Patna Police,' the driver replied with confidence.

Confused, the policemen let them pass.

Just after they crossed the bridge, another policeman flagged them down.

'Now what is it?' the driver murmured.

'Where are you going?' the policeman asked the driver.

'We are on our way to Bhagatpur,' the driver replied.

'So, you will pass through Tailorgunj. Drop me to the police station there,' he said.

The driver looked towards Gautam, who nodded.

'What's your name?' Gautam asked the policeman who came aboard his vehicle.

'I am ASI Ratan Lal. I am in the STF,' he answered as if to stress his importance.

'You mean the Special Task Force to fight the MAF?' Gautam asked again.

'No, STF to guard Ganesh Rai.'

'You have formed an STF to guard a person in jail?'

'You see, his father was killed in jail when he was there. This time we have been posted to ensure his safety. His life has been threatened by many people, including the MAF.'

'You must be having a tough time then.'

'No, he is very kind to us. Last week, he celebrated his birthday in jail and we were showered with gifts. That woman, Nisha, will have to pay for getting him behind bars.'

'Ganesh Rai is looting your natural resources and making you poor day by day and you still love him just because he showers you with presents?'

The policeman did not seem to be happy hearing this.

'It is none of your business. You keep to your work,' he answered, irritated.

All of them kept silent. The vehicle was nearing one fuel station.

The driver said, 'Sir, we will stop here for diesel. You can have some tea in that dhaba nearby. The samosas in the shop are very famous here. Try some.'

'There is still some diesel left. Why don't you fill the tank later?' demanded Gautam.

'This is the last fuel station of this area. After this, for the next 50 km there are none.'

'Why? Do the people of Bhagatpur not need fuel?' asked Mohan.

'There, the diesel is sold by paan shops in containers at a higher price. After a few kilometres, the mining area starts and that is also an MAF core area. No one dares open any business centre inside it. Here, near the dhaba, is the company headquarters of SPCCL. From here till Bhagatpur you will find numerous stone-crushers, all maintained by SPCCL. Behind the river, above the slopes of the hill, lies the MAF area. Both the MAF and Ganesh Rai's men dominate the area from here to Bhagatpur.'

Gautam and Mohan got out from the vehicle.

'If you need anything else, you will find it,' said Raghu, gesturing towards a nearby hut.

'What did he mean?' Mohan asked.

'Do you feel the need to consume alcohol?' Gautam asked.

Mohan looked at him with a sullen face and shook his head.

'Then forget about what he said.' Gautam moved forward to the cigarette shop. Ratan Lal followed him and asked for paan. When the shopkeeper asked for money, though, he fumbled in his pockets but could not find any.

'No problem, I will pay,' replied Gautam, sensing his predicament.

'Thank you. I will walk to the police station. Thanks for the lift,' Ratan Lal told Gautam.

'Where is it?'

'There,' the policeman pointed to a fort situated on a cliff, at a height of approximately 500 m. Four dilapidated canons faced down from its corners.

'That fort houses your police station?'

'Yes, sir, this is Fort Vikramgarh and was built by the Raja of Bhagatpur in the 14th century. The police station is situated at its centre, probably the poorest in the world and with only the crumbling walls around it to defend us. There is also a mobile tower there.'

As soon as Ratan Lal turned away, the shopkeeper started abusing the police force for doing nothing but extracting money from shopkeepers and other hapless people.

'How far is the Bhagatpur police station from here?' Gautam asked him.

'Sir, beyond this point you will not see any evidence of police or government. A few days ago, they started a police outpost a few kilometres away but it was blasted by the MAF. They say this is the *liberated zone*,' the shop owner replied.

A board informed them that the 'SPCCL Company' was across the road, opposite the dhaba. There was a legion of trucks with 'SPCCL' written on them parked outside the compound.

'Sir, why is this place called Tailorgunj?' Mohan asked.

'I can only guess that it's been named after the British commissioner of the area who was killed in the Birsa Munda uprising, Robert Taylor. Come, we will have some samosa *chaat*,' replied Gautam.

The people inside the dhaba were engrossed in talking about the local politics and the MAF. They were discussing the rumours of Nisha contesting the elections and her chances of winning here. It seemed like everyone there was a political analyst.

While Gautam and Mohan were having tea, two vehicles pulled up for petrol. In one of them, Gautam could see a woman in her 30s, wearing jeans and a T-shirt, engrossed reading a magazine.

He heard murmurs among the people sitting beside him. 'I think she is Kavita Sethi,' someone whispered.

Gautam looked at the woman again. 'This doesn't look like the woman I saw in the photograph. Kavita has longer hair and a sharper nose,' he thought.

As soon as the vehicles began pulling out of the filling station, a burst of gunfire brought them to a halt. The drivers tried to race away but two grenades thrown from somewhere behind the bushes lifted them a few feet above the ground.

Crouching beneath a cot, Gautam could see five attackers with their faces covered taking aim from behind the bushes. They were firing from AK-47s. Gautam wondered whether they were the same men they had met a while ago.

The firing continued till the attackers ensured all the occupants of the vehicles had been killed. Gautam saw the woman on the front seat slumped forward. The men emerged from behind the bushes, calmly moved towards the vehicles and picked up the guns of the slain guards, then vanished into the jungle. Gautam looked in the direction of the police station. He could see the silhouettes looking at the direction of the blast but none dared to come to the rescue.

The driver came running towards Gautam and said, 'We need to get away.'

'But we should help them,' said Mohan.

'No one is alive. Don't help victims of the MAF unless you want to be among them. Now, come along or be left behind. I am going.'

'Okay, okay, we are coming.'

The taxi sped towards Bhagatpur.

'Where do you want to go in Bhagatpur?'

'Take us to any good hotel.'

'There is only one hotel in Bhagatpur, Hotel Mahendra. It has good rooms. I will drop you there.'

After an hour, they pulled up at a two-storey building.

'Raghu, will you be my driver and guide while I am here?' asked Gautam.

Raghu hesitated for a moment. 'It will be 500 rupees per day, plus fuel for the vehicle.'

'Okay, be here tomorrow morning at eight.'

Hotel Mahendra had about 50 rooms and a reception counter on the first floor. Gautam and Mohan kept their luggage at the bottom of the staircase, went upstairs and knocked at the door. The desk attendant was busy watching songs on television. Another man was sleeping on the couch. After a few knocks, the desk attendant looked at them and said, 'Want booking?'

'Yes.'

He gave them a handwritten note containing room rates. They opted for the luxury room which had the highest tariff.

'Who is this hotel's owner?' Gautam quizzed the bellboy.

'Mahendra Pratap Singh, the man who retired as General Manager of the Railways. He lives in Delhi. The hotel is looked after by his manager, Suraj,' the boy replied.

The room which they got was an old-fashioned room reminiscent of the British era. The only sign of modernity in it was an AC which seemed to stop working as soon as they stepped in, and the television in the room only showed a blue screen. The wall hanging had the drawing of a snow-clad landscape with the caption—*Take time to enjoy the present.* There was a huge wall clock hung above the door and the floor had a thick red carpet which didn't look like it had been cleaned in the recent past. This was the costliest room of the hotel.

While they prepared to catch a few winks, they were startled by the harsh ring of the doorbell. Mohan opened the door to see a paan-chewing lad standing at the door, grinning at them.

'What is it?' Mohan asked.

'I wanted to ask if you need anything,' the lad replied.

'Oh! You are from room service. I was looking for you. Why is the intercom not working?' he asked.

The lad stared at him.

Mohan pointed his finger at the phone and said, 'Not working.'

'Oh! You mean the phone.'

'Phone or intercom…whatever! Why is it not working? How will I contact room service?'

'I will have to change the batteries in the phone.'

'I think you have charged us for an AC room where the AC is also not working. Does that run on batteries too?'

'Oh, no sir. The power supply has just tripped and will return after two hours. That's why the television and AC are not working.'

'Don't you have backup generators?'

'The generator is switched on only at night. During the day, we work with invertors.'

'The hotel is run on invertors? Wow! Anyway, bring us two cups of tea and water,' he said.

'Mineral or regular?' the boy asked.

'Mineral,' Gautam replied.

The power supply was restored sooner than the bell boy had predicted. The tea came after half an hour.

While they were drinking the questionable brew that had been served, Gautam asked, 'Mohan what do you think of today's attack?'

'I don't know what to say. Everywhere we go, someone is killed. I hope the attack was not connected with our arrival here.'

'Switch on the television. Maybe, we can find out more.'

A couple of local TV channels were following the story. 'Today, suspected MAF rebels blew up the vehicle carrying Rekha Mishra, wife of Special Magistrate Ajay Mishra, who was returning from Patna. Her security guards and the drivers of the two vehicles in her cavalcade have been killed. The motive of the attack is unclear. However, in a communication to the channel by an MAF spokesperson, the vehicle had been blown up by mistake. The MAF took Rekha Mishra to be Razia Regiment leader, Kavita Sethi. They have categorically stated previously too that they never kill civilians.

The police has refuted this claim and said that the MAF targeted the officer's wife as he is here to oversee the construction of the power plant. Eyewitness claim that no one from the police station, located barely 100 m away, came to the rescue, however the DSP of Tailorgunj said the police force responded immediately but before they could reach the ambush site the attackers fled.'

'Switch off the television. They are talking rubbish. There weren't any policemen at the site. The MAF could be right, that lady was dressed exactly like Kavita. I have seen her photographs.'

'But why would they attack Kavita?' Mohan asked.

'This only she can answer. But the MAF has attacked the RR camp earlier. I have read it in the file provided by Subhash Joshi. I think Charulata nurses a personal grudge against Kavita. So, on our first day in Bhagatpur we have realised just how dangerous this place is.'

'Where should we begin?' Mohan asked.

'Tomorrow, I will meet Nisha. She will be the starting point of our investigation and we shall proceed from there.'

23

19 February 2013, 8 A.M.

In the morning, the harsh ring of the intercom disturbed Gautam's sleep. 'Yes.'

'Sir, your vehicle has come,' the reception informed him.

'We are coming.' Reaching out for a cigarette, he went to stand by the window which had been left open all night. Electricity had played truant the previous night and the air conditioners could provide no respite from the heat. The air outside had been pleasant but the red spots on his body testified that mosquitoes had had a field day (night perhaps!).

The hotel, situated some distance away from the main market area, was surrounded by fields on two sides, a railway track on one side and a road on the other. As Gautam looked out of the window, he could see people walking with plastic bottles towards the bushes to relieve themselves. A peacock was in a jubilant mood, dancing away to glory. Alas, he had no time to admire nature's beauty; his heart was beating with newfound trepidation. His new mission that he'd embarked on would perhaps change the meaning of his life.

After his morning ablutions, he went to Mohan's room.

'Are you ready?'

'Yes, sir. I shall take a few more minutes.'

'Come soon, the driver is here already.'

They locked their respective rooms and went outside where Raghu was waiting.

'You know the NS2 office?' asked Gautam.

'Master*ni*'s office? I will take you there.'

Nisha was in her office, busy writing letters to the UN office in New Delhi requesting for funds. The NGO had expanded exponentially in the last few years, but, she was struggling to get enough sponsors on board. The UN had sought a report of her activities and the accounts of the last two years for verification purposes.

Someone approached her desk and stood silent. The shadow of the person fell on Nisha, and she felt a strange sense of familiarity. She put down the papers and looked up, and the sight made her exclaim in astonishment.

'Gautam,' she said while jumping off her seat.

'Yes.'

'I can't believe it.'

'How are you?' Gautam said.

'How come you are here?'

'It's a long story. Can I sit down?'

'Yes, of course. I still cannot believe you are here.'

Gautam leaned towards her across the table and touched her hand.

'Now, do you believe I am here?'

'You have not changed!'

'But you have,' he said, while looking at her from head to toe.

'Yeah, it is all destiny,' she said.

'I did not know you believed in destiny.'

'I started believing in it only after I came here. What have you done to your eyes?'

'You mean my spectacles?'

'Yes.'

'Lenses. I wear lenses now. See,' he leaned towards her.

'So, how is life going on here? I have read about you. How have you adjusted here?' Gautam prodded further.

'It seems tough from outside, but, for me it is the usual life. What do you do?

'I am a journalist and he is my colleague Mohan,' he said pointing towards Mohan.

Mohan said 'hi' to Nisha.

'We are doing a story on Bhagatpur and that is why we have come here.'

'I thought you were interested in police service. You used to tell me you will try for the Indian Police Service? How did journalism happen?'

Mohan coughed.

'We do not always get what we dream. You also wanted to go in for research but landed up here,' said Gautam.

'Yes, sometimes destiny charts our course in life.'

'Destiny! I think your great work shows you are upholding your ideals.'

'Ideals? Today's idealism is tomorrow's pragmatism. Who knew the ideal non-violent struggle of Mahatma Gandhi would become the path of India's Independence.'

'How philosophical.'

'I just want to carry forward my father's dream. Now, it is my dream too.'

Saroj brought tea and biscuits for them.

'Saroj, this is Gautam, my college friend, and this is Mohan, his colleague. They are journalists and have come here to write about Bhagatpur. Saroj is my childhood friend. Her father, Shyam Lal was a close friend of my dad. She also used to study in Delhi.'

'Really! We never met there?'

'I did not know she was in Delhi either. I left Bhagatpur after Papa began working for the CBI, when I was 10. We did not meet after that. It was only when her father was killed during protests against land acquisition, did she return here. That's how we met again. We decided to make the agitation against land acquisition a part of the NS2 movement.'

'Nice to meet you, Saroj.'

'Are you in touch with anyone else? Seema, Manu, Rajesh, Chetan or anyone else from our group? Where are they?' asked Nisha.

'Off and on through email. But, I haven't met them after college. Have you?'

'I am not on any one of the social networking sites.'

'Okay.'

'How do you intend to start the research for your story?' asked Nisha.

'Well, I would like to meet all the people concerned and note their views. I will start with you.'

'That's a good idea. Tomorrow, there is a public hearing at Ajay Mishra's office. Why don't you come along?'

'Where is the public hearing?'

'At his office.'

'But, this should be at some neutral venue.'

'He has cited security reasons for holding the meeting at his office. You know about the attack on his wife?'

'Yes. Poor lady!'

'This is the last order of business he has before he goes on leave.'

'All right.'

24

20 February 2013, 10 A.M.

The next day, Nisha, Saroj, Gautam, Mohan and some villagers went to Ajay Mishra's office for the public hearing. The office was being guarded like a castle. The guards at the gate stopped them.

'You can't go in. A public hearing is going on inside,' they said.

'But, we are also here to attend,' explained Nisha.

'Sorry madam, only 50 villagers are allowed inside.'

'Who are the men inside right now?' Gautam asked.

'They will obviously be the ones who support the government's land acquisition, probably plot owners. Ajay must have chosen them especially for the hearing,' averred Saroj in contempt.

'But, this is wrong. Gautam, see how these people operate here,' said Nisha.

Even after half-an-hour of cajoling the guards, they were not allowed inside. The villagers accompanying them were growing restless and started shouting slogans against Ajay Mishra. After the commotion reached cacophonic levels, he was forced to come out and face them. 'What do you want?' he asked, irritated.

'We have come here for the hearing,' replied Nisha.

'The hearing has concluded and the people are in agreement with the offered compensation.'

'But this is illegal. Only 50 people cannot decide what thousands want,' asserted Saroj.

'Why is it illegal, just because it doesn't suit *you*? These people are representatives of all the 50 villages here. Who has given you the mandate to represent them?'

'But sir, these dealings should be more transparent. It is a *public* hearing after all,' intervened Gautam.

'Who are you?' Ajay looked at him suspiciously.

'I am a journalist,' he replied.

'So, you people have called the Press as well. But you are too late as the decision has already been made. If you disagree, you can go to the court. Now, please go. I have urgent work to take care of.' Ajay left the venue in his vehicle surrounded by guards.

The public gathered outside his office grew extremely restless and Ajay's parting words had only served to fuel their frustration. The police began lathi charging, they did not spare Nisha and Gautam. The villagers who had been inside for the hearing also joined in the melee.

'Nisha, there is no use staying here. Let us move away,' Gautam advised her.

Nisha asked the villagers to reassemble at NS2, where she announced a press conference.

'What will happen in the press conference? We had journalists with us. They didn't spare them either. They respond to only one language,' said Saroj.

'Saroj, calm down. We should try to get wide coverage for our cause and if need be we will launch a Satyagraha.'

'Nothing will come out of your Satyagraha and press conference. I am going.' Saroj left. She was followed by the villagers, leaving Nisha dejected.

Gautam turned to her. 'Do you think your methods will work here?'

'Do you doubt me too?'

'I do not doubt you but your methods. Today's incident has convinced me that your methods will require time to bear fruit, which I think this place does not have. Ajay Mishra has ignited the fuse and gone away.'

'That is why I wish to join politics.'

'Are you sure you want to contest the elections?'

'Yes, I am. That will be one of my announcements in the press conference.'

'Do you know the MAF has turned against the elections? They will also become your enemy. Why do you want to risk your life?

'They were never my friends. I will handle it.'

'And Charulata?'

'I don't know anything about her. In fact, no one does. She could be a legend the MAF has floated to serve their purpose.'

'I wish to meet her for my story.'

'It is difficult but you can meet some of the MAF men in their camps.'

'Really! Can you arrange for that?'

'I can ask Swami*ji*. But, in the meanwhile, keep a low profile. The MAF do not like strangers,' Nisha added.

'I understand your concern. This story will be the story of my life and I will take the risk.'

'Okay. As you wish. Be ready for the press conference tomorrow.'

~

The next day, Nisha came dressed in a khadi *salwar kameez* for the press conference. Gautam and Mohan took the last row seats and observed the press conference.

'I have called you all here for an important announcement. It has been almost four years since we started, Nai Soch-Nai Subah, and that is how long we have been fighting against the evils that prevail in Bhagatpur. But despite all my efforts, the issue of compensation remains unresolved. We have lost the court battle and the government has started constructing the power plant. Yesterday, the public hearing was a farce for they had handpicked only their supporters. But, I have decided not to accept this lying down. I wish to inform you all that I have decided to contest the upcoming elections.'

There was a flutter in the gathering and many voices tried to interrupt Nisha.

'Madam, which Party are you contesting from?' one of them asked.

'Indian National Party.'

'But madam, we have heard the Party has appointed the home minister to lead the campaign. Are you comfortable with him, given the recent corruption controversies?'

'See, I have joined this Party as I agree with its principles. One person does not define its ideologies. I have faith in the law of the land. If proven guilty, he shall be punished.'

'Do you think you will change the policy regarding the power plant if you win?'

'I believe in democracy. I will fight.'

'What are your views on the MAF, who is also fighting against the same?'

'I appreciate their purpose, but, I do not think violence is the solution. I request them to come forward and engage in a dialogue.'

'But, we have heard that you support the MAF. You had filed a PIL against Ganesh Rai which helped them. It is also rumoured that the MAF protects you as they killed Jagdish, the man who threatened you at your office premises.'

'It is all rubbish. I have never supported the MAF and it is not protecting me. I had filed the case as I felt it was my duty as an Indian citizen. Who killed the person or who threatened me is a matter of police interrogation and I would request the media not to pass the verdict on the issue.'

One of the journalists noticed that Saroj was not present.

'Madam, why is Saroj not here for this important announcement?'

'She is busy with some other work,' replied Nisha.

The journalists posed some more questions, which she patiently answered.

'Let us hope we are going in the right direction,' Gautam told Mohan after the conference.

25

22 February 2013, 9 A.M.

'What is our informer up to? Why does he not meet us?' asked Mohan.

'I have no idea, Mohan. Maybe, he is afraid. After all, he is also on a secret mission. Of course, there is always the possibility that he is playing games with us,' Gautam said.

'What games you are talking about, sir?' asked the hotel manager, Suraj, who was also in the dining room.

'Oh! Last night's cricket match. We couldn't watch it fully because the electricity kept coming and going,' replied Gautam.

'Sorry, sir, these days the electric supply has become erratic. The onset of summer means frequent power-cuts. What to do? We are in a power deficit state. I hope this power plant solves our problems,' he replied.

'But, there are so many battles going on around its construction.'

'Yes, it is true. But it is also true that the state badly needs more power stations. Anyway, did you like the mango, sir?' he asked Mohan.

'Yes. What kind are these?'

'Sir, this is called Malda mango.'

'Isn't Malda a town in Bengal?' enquired Gautam.

'Yes, sir, but it is grown around here as well. It is one of the fruit's sweetest varieties.'

'For how many years have you been here?' Gautam asked Suraj.

'Five years.'

'Do you have a coal trading point here?'

'No, sir, why do you ask?'

'I have seen many coal sacks going into the cellar.'

The manager looked left and right after hearing the question and answered.

'Actually, sir, our staff takes some of the coal that passes through the area and keeps it to be used in our kitchen.'

'But, that is illegal.'

'Yes, sir. I have asked them to stop, but, they carry on and give our hotel a bad name. Sir, if you don't mind, could you tell me for what purpose you are here?'

'We are journalists and we are researching for a story on the power plant and the issues it has brought along.'

'How long are you planning to be here?' he asked.

'A month, perhaps. Is that a problem?'

'No, sir. It is my honour. Kindly write about my hotel also and please do not mention this coal part. I assure you it will be stopped.'

'Sure. I will also write about the mangoes,' he said, glancing at Mohan.

'Will you be going out today?' asked Suraj.

'Yes, we will go towards the villages and return by evening. Please check if our driver has come.'

Suraj went towards the reception and returned with Raghu, who was grinning.

'*Johar*, sahib,' Raghu said.

'Good morning, Raghu. Please take us to the villages today. I wish to talk to the people about the power plant,' Gautam asked Raghu.

Raghu took the Tower Chowk route but after a short distance, they reached an unmetalled road which diverted them to a temple. Beyond this, the road was so narrow that the taxi was not able to move on. They disembarked and began walking. A small crowd had gathered near the temple.

'What is going on there?' Gautam asked Raghu.

'The supporters of Ganesh Rai have gathered for a puja and sacrifice for his release,' he replied.

The priest put vermilion and wet rice on the deity while chanting mantras. Then, he walked towards the goat tethered near the temple and pulled its ears. The animal let out a mournful noise. It was then picked up by two men, who pulled its legs back while fixing its neck on the altar. One of them raised a long sword and chanted—'Chandika Maharani *ki jai*,' and pressed the sword on the neck of the hapless goat, severing its head.

'Poor animal!' Mohan murmured.

When they walked on and entered the village, the priest stared while children ran behind them, shouting and giggling. Their parked vehicle was a source of great amusement. They were shooed away by the priest.

The village was based on a radial pattern where the central part was occupied by a pond. One side of the pond was the residential area while farms were located on the other side where the villagers worked. The roads radiated away from the pond in all directions at regular intervals. There was a dilapidated bathing ghat on its banks where some women were seen washing clothes. Even buffaloes seemed content to be under water in the scorching heat. Further away, a group of pigs was hunting for food.

Ganesh Rai's bungalow was near the pond, where no one else from the village stayed. His residence seemed to demarcate the rich from the poor. The pond was lined with palm trees which had toddy pots hanging on almost all of them. The farms were small and rice and sugarcane were the staple crops. The main occupation, however, was animal grazing and collecting products from the forest, situated a few kilometres away near the river Bhagat. Jhum cultivation was the dominant form of agricultural practice wherein the villagers cleared a patch of forestland to cultivate for some years, and then move on to another patch when fertility dwindled. However, Ganesh Rai owned a large chunk of land where he employed villagers as tillers, following the informal *ryotwari* system, but he would get a sizeable rent, much above the state norm. Raghu told him that the forest was infested not only with the MAF, but, also wild animals and he that animal attacks had afflicted many villagers.

I feel bad for them. They are sandwiched between the RBS, the MAF and the police force on one hand and the wild animals on the other. I don't know whether to believe all of Raghu's tales, though, thought Gautam as he looked around.

The frail old hut owner sitting on the mud floor was perplexed when he saw them.

'*Johar*,' he said by way of greeting.

'Sahib is from Delhi and he wants to ask you a few questions,' Raghu told the hut owner.

The old man nodded, pointed to a tattered cot made of bamboo strips and asked them to sit.

'Are you happy with this power plant?' Gautam asked.

'Sahib, they have taken our land. How can we be happy?'

'But, they have provided compensation.'

'We want our land back. Please ask the government to give us our land.'

'I will do that. For how many years have you lived here?'

The old man replied, 'Sixty.'

'Do you know every villager here?'

'I know the villagers of not only this village but all the 50 villages in the Tailorgunj subdivision.'

'Do you know about the MAF?'

He didn't say anything.

Raghu whispered in Gautam's ear, 'Don't ask him this question. Nobody here will talk about the MAF.'

Gautam persisted. 'Why don't you help the police deal with the MAF?'

'Why should I? The police killed my only son in a fake encounter and carried his body on a bamboo stick, displaying it as a trophy. It was a Maoist killed by the police in an encounter which would 'honour' the latter the rewards. The police is cruel here, sahib.'

'Do you know who Nisha is?'

'Yes, sahib. She is a very nice lady who is fighting our cause.'

'What about her father?'

'He was also a good person. It is unfortunate that he was killed.'

Map of Bhagatpur

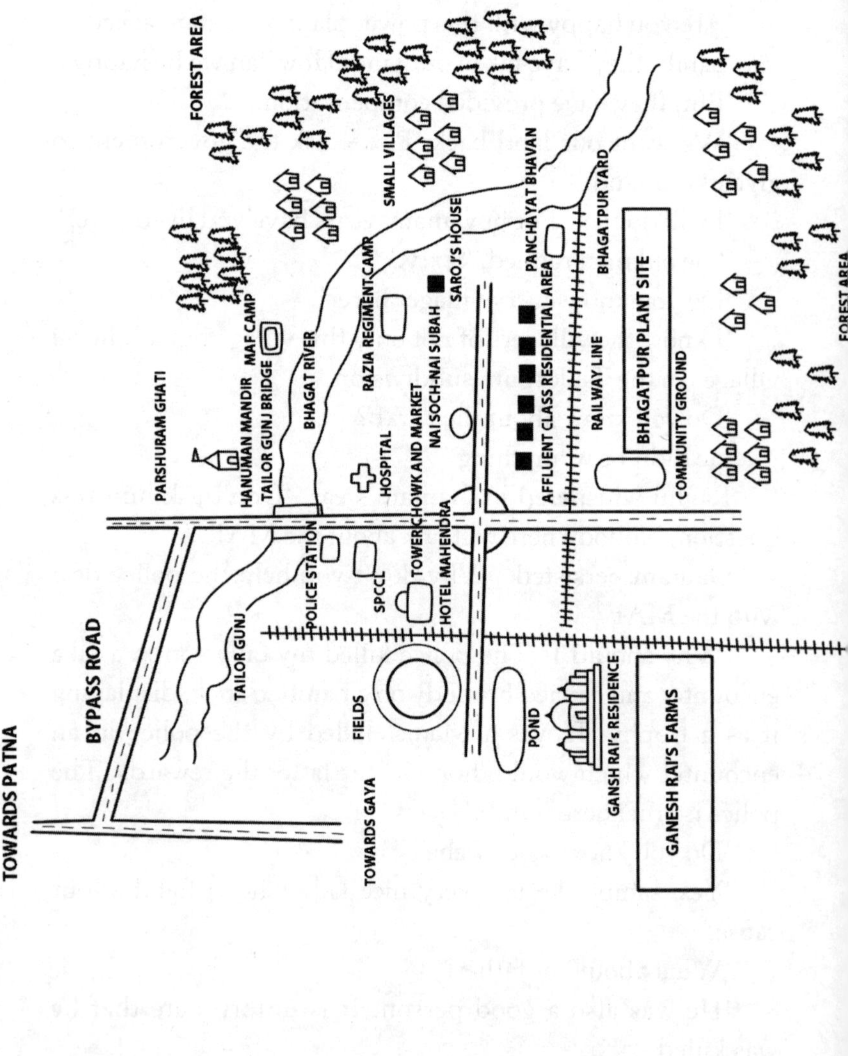

'By whom?'

'I don't know, sahib. Some say the MAF killed him; some say Ganesh Babu had him murdered. We are poor people, sahib, we do not know much.'

'Thank you for talking to us. We will take your leave. I promise to write all this in my article so that people know your pain.'

As they came out, Mohan said, 'Sir, what rubbish was he talking about? I don't believe that the police were so brutal to his son.'

'It must be true, sahib. The police and the MAF, both are equally brutal. No one can be believed. The land means so much to them, far more than human lives,' said Raghu.

'The land is their entire livelihood. That is why all issues regarding its ownership and alienation can lead to caste wars in this area.'

'What you are saying is true, sir, but asking them about the MAF is futile,' said Raghu.

Oblivious of the fact that two persons were watching them from behind the palm trees lining the pond, they continued their discussion.

'Raghu, can you show me the other side of the village?' asked Gautam.

'Yes sir. Come this way,' Raghu replied.

After they had travelled a short distance away from the village, the taxi screeched to a halt as two vehicles seemingly appeared out of nowhere, blocking their way. Fifteen armed persons alighted and dragged them out. Gautam and Mohan were too stunned to speak but Raghu began screaming for help.

'What are you doing?' he screamed.

One of the assailants took out a knife and slit his throat. While he lay gasping for life, his passengers looked clueless, but, were aware that they had to be quick with their next course of action. As soon as Raghu's killer moved towards Gautam, he kicked the man with his leg and when he stumbled, he held in a vice-like grip and pinned him to the ground. Next, he punched the man who was holding Mohan and signalled his friend to follow him while the assailants tried to recover from this surprise counter-attack. The police officers in plainclothes ran for their lives, jumping into the sugarcane fields while the bunch of attackers quickly regrouped and began chasing them.

'Why do they want to kill us?' panted Mohan

'Do you want me to stop and ask?' snapped Gautam.

'NO!'

'Keep running.'

After 15 minutes, Mohan stumbled on a stone and fell to the ground. Gautam stopped to help him up but by then they were surrounded. One of the men took out a long sword and moved towards them. Gautam's hand tightened at his service revolver concealed beneath his shirt.

'Stop,' the stern voice halted his step.

The assailant looked up to see the pujari of the temple standing by Gautam.

'What is it pujari*ji*? Why are you saving these police informers?'

'How can you say they are police informers?'

'They were with Raghu who we know is a police informer.'

'We did not know about this,' Gautam mustered courage to speak.

'These people are journalists. They have come to write about this place. We have seen their resolve during the public hearing when they suffered lathi blows for us. '

Soon, they saw the police jeep arriving from a distance.

'Who called the police?'

'I called them,' the pujari said.

'Pujari*ji*, this is not correct. We people are fighting for you and you are siding with the police?'

'We are not siding with the police. But, we want to save these innocent people.'

The assailants retreated.

One of the men in the group was staring at Gautam when the leader called him—'Babu Lal?'

'Yes, commander,' he returned.

Gautam and Mohan watched them leaving.

'Mohan, I have heard that name somewhere.'

'Where?'

'Perhaps, from Subhash Joshi. I'm quite sure that when we raided the hotel, this man was in Delhi.'

The policemen arrived within minutes and took custody of Raghu's body. They also asked Gautam to come to the police station, where he proceeded to narrate what had happened.

'There is nothing we can do,' the SHO, Kanahiya Paswan, said helplessly.

'Poor fellow. He died because of me,' said Gautam.

'Forget it. You could not have done anything.'

'By the way, sir, are you the one who was kidnapped by the MAF few months back? Can you tell us about it? It will be a good story for our article.'

'Which newspaper do you work for?'

'*Janshakti*,' Gautam replied.

'We had gone to inaugurate a football match in the village. As soon as I reached the dais, a series of gunshots was fired. My bodyguard was hit and another constable and I ran towards my car for cover. We raced towards Tailorgunj, but, as soon as the car reached the forest stretch, a boy with a gun blocked my way. The constable wanted to fire but I restrained him as I knew it was useless. The boy came up to us and asked if I was the SHO. They took me away.'

'Where did they keep you?'

'They kept moving me from village to village. Beyond the river Bhagat, among the forest, there are scores of villages which are among the core supporters of the MAF. They never kept me in a village for more than a day. Mostly, they made me travel on foot but sometimes they used a bike for transportation.'

'You lived with them for almost two weeks. You must have talked to some of them. What is their mission? What are they fighting for?'

'They are against the system. They do not believe in democracy but want to form a socialist government. They are ready to die for their cause. All of them are loyal to their leaders—Gireesh and Charulata.'

'Why did they release you after taking such pains to kidnap you?' asked Mohan, who was taking notes.

'A few days after my kidnapping, when I had all but lost every bit of hope, Narendra Nath mediated on my behalf.'

'The yoga guru? How did he come into the picture?' asked Gautam.

'My wife is his disciple.'

'But why would the rebels listen to him?'

'I also found that intriguing. It seems they respect and listen to him.'

'Strange. So, they released you without any trade-off?'

'As far as I know, yes.'

'But, why did they kidnap you in the first place?'

'I had arrested Gireesh as part of my PRM (People's Resistance Movement) duties, back when it was still functioning. They were avenging that.'

'How did Gireesh get out then?'

'Charulata freed him. That's why they call her *the ghost*.'

'How did she do that?'

'I cannot talk about the incident as it is classified information. Now, no more questions, please. My vehicle will drop you to your hotel. Please be careful in future.'

'Okay, sir. Thank you. We shall go now,' said Gautam.

As they left, Gautam told Mohan—'Strange, is it not? Narendra Nath knows so much about the MAF. He can even go where the police dare not venture.'

'Shall we meet him?'

'Not yet. We better not push it or our cover will be blown. Terrorist groups also have sympathisers just like the pujari we saw today.'

When the vehicle dropped them to the hotel, it was 7 p.m. and there was no electricity, again. Everything was unusually quiet. Gautam could not sense the movement of any of the staff at the hotel. Even the gatekeeper was missing. For some reason, Gautam felt wary.

'Mohan, light a matchstick,' he asked Mohan, giving him his matchbox.

Gautam drew out his pistol and went near the room. He put the keys in the lock and turned it. Mohan lit another matchstick. To their horror, the room had been ransacked with their luggage strewn all around.

Just then, the electricity resumed. Gautam called out to the hotel manager, furious. 'How can this happen?'

'Sorry, sir, there hasn't been any electricity since morning and our watchman has gone on leave. I will change your room.'

'Do it now.'

'Sir, who do you think is behind all this? Why did they target Raghu? He was a poor man,' asked Mohan, once they had moved their luggage and belongings to the new rooms.

'It seems someone does not like our presence here and even those associated with us are in danger. From now on, we will not take any accomplices. Everywhere we go, someone is killed.'

'What about Nisha?'

'On the contrary, I think she is our shield here!'

'How come?'

'First, she is an important person here. People admire her; and the MAF cannot risk people of Bhagatpur going against them. Second, you have seen how important Narendra Nath is to the MAF. Narendra Nath is Nisha's uncle.'

'So, what shall we do now?'

'Let us see how tomorrow unfolds.'

After Mohan went to his room, Gautam sat on the chair beside his bed and lit a cigarette.

I wonder what stopped that man from attacking us. It is strange that we were left unhurt. I must discuss this with Nisha.

26

23 February 2013

In the afternoon, while Nisha was preparing for her class, she noticed Saroj standing at the office entrance looking at her rather strangely. It was as if she was upset about something but wasn't quite sure about expressing it.

'Madam, I want to talk to you,' she said, finally.

'What is the matter, Saroj?'

'Was Gautam a good friend of yours in college?'

'Yes, why do you ask?'

'Are you sure he is a journalist?'

'Yes, of course. By the way, Saroj, why were you not at the press conference when I announced I would be contesting the elections?'

'I don't think elections will help.'

'Why are you against them? India is a democratic country.'

'I don't believe in democracy. I believe in radical change. I think you will also become a cog in the wheel, crushing the poor in the name of development.'

'I'm not like others, Saroj. You know me very well. My greatest wish is to do anything and everything for the people of this area. Right now, I feel politics will be the right move.'

'Anything? Will you take up arms as the MAF did?'

'Yes, if it is for the people.'

'Then, what is the difference between the MAF and you?'

'The MAF feels violence is the only solution and I feel violence is part of the problem. Only a peaceful political movement will change the face of this place.'

Hearing this, Saroj simply gave Nisha a piercing look and rushed out of the room.

Gautam and Mohan entered just as Saroj was on her way out.

'What happened?' Gautam asked.

'I don't know. But something is up. Since the MAF issued a warning opposing the election, she turned against it too. I did not know she would abide by their every decision. She also doubts your credentials. She is clearly an MAF sympathiser.'

'Something happened to us also.' Gautam narrated the incident.

'What? I hope you are not hurt.' She sprang to her feet.

'Then, we returned to our hotel and found that someone had vandalised our rooms. Curiously, they did not take anything.'

'Do not venture around the village. If necessary, take me with you,' she said.

'Forget that. What has happened to Saroj? Do you trust her?'

'I do, but lately she has been behaving erratically.'

'Where has she gone now?'

'Probably to her house.'

'Where does she live?

'Her house is at the corner of the village in a very isolated place. I asked her many times to live with me but she likes staying there. She is a brave woman. Anyway, listen, before anything else untoward happens, please let me talk to Swami*ji* so that you can have direct access to the MAF.'

'I will take care. Ask your uncle. Till then, can you arrange a meeting with Kavita?'

'Yes, I talked to her about you. You can meet her next week.'

'One week! We will wait.'

'Come, I will drop you to your hotel.'

Gautam sat in the passenger seat of her car while Mohan got in the back. After half-an-hour, they reached the hotel.

'Thanks.' Gautam remained standing near the car. Mohan, meanwhile, moved towards the hotel but after a while realised that his colleague had not joined him.

'Sir, shall we?' he interrupted.

'Yes. Call me if you get something,' said Gautam, blushing, bidding Nisha goodbye as she drove off.

'We are jobless for a week. What do we do now?'

'Sir, I have discovered something.'

'What?' asked Gautam.

'There is a stall at the corner which serves better tea than this hotel. Let us have our morning tea there tomorrow and take a walk around. Let us explore nature's bounty.' said Mohan.

'Okay, we will meet in the morning.'

Both of them retired for the day.

27

24 February 2013, 7 A.M.

Gautam and Mohan were perhaps the first customers at the tea stall. They were offered two plastic chairs near the drain flowing by the shop. After preparing a cauldron full of tea, the stall owner put a glass on a saucer and poured tea in it till it spilled over and filled the saucer as well. He moved away from them and poured the tea on the ground and offered prayers before returning to the cauldron. Then, he put the tea on his palms and tasted it. Not satisfied, he added more tea leaves and seemed content after another round of sampling.

'The taste is good. Your discovery is not in vain.' Gautam looked at Mohan and smiled. 'Come, Mohan, we will take a walk and start a healthy life.' He handed a 10-rupee note to the shopkeeper, who handed him the change along with a scrap of paper. Confused, Gautam opened it while they walked away.

'What happened, sir?' Mohan asked.

Gautam handed him the paper, which read—*10 a.m., Hanuman Mandir at the Ghati.*

'What is this, sir?'

'No idea.'

'What if it is a ploy to attack us?'

'We have to take a chance. Have you brought your revolver with you?'

'Yes, sir,' he said, feeling the revolver tucked under his shirt.

'Good, let us go. We will walk. If anybody asks, say we are going to pray.'

At 10 a.m. sharp, they were at the temple and wondering what their next step should be when a voice behind them uttered—'How is the climate in Delhi, sahib? Don't turn around. Go and wait for me behind the temple.'

They did as they were told and Gautam finally got the chance to look at the owner of the voice. He was middle-aged, bearded and not very tall.

'Is your name Babu?' asked Gautam. 'You are the informer. What were you doing till now?'

'I am the one who should ask this question. No one contacted me. Did you people send me here to die?'

'Listen, there was a communication gap. The officer you were in touch with, Sudhakar, was killed.'

'I know. But someone else could have taken charge.'

'Sudhakar did his best to protect you and destroyed any evidence that could have led the MAF to you. How could we seek you out when you did not exist on paper? Tell me, why have you called us here?'

'I was sent with our commander Samir to accompany comrade Gireesh to Delhi. There...'

'Why did Gireesh go there in the first place?' Gautam intervened.

'Rohit Kumar asked the arms handler, Guhar, to call the senior leader of the MAF to collect the ammunition. Sensing the enormity of the task, Gireesh decided he would go himself. Then, Rohit asked Soumit to alert the police. He thought this would implicate Gireesh and get us caught.'

'Your people killed Soumit.'

'The MAF did not kill him. We had strict instructions not to indulge in violence in Delhi. He was probably killed by Rohit himself. I read about you and the encounter in Delhi and thought you could be helpful.'

Gautam seemed alarmed. 'If you know about me then maybe Samir, who was also with you, also knows who we really are.'

'He hasn't realised it yet. If he knew, you would have been dead by now.'

Why didn't you contact your bosses in the IB or the local police here? Wouldn't that have been easier?'

'The local police are useless. In Delhi, I tried contacting the IB, but, Samir was always with me.'

'But, you could have contacted Kavita. You knew she was also part of *Operation India One?*'

'I have no idea about *Operation India One*. Sudhakar only told me that I was operating alone and I have to report to him. In any case, the MAF has kept a strict vigil on Kavita and RR. Anyone found interacting with any of the RR soldiers are eliminated. Raghu had transported some RR soldiers to their camps a few weeks back. So, I decided not to contact Kavita.'

'How did you manage to infiltrate the MAF?'

'I posed as a landless labourer from Ghaziabad who was hounded by the police. I lived in this temple for almost a month and befriended the priest. He is an MAF sympathiser and recommended me to them. I am in comrade Samir's group.'

'How many groups are there?'

'There are three groups—one led by Samir, the other by Chakradhar and the third is under an unknown comrade who lives in Bhagatpur under disguise. Charulata is the overall commander of the group.'

'How do you not know who the third leader is?'

'Cadres of one group are not allowed to mingle with the other. We only know the overall structure of the group but not the members of the other groups.'

'What about Charulata?'

'She only meets Chakradhar and Samir. When she does come out to speak to us she always has her face covered.'

'Why did you try to kill me?'

'We got the news that two outsiders were enquiring about the MAF in Bhagatpur along with Raghu, your driver. The MAF had an apprehension that Raghu was a police informer and was helping you gather information about us. We were asked to kill you and the comrade in Bhagatpur was asked to ransack your room.'

'They did not take anything from my room.'

'I am not aware.'

'You called me here and you also tried to kill me. How can you do that?'

'I have to do what is being instructed otherwise I would be labelled a traitor and killed in a *janadalat*. I knew you would have done something to save yourself.'

'How did you contact me?'

'I could call you here because the tea stall owner is my friend and I had seen Mohan there earlier. I asked him to give that paper to you.'

'Can you give us any information about what the MAF is planning next?'

'A huge consignment of arms is expected. Guhar will deliver the consignment himself to prevent any mistake. He will be at the New Delhi railway station tomorrow.'

'Who will supply the consignment? How is it being transported?'

'I don't know much. Guhar will transport it from Delhi to Dhanbad by train. One of our group members will take the consignment from him. Only our leaders know how it will reach here.'

'After Guhar asked Gireesh to come to Delhi, they still trust him?'

'Guhar is our main arms supplier and this time the MAF is in dire need of ammunition for the new rifles we acquired in the last deal. Besides, Guhar has already clarified to Charulata he was unaware of Rohit's gameplan.'

'All right. I will alert out forces. But what do you intend to do?'

'I wish to return to Delhi, sir.'

'We will make sure that happens. But first, we must nab this Charulata.'

'She is very secretive and after Gireesh's arrest they have become more vigilant. Sir, I must go now or they will suspect me.'

'One minute. What is your real name?'

'Ravi Chaurasia.'

As soon as he left, Gautam let out a sigh of relief.

'Mohan, go to the market area and call Rajesh in Delhi. Ask him to nail Guhar.'

28

25 February 2013, 5 P.M.

A poker-faced man carrying a heavy suitcase was walking on platform No. 10 at the New Delhi railway station. He seemed to be headed in the direction of the Dhanbad train which was due to leave shortly. In his haste, he accidentally bumped into a woman striding towards him and the suitcase fell to the ground with a thud as a result.

'Sorry, madam,' the man apologised.

'What sorry? Can't you see where you are going?' She was in no mood to relent and a commotion ensued. Two policemen patrolling the platform with a sniffer dog came towards them to look into the matter and while they were in the process of pacifying the woman, the dog began clawing at the suitcase.

'What is in there?' they asked the man.

'Just clothes,' he replied.

'Open it.'

'There are only clothes inside.'

When the officers moved to open it themselves, the man made a run for it. In a bid to cross the platform, he jumped in front of a running train and in another split second, his badly mangled body was thrown in front of horrified onlookers.

'Oh my God!' the woman shrieked.

The authorities immediately set to work clearing the platform while the police called for the bomb squad to investigate the contents of the suitcase. DCP Rajesh Kumar, accompanied by Subhash Joshi, also reached the site and attempted to make sense of what had just happened. Meanwhile, the bomb squad found the suitcase stashed with ammunition for AK-47s and other sophisticated rifles.

'Gautam was correct. The dead man is Guhar. The weapons, mainly ammunitions recovered from him were meant for the MAF,' said Rajesh.

'Check his phone records,' Subhash Joshi asked his subordinate. When Rajesh did so, he found something that shocked him. 'Most of the calls are from Kashmir but a few are from Bihar. It looks like the MAF is involved. But one phone number belongs to Delhi Police ASI Aslam Khan!'

'Your man? Some of your men are involved? I cannot believe it,' Subhash exclaimed.

'I am surprised too, sir. We will keep him under surveillance.'

'Tell me how much this man knows. Does he know about Gautam and his mission?'

'No, Aslam knows nothing. But—'

'But what?'

'Aslam was with Gautam when he raided the hotel to arrest Gireesh. That night, we failed to arrest Vikas. I think Aslam may be behind his escape. As per our team's report, Aslam frequents a house in Lakshmi Nagar.'

'The satellite phone location of that night was also Lakshmi Nagar. Rajesh, don't wait, raid the house immediately. Supervise the raid yourself. I do not want any mishap.'

Rajesh and his team of 10 STF (Special Task Force) commandos immediately set off for Mahendra Mansion, which was the address of the Laxmi Nagar house. While the commandos surrounded the house, Rajesh barged in through the front door.

Aslam was inside, having a drink with a visitor. His face went ashen on seeing his senior.

'Your time is up, you traitor!' growled Rajesh.

'I have not done anything, sir,' he said, stealthily moving his hands towards his back, probably fumbling for his gun.

'Don't do that unless you want me to fire. This house is surrounded by commandos and you are no match. Put your hands up.'

Aslam knew the futility of putting up a fight and surrendered.

'What is your name?' Rajesh asked the other person.

'Vikas.'

~

Rajesh and Aslam met in the interrogation room.

'Aslam, what did you do for them?'

Aslam was silent.

'You have worked with me. You know I am rather infamous for my third-degrees. Do you want to talk after I torture you or now?'

'My job was only to alert them about any probable police action. It started with IB and not with Delhi Police.

I was briefly attached with Sudhakar Bansala who was on deputation to IB and who was in charge of planting a mole in the MAF. We received a tip-off about an arms deal going on near the UP border. I raided the place along with five constables. All of them died in cross firing. Vikas who was supervising the arms deal there told me he would let me go if I spy for them in IB and would provide good money too. I accepted the proposal. Few days later, Sudhakar shared a plan with me to send a mole in MAF. He did not tell me anything more. I passed on the information to MAF. They accosted him and tried to get information about the mole, but, he refused to divulge any details and died. He destroyed all information about the mole. Subsequently, I was transferred back to Delhi Police and call it a coincidence, my association with Gautam got me thrown into this case all over again.'

'You sold your soul for a few rupees. You will pay for it.'

After interrogating Aslam, he turned towards Vikas.

'You are the main fund organiser for MAF here in Delhi. Tell me how you transport arms for them?'

Vikas spilled the beans.

'The arms are first procured from Pakistan and shipped to Mumbai. From there, it is brought to Delhi where it is stored at the Mahendra Mansion. Then, it is transported to Dhanbad, and in collusion with the railway and the police, it is put inside the coal racks that pass through Bhagatpur. When the train passes through Bhagatpur, it slows down and the MAF operatives take out the weapons and ammunitions hidden beneath the coal. They operate like petty coal thieves but with the coal, they carry the ammunition to the cellar of Hotel Mahendra where the weapons are stored before being sent to the MAF forest camps. Hotel Mahendra and Mahendra Mansion are owned by the same person—Mahendra Pratap Singh.'

The owner of the hotel, Mahendra Pratap Singh, was inevitably arrested. Jehenabad police was informed which raided Hotel Mahendra for any more arms and ammunitions. The hotel was not sealed but the management was served a notice to reply within a week about their involvement.

'My God, I have never heard of such ideas. Congratulations, sir, our plan is working,' Rajesh told Subhash.

29

1 March 2013, 10 A.M.

A bus stopped at Tailorgunj, and 15 women got on board. A watchful hawker selling fruits began walking towards a telephone booth as soon as the bus moved away. Two hours later, as it reached the highway towards Gaya, an explosion ripped it apart. The bus was thrown 15 ft. into the air and a crater was formed at the place. By the time any semblance of help could be arranged, most of the occupants had been killed.

At the MAF camp, a messenger relayed the event to Charulata. 'Fifteen RR soldiers died in the bus explosion.'

Samir, who was with her at the time, spoke to Charulata—'This will send out a message to the government and tell them what happens when they arrest one of us.'

'But Charulata, there were more civilians on the bus than soldiers. I think it was wrong to kill them. We will be criticised as murderers,' said Chakradhar.

'But we had to send out a fitting reply,' retorted Samir.

'That doesn't mean we just go and kill civilians. I am not in agreement with your methods. We have to provide an apology.'

'No, we will not send out any apology. But yes, I agree, the blood of innocent people should not be shed,' intervened Charulata.

'Commander, moving on to another order of business, we have made up a detailed plan for kidnapping Ajay Mishra,' said Samir.

'Not again, comrade Samir. Why are you bent on destroying our image? Moreover, Ajay has not returned from leave and he is a guarded man. We can have causalities.' replied Chakradhar.

'We have got news that Ajay is returning and we shall kidnap him while he is on his way sans tight security. For ransom, we will not demand cash but the withdrawal of the power plant project. He is a senior officer and I'm sure the government will be forced to comply,' said Samir.

'There must be no civilian causalities this time,' asserted Charulata.

'Let me handle this,' said Chakradhar.

'Why do you not have faith in me?' asked Samir.

'There are voices saying that your men engage in extortion. See what happened when you went to Delhi with Gireesh. It has also come to my attention that one of your people was in the Bhagatpur Hanuman Mandir yesterday without any reason. You know our men should not go beyond river Bhagat in the village without any valid purpose.'

'Are you doubting me?'

'I am not. But, who is the man you are talking about?' asked Charulata, concerned.

'His man—Babu Lal,' replied Chakradhar.

'Isn't he the one who went with you to Delhi to escort comrade Gireesh, Samir?'

'Yes, but he was with me all the time.'

'He did not have anything to do with what happened there because Gireesh's arrest was planned by Rohit. But, have you noticed that it was after that incident that a traitor was born? Someone is informing the police about our activities since then. Chakradhar, get Babu Lal under surveillance. If he is the culprit, we will make him pay. '

'Okay, commander.'

'Have you checked the antecedents of those two journalists who Swami*ji* asked us to meet?'

'Yes, they are working for *Janshakti*, a newspaper in Delhi, and the main man, Gautam, is Nisha's college friend. Nothing suspicious,' replied Chakradhar.

'Arrange for them to come here. Since they are journalists, they can write about our views too. I would like to meet Nisha too. She has many doubts about us.'

'Okay.'

'Make arrangements for kidnapping Ajay but only after we have met Nisha and Gautam. And Chakradhar will handle this. Is this fine by you, Samir?'

'As you wish.'

Charulata soon retired to her room.

Who is the traitor here? Can it be Samir? Chakradhar is an old friend of Gireesh since the Eklavya Sena days. Samir joined our cadre five years back. I will have to be more vigilant, she thought.

30

3 March 2013, 8 A.M.

'Sir, there is a note for you.' The hotel manager handed Gautam a sealed envelope.

'From?'

'I don't know. It was delivered here anonymously,' the hotel manager shrugged.

Gautam went to his room and opened the note, which turned out to be handwritten. It contained the following message—'Be there tomorrow with your friend and Nisha at the Hanuman Temple after sunset. Go to the pujari and offer him some laddus. He will give you a note.' It was signed—'Charulata'.

'Sir, shall we inform our superiors? They can find out Charulata's location by tracking us.' Mohan asked.

'Their location is not secret. Their mission is. What do they want? First, *we* will find out.'

When Nisha was informed, she was furious. 'I do not want to meet these murderers.'

'I thought you were an MAF sympathiser,' Gautam said.

'This is not a way to lead a revolution. They have killed civilians in that bus.'

'That is why we are going there. Come with me. Let us find out how they think.'

Reluctantly, Nisha agreed, and the next day, they duly reached the place they had been asked to. The pujari handed them a note which asked them to board a blue coloured boat and ask the man steering it to row them to the other side. This man then handed them another note which asked them to walk into the forest in a straight line without looking back for about a kilometre. As they walked, four gun-toting teenage boys came out of the bushes and walked with them. They were face-to-face with their perceived enemies for the first time, and Gautam was amazed by what he saw. The boys who were grouped along with the hardliners could pass off as ordinary youngsters.

'*Lal Salaam,* comrade. I am Krishna. You can call me Krish,' said one of the boys. He was holding a bag full of biscuits, a water bottle and an AK-47. The others looked slightly older than him.

Are these young boys the greatest security threat to the nation? Gautam thought.

'It is a long walk, comrades. So be prepared,' said Krish as they continued towards the interior of the forest. There was no road and small craters emerged now and then which the group said were marks of IED blasts. Most of the trees had bullet marks on them. As they walked, little hamlets gradually began to emerge and the feeling that this was no ordinary cluster of huts grew distinctly stronger.

The village seemed spacious, the houses scattered far away from each other. Some houses were deserted and a close look revealed that they were just skeletal structures, all burnt.

'These houses were burned during the last PRM raid,' said Krish.

'I had no idea. This was never spoken about in the mainstream media,' said Mohan.

'Yes, this kind of news is usually suppressed. In fact, before the formation of the RR, the government sent the PRM here. They burned our villages, raped our women and killed everyone they could lay their hands on. But, we also responded bravely and due to the mounting causalities they withdrew after a while,' said Krish.

They entered a house, where a few people were sitting around a fire. The lady of the house greeted them inside and served dried vegetables and red rice.

'You rest here. Tomorrow, some people will arrive from the camps to pick you up. Our job was to transport you till here. The village level militia will take you to the edge of the camps in the forest and from there the higher level cadres will take care of you.'

'There is hierarchy here too. Nisha, are you all right?' asked Gautam when they had been left alone.

'Yes. I am. But I am shocked to see such young boys handling guns with such ease!'

'Yes, it is surprising. I cannot stop thinking about the raids on the villages, though? Were you aware of it?'

'No. I am sure the government is hiding more secrets here.'

They rested that night on thin sheets of bamboo laid over the mud floor.

The next morning, 10 young people arrived—girls and boys in their teens and probably, early 20s. Krish explained that this was the village-level militia, the lowest rung of the MAF military hierarchy. Dressed in different kind of attire, from saris and lungis to frayed olive-green fatigues, each of them had a muzzle-loading rifle, which had probably been looted from the PRM. Some carried knives, axes and bows, and arrows. After breakfast, which was leftover rice from the previous night's dinner, it was time to move. Without much talk, everybody fell in line. Leaving the village and walking in single file into the forest, they halted only in the afternoon near a small pond, which was the last stop before the camp.

After lunch it was a few hours' walk to the camp and it was already dark by the time they arrived. There were several layers of sentries and concentric circles of patrolling, about a 100 comrades lined up in two rows, all of them armed. They began to sing—*'Lal Salaam, Lal Lal Salaam, Aane Vaale Saathiyon ko Lal Lal Salaam'* (red salute to the comrades who have arrived).

Samir greeted them at the Parshuram Ghati, where all the people they saw were equipped with highly sophisticated weapons—AK-47 and INSAAS.

'*Lal Salaam*, comrade, I am Samir.'

This is the same Samir who had accompanied Gireesh to Delhi! thought Gautam.

'*Lal Salaam,*' he said out loud.

'Welcome Nisha. We have heard a lot about you.'

'Likewise.'

They were led into a cave-like structure, which actually turned out to be quite a comfortable dwelling. Inside the cave, some rooms were carved out of the stone. All these rooms had no doors. Only, the last room had a door which was closed that time. They were allotted two such rooms—one for Nisha and another for Gautam and Mohan. These rooms were sparsely decorated with oil lamps. One small window was carved out that opened towards the forest which was cleared of all dense tress to allow sunshine during the day. Plastic sheets were laid on the floor for bed. A thin mattress and a blanket, and a pillow made of jute stuffed with used clothes, were spread on the bed.

'Rest. We will meet later,' Samir said.

Dinner was organised at the open space outside the rooms. It seemed this space was their meeting room.

At dinner, Chakradhar explained to them the structure of their organisation.

The villages under their control were administered by an elaborate structure of janta sarkars (people's governments). The organising principles came from the Chinese revolution and the Vietnam War. A group of janta sarkars came under an Area Committee, of which there were two, headed by Samir and Chakradhar respectively. Charulata was the overall commander. Gireesh was their main fund collaborator.

'Do you receive funds from foreign countries?' Gautam asked Chakradhar.

'No. All our funds are generated internally,' replied Samir.

'The media said Gireesh was going to receive funds mediated by Chinese influence?'

'That is police propaganda.'

Mohan shifted his legs. He thought, *Was it our propaganda?*

They went on to elaborate the work done by janta sarkars in the villages. One hour later, Gautam saw the closed door open and a woman walked towards them. It was Charulata. They all rose.

'Good to see you, Nisha,' said Charulata.

'Me too. You are the Robin Hood of this area,' she replied.

'And you, I presume, are the Gandhi of this area.'

Gautam was studying Charulata's face. She had a dusky complexion and was quite short. There was a deep gash under her chin.

'*Swamiji* told us you want to meet us. What do you want from me?' she turned towards Gautam.

'As you know we are working for—'

'*Janshakti*, I know you have joined some days ago and I also know you were in the same college with Nisha.'

'You know so much about me. I thought we should also know about your ideologies.'

'After the arrest of Gireesh, the media and police have circulated many rumours about the MAF and myself. I thought the time has come to move past these rumours. So here I am. Ask whatever you want.'

Mohan took out a pen and paper as Charulata settled on the ground before them.

'First, let me know about your motto? What are you fighting for?'

'A government free of a tyrannical rule.'

'And this is your way? Armed revolution?' Nisha intervened.

'What do you propose? We go to Jantar Mantar and sit on a fast unto death or we get lathi charged by the government and do not do anything?'

'You can't ridicule non-violent methods. That was how we got our freedom.'

'That was not freedom. It was transfer of power. Now, the situation has changed. Your non-violent methods will not yield anything. The court battles you have yourself seen.'

'But, there is always a way.'

'You do not know life here; you have been here just for a few years. It is because of us that the police or forest departments dare not touch the villagers. During the PRM days, the police used to raid our villages and rape our women. They took everything they could lay their hands on, killed innocent people and dressed up the corpses as MAF operatives to win awards. They call this area Naxal *infested* as if we are a breed of infectious virus contaminating this place.'

While Charulata showed them photographs of the victims of the police raid, Gautam recalled the contents of the file provided by Subhash Joshi that had similar photographs conveying tales of horror and tragedy. That had been equally macabre. The propaganda machinery of both sides ran a malicious campaign against each other.

While Nisha was chatting with Charulata, Gautam looked around the room. It was sparsely adorned with red flags and photographs of revolutionaries. There was a photograph of Chairman Mao, up on a red cloth screen. Marx had been featured too, along with Charu Mazumdar, the founder and chief theoretician of the Naxalite movement. His romanticising of the armed struggle had led many youth in the war against the government. Charulata had clearly been deeply influenced by him.

'Have you led the movement elsewhere?' Gautam asked her.

'I wanted to be a revolutionary right from childhood. My parents were butchered in a police raid in the Dandakaranya region. At the age of five, I knew how to fire guns. We fought there in the Dandakaranya forest. There, I led one of the area committees under the command of Dandakaranya Communist Party (Maoist). Cadres of Eklavya Sena used to take shelter in our area when they were persecuted here and in Jharkhand. Hearing their plight, my Party instructed me to take up the cause of Eklavya Sena. I came to Bhagatpur and formed the MAF with Gireesh.'

'Have you had any dialogue with the government?'

'We wanted to have dialogue with the government but only when they stopped killing us. By arresting Gireesh and Vikas, they have clearly shut all doors to negotiations. Now, we will not have any meeting with the government unless they release Gireesh and Vikas.'

Suddenly, there was a commotion. A group of people led by Chakradhar were dragging a person who was bound. Gautam looked at the man with horror.

'Babu Lal!'

'Commander, he is the traitor,' Chakradhar told Charulata.

'Do you have any proof?' Charulata asked.

'Yes, I had him under surveillance and have enough evidence.'

'We will try him in the people's court.'

'What is that?' Gautam asked Samir.

'When we get hold of a person who acts against us, a trial is held at the people's court which is attended by hundreds. They listen to the whole story and a collective decision is taken by the people. Some are sentenced to death; others are warned and let off. Even with informers—they are becoming a nuisance—the people decide. The Press always reports about informers who are killed, never about those who are let off. So, everybody thinks it is a bloodthirsty procedure in which everybody ends up being always killed. It is not about revenge, it is about survival and saving future lives. Of course there are problems, we have made terrible mistakes, even killed the wrong people in our ambushes thinking they were policemen, but the brutal manner in which we have been portrayed is unfair.'

'The dreaded *People's Courts*. How can we accept this rude form of justice?' asked Nisha.

'What about *encounters*, fake and otherwise, that get policemen and soldiers bravery medals, cash awards and out-of-turn promotions from the Indian government? The more they kill, the more they are rewarded. They are called brave hearts and *encounter specialists*. Anyone who dares oppose them is called anti-national.' Charulata's voice had gone up by a few decibels.

'Let me know to whom he was supplying information,' said Samir, walking off towards Babu Lal.

Charulata put on a white cloth on her face. She hid her face at all times.

Gautam and Mohan were growing nervous. What if he mentioned them?

Babu's hands were tied and he lay on the ground while the MAF cadres rained blows on him.

Nisha could not bear the sight and ran inside the cave room. Gautam and Mohan sat quietly. Looking at the way Babu was being tortured, Gautam was convinced he would open his mouth. In his mind he was readying an escape plan. However, seeing the number of cadres around, it seemed impossible to flee. He felt sorry for Nisha.

Suddenly, a gunshot rattled the atmosphere. Charulata, Gautam and Mohan ran towards the crowd.

'What happened?' Charulata asked as they saw Babu lying on the ground soaked with blood.

'He snatched my gun and shot himself,' Samir replied.

Gautam was dazed.

'He was guilty, so he committed suicide,' said Samir.

After they took the body away, Charulata moved towards Gautam.

'Sorry. These things happen here.'

Nisha reappeared at the cave entrance, visibly shaken.

As Charulata went near her, she asked, 'Charulata, do you think your methods will bring about any development here?'

'I am not against development, but, I also believe that this power plant will not succeed till proper compensation and rehabilitation are promised.'

'That is why I am agitating against it. But, I do not approve of your methods.'

'You do not approve of our methods but you recognise we are fighting for the people, as are you. Our methods are different but our goals are the same. I will fight for them till the end. I hope you will too.'

'I promise that I will. I admire your courage but remember we can never be on one side.'

'We can never be. You are going to join a political party. We do not approve of elections under these circumstances. If you indeed enter the arena of political battle on the polling day, you will find me opposing you.'

'You are threatening me!'

'No I am not. If I had to kill you, nobody could stop me, I am just warning you. We will never allow the elections to happen.'

'We will see what happens on the polling day.'

'As you wish, Nisha. And our journalist friends, I hope you got the replies to your questions. Be my guest tonight and tomorrow you all can leave. I have to go now.'

'We are honoured to have interviewed you,' Gautam expressed his gratitude.

After Charulata left, Mohan said, 'There is so much violence among them too. They are indulging in atrocities, but, they do have a cause. I don't think they can rightly be labelled terrorists.'

'They are rebels,' said Gautam.

The next day, they were bid farewell with a song sung by the cadres at the camp.

'Lal Lal Salaam, Lal Lal Salaam, Jaane Wale Saathiyon ko Lal Lal Salaam.'

The trio was escorted to the same village from where they had been left by Krish. From there, Krish and four more boys led them to the river.

31

5 March 2013, 6 P.M.

At the Razia Regiment camp, Kavita was in her chamber when a strange sound caught her attention.

Beep beep beep.

She looked towards her study table from where the sound was emanating and immediately rose and locked her chamber from inside. She then went towards her table and pressed a lever which moved a section of the desk, revealing a transmitter which was emitting continuous beeps. She took the transmitter. 'Tiger den. Over.'

'Grey Wolf calling. Some movement towards the river. Armed men going towards Bhagatpur. Over and out.'

She immediately put the receiver back in place and took out another transmitter. 'LRP1 (Long Range Patrol1), some movement noticed towards the river. Move in quickly.'

While Gautam, Nisha and Mohan were escorted by four armed men or rather boys, led by Krish, a messenger came running behind—'An ambush patrol is waiting near the river. Retreat.'

But firing had begun from the opposite side. The cadres fell in line and started firing towards them.

'What is happening?' Gautam asked.

'Someone has informed them of our movement,' Krish replied while firing his AK-47.

'Another informer! Who is he?' Gautam thought.

After 15 minutes of continuous firing, Gautam saw a bullet ripping through Krish. He fell to the ground.

'You people retreat. Leave us,' Gautam pleaded with the group escorting them.

A bullet hit Gautam's arm.

'Watch out, comrade. Lie low,' someone told him.

'Gautam, are you okay?' Nisha shouted.

'I am, but remain where you are,' he responded. 'Go from here. Give me your guns. We will keep them engaged,' Gautam advised the remaining boys of the escort.

'You can fire this weapon?'

'Yes. We have seen you people operating the guns. We will stop them. Go.'

Gautam and Mohan took the guns and started firing in the air while the MAF contingent retreated. After a few minutes, the firing from the other side stopped and soldiers started moving stealthily towards them.

Gautam, Nisha and Mohan put their hands up and got out.

'Who are you?' Gautam replied.

'RR soldiers. Do not move or you will be dead.'

'Listen, you are mistaken. I am Nisha, you people know me. They are my friends,' she said.

'This terrorist was your friend?'

'He was not a terrorist. He was only 16,' Gautam shouted.

'You people have helped them. You are under arrest,' the leader shouted.

'I wish to talk to your officer, Kavita. She knows me,' Nisha said.

The commander of the battalion phoned Kavita. 'Madam, we have nabbed three persons, one of them calls herself Nisha. She wants to talk to you.'

She passed the phone to Nisha. Kavita recognised her. Nisha explained her journey. Next to her, Gautam fainted due to the blood loss inflicted by his wound.

'Officer, take them to the hospital. They have mistakenly been fired at,' Kavita ordered the battalion commander.

At the hospital, Gautam regained consciousness after a few hours. Nisha was anxiously waiting by his bed side.

'How are you?' she asked him.

'I am fine. Is everything all right?'

'Kavita helped us. But you cannot live by yourself now. Both of you come and stay with me. In any case, the police have decided to seal the hotel. I have a guest room.

'But...'

'Dangerous things are happening. You are not safe elsewhere.'

'What is the guarantee that we will be safe there?' Mohan asked.

'It is my guarantee. While I am living, you will be safe there.'

32

15 March 2013

For the next few days, Gautam stayed with Nisha and helped her run her classes. A week after, Nisha received a call from Kavita saying she wanted to meet them. Nisha informed Gautam and they decided to go that very afternoon.

'Saroj, we are going towards the RR camp. Take care of the classes. I will return by evening.'

Saroj's gaze followed them as they walked away from her. Nisha, Gautam and Mohan got into the car and drove towards the RR camp.

Among the quiet surroundings, some distance away from the river, a red building emerged. The signboard read—*Razia Regiment (RR)*. The plaque inscribed near the entrance also announced, 'India's first all women commando force'. A life-size statue of the legendary medieval era queen, Razia Sultan, charging forward on a horse, graced the entrance. The building was protected by a fence and numerous tents and small rooms dotted its precincts. At the gate, they were greeted by a young lady who introduced herself as Shweta

Bhatnagar, the Assistant Commandant of the RR. She took them for a tour of the camp.

They passed the training ground where 10 woman commandos, dressed in black dungarees, were practising shooting with sophisticated automatic rifles. They disassembled the weapons, blindfolded themselves and reassembled the weapons with ease. Other commandos were practising rope climbing. There were watch towers all around which were being patrolled by women guards.

Gautam said, 'Now, even the CRPF (Central Reserve Police Force) and the Indian Army have raised all-woman commando forces. More women are joining the armed forces in combat roles. I have no doubt about their capabilities. They may be even better than their male counterparts.'

'Yes, of course! Women are no less than men. Kavita is a shining example.'

'You are also an example!'

Nisha blushed.

They climbed up to the first floor of the red building which served as the headquarters. The first floor was where the chief commandant lived.

They were met by a woman in her 30s with a complexion so white that the blue veins on her arms could be seen. She had sharp features. She was dressed casually, in jeans and a T-shirt.

'How are you, Nisha?' said Kavita, giving her a hug.

'I am fine, how are you?'

'As always. Is this your friend?'

'I am Gautam, and he is Mohan,' Gautam introduced them.

'Nice to meet you. Sit down please,' she said, gesturing towards the sofa in the room.

Gautam apprised her of his news report about Bhagatpur and his meeting with the MAF.

Kavita listened to him with rapt attention and said, 'What do you intend to find out? You want to know who is the evil here? Or, why we have failed? You will not find anything. I have been stationed here for the last five years. We have been able to pinpoint their locations. But unfortunately, we have to work under the direction of the State Government which does not want to wage a finishing battle against the MAF. I had asked the State Government several times to give us permission for assault on MAF bases. But, the State Government has not consented'.

'You know their locations?'

'Look at the hill there.'

She pointed to the hill outside her office across the river.

'Behind the Parshuram Hills is the camp of the MAF Ultras. That is where you had gone. We know where they are but cannot do anything. We have been asked to fight with our hands tied behind our backs. This whole issue is seen as a law and order problem and that is a state subject,' she continued.

'But, you have done a commendable job. It would not have been easy for you to motivate the women of this place to be commandos,' said Gautam.

'It was tough. But after the PRM failed, this was a brilliant idea which was sanctioned by the Central Government within weeks of me drawing up the plan. I handpicked 100 women from the camp and sent them for training to CIJW (Counter

Insurgency and Jungle Warfare School) Mizoram, so they could learn guerrilla techniques. The batches have now returned.'

'There was an attack on your camp last year. Can you tell us about that?' Gautam asked.

'Yes, I remember the day. It was the midnight of 26th June 2012. It had been raining since morning. The sounds of river water swirling and gushing with full force could be heard in the camp. Most occupants were sleeping or preparing to go to bed. I was at my desk in this room studying a report in the local newspaper about my camp when a deafening noise startled me. Lights came on everywhere. I jumped up from my seat and rushed to the window to see smoke at the entry gate. We had been attacked.'

'What did you do then?'

'I immediately reached for my service weapon. The guards at the gate took positions behind the sandbags and began to fire in the direction of the gate. The constables at the barracks ran to the armoury to collect their INSAS (Indian Small Arms System) rifles and ammunition. The group of people gathered outside the gate entered the camp and began to shoot in all directions. The staff quarters and tents at the entrance bore the brunt of the attack. After our commandos recovered from the initial shock and took positions, they began fighting back. The gunfire raged for two hours. A small group of the attacking force led by a woman reached this building. They surrounded my office and fired indiscriminately towards this room where I was holed up. When they presumed I would be dead, the woman leading the group entered the room. I guessed she was Charulata. By then, reinforcements arrived and they engaged the terrorists outside. I fired at Charulata. Seeing me alive, she tried to flee but I caught hold of her. A fist fight ensued between us. I tried to take the veil off her face but she resisted and jumped out from this window. They retreated after they realised we had assumed supremacy.'

'That girl was Charulata?' Gautam asked.

'Perhaps!'

'Why does Charulata hate you so much?'

'Our animosity is more than a decade old. As Jehenabad's SP, I had arrested Gireesh. It is another matter he managed to flee. We had regular skirmishes with the MAF during the time I was working for People's Resistance Movement (PRM). I am the only one—and I am not exaggerating—who can prevent Charulata from creating a Red Corridor.'

'Why is the police force so helpless here? We had noticed their helplessness while MAF killed Rekha Mishra,' Mohan asked.

'That police station is only meant to secure a ground for the government to launch a full-fledged military operation in the future. The government also knows that the police force is no match for the Ultras here.'

'Even if the police force is no match to their firepower, your force is well trained. If you cannot attack their bases, you can at least prevent them from coming out in the open. While coming to Bhagatpur, we saw them roaming near the highway, they killed Rekha Mishra, they killed Raghu. Even in their camps I did not feel even an iota of fear in their minds.'

'You are correct. We are capable of fighting them but the basic problem is of—HIG.'

'HIG?'

'Yes—Human Intelligence Gap. We have practically zero human intelligence. Since this place has seen a lot of fake encounters, people generally do not trust security forces. Our women commandos have some respect here but we are far away from being recognised as a credible intelligence service. The news regarding your movement to the river was one of the first bits of information.'

'But, the MAF must have infiltrated your organisation too as they received the message as soon as you did.'

'No, we do not have traitors. It was my mistake. In my zeal to respond I used an unsecured radio frequency to relay my message.'

'They have such sophisticated equipment so as to intercept your message on a radio transmitter?' Nisha asked.

'They have some. It has all been looted from the police force. But, why did you go there? What was your purpose?' Kavita asked Nisha.

'Gautam wanted to go there and they would allow only on the condition that I accompany him. That turned out to be a good decision.' Nisha said. 'What do you think of the attack on Ajay Mishra's wife? It was supposed to be an attack on you.'

'Yes. I know they wanted to kill me. Fools! What did they think? I am Kavita Sethi, their nemesis. They will soon get a reply from me.'

'Are you contemplating some kind of military retaliation?'

'They understand only one language—the gun. One day my gun will do the talking.'

'Many find your methods inappropriate.'

'I am not using brute force against civilians and that is my strength. I admit the People Resistance Movement was a bad idea, but, the RR is a novel one. But then, the negative propaganda by vested interests has maligned our image but that does not bother me much. I always focus on the larger picture. The aim is to finish the MAF and the RBS. Till then, I will have to fight these human rights violation cases. I am personally fighting around 10 cases against me in various courts here,' she said.

'Maybe, but this makes the situation complex.'

'Yes it does. You may also have understood how locals are divided in their opinions. Some support us and join us in our battle but the majority likes to align their faith with the MAF and its methods. The administration and government have failed to garner the peace-loving people's support.'

'But, why are they not able to see the writing on the wall? This violence will lead us nowhere.'

'The political short-sightedness blurred the vision of the policymakers and that resulted in the mishandling of this sensitive issue. The issue needs the carrot-and-stick policy. I am ready to wield the stick, but curiously enough, the carrot is eaten by the policymakers themselves. For the last five decades, this place has not understood the meaning of the term *development*.' All the money in the name of grand schemes has been siphoned by politicians and bureaucrats. Naturally, people are angry. This leads them to the MAF camps.'

'We have learnt a lot today. We will leave you to your work now. It was nice talking to you,' said Gautam.

'Best of luck.'

33

14 March 2013, 7 P.M.

Gautam was drawing a picture on a white sheet when Mohan entered his room.

'Sir, what is this?'

He found Gautam sketching a portrait of Charulata.

'Go to Jehenabad tomorrow and fax this photo to Subhash Joshi,' Gautam asked Mohan.

They were distracted by a sound.

'What is happening?' Gautam asked.

'Nothing, sir. Saroj is locking up and preparing to go,' Mohan replied.

'Where is Nisha?'

'She is reading a book.'

'Come with me,' he asked Mohan, who followed suit. Keeping a safe distance from Saroj, they began tailing her. She took the road towards the village and moved past the Panchayat Bhavan to the banks of the river Bhagat. Her hut was the only one-storey building in the area. The bricked walls were plastered, unlike the mud walls for most of the villagers. An electric wire hung to her house from the nearby pole. Her house was one of the privileged few in Bhagatpur which is equipped with an electric connection and a landline.

'Sir, why have we come here?'

'Quiet, Mohan, I have a doubt that our friend Saroj is part of the MAF. Our informer had told us there was one more person at Bhagatpur who was working in disguise. Saroj seems to be very supportive of the MAF and she goes missing whenever there is an encounter with the MAF. Moreover, analyse the location of her house carefully. If she indeed is the espionage leader of MAF, this place is ideal to intercept radio transmission signals from the Razia Regiment camp. The RR camp is in Line of Sight(LOS) communication distance from this region.'

They set up watch outside her house but nothing significant occurred even after a lapse of three hours.

'Let us go back. It seems we are assuming too much,' said Gautam.

'I told you so. Saroj hardly fits in as an MAF operative.'

'I may be wrong but still I believe she has something to do with Charulata.'

As both of them were returning they saw a truck plying towards the Parshuram hill.

'A truck in the middle of the night?' Mohan asked.

'Maybe it is going to Gaya. Let us go back now. Nisha must be getting worried.'

As they moved towards the NS2, the truck silently moved on the serpentine road winding towards the hillock. Its contents were covered by a tarpaulin. The front panel had *Raju Transport* written in bold. The cabin light was left switched on to give an impression that it was a civilian vehicle. This was the standard practice here so that the MAF rebels or RBS cadres did not mistake it for a police vehicle. The murmur of the engine pierced through the eerie silence of the night. As the vehicle reached the giant Hanuman statue, the driver bowed his head in obeisance and continued driving.

'*Bajrangbali* is the only saviour in this lawless land,' he murmured.

The Hanuman temple was the starting point of the Hanuman Ghati. Despite the wind, the driver was sweating profusely even in the pleasant weather. As he neared the police checkpost, which had been set up by the local police after the attack on Ajay Mishra's wife, he slowed down. All the drivers plying up the Parshuram Hills towards Gaya bypass were issued a pass by the Tailorgunj police station. The vehicles were allowed to go further on the basis of this identification. This ensured that no arms reached the MAF rebels who had bases in the forests bordering Hanuman Ghati.

The guards manning the outpost had seen the truck coming. The leader looked at his watch.

'It's 3 o'clock. Who is coming at this hour? Take a look,' he asked one of the guards.

The sentry looked at the list of passwords lying across the table, stepped out with an SLR in his hands and asked in a sceptical tone—'Hand me the pass.'

The truck stopped, but, nobody emerged from it.

The sentry repeated himself, putting pressure on the trigger.

The driver opened his cabin door and handed him a piece of paper.

The guard matched the pass with that with him. Satisfied, he put the SLR aside and went to the truck and asked, 'What are you carrying?'

'Items for local *kirana* stores, sir.'

The sentry flipped the tarpaulin of the truck and found nothing except sacks and bundles in different sizes.

As soon as the sentry ordered the road block to be removed, the driver mopped the sweat off his forehead and pressed the accelerator. As the truck moved around the corner of Hanuman Temple and pushed forward, the vehicle slowed down again. The tarpaulin sheltering the back of the truck flipped over and a figure deboarded from it. It quickly moved towards the scrubs at the foothills. One by one, 12 people disembarked. The driver felt a thud and he sped thereafter. All the 12 figures assembled at the base of the hill. The leader of the group, Kavita, stepped ahead and spoke in a hushed tone.

'Friends, we have assembled here to mount the biggest operation ever undertaken by our forces against the danger we have been fighting against for the past few years. The time has come to give them a befitting reply. Now, listen to me once again. Put on your night-vision devices. We will divide ourselves in groups of two and fan out in all directions. The ascent is 700 m. It will take around two hours to reach the top. Beware, the area is mined. Use the mine sensor to detect and steer clear of them. There are three watchtowers to inspect for any intruders, the exact locations of which are indicated on the map. We have to neutralise the watchtowers first. Remember, surprise is the key. Our other teams have reached their positions. We will succeed in our attempt.'

The listeners raised their hands in the air to show solidarity.

The battalion moved stealthily upwards. There were four, not three, watchtowers looking all around. However, they had come prepared for any such surprises. Four clean shots from the sniper rifles took care of the guards at the watchtowers. The commandos fanned out at the summit of the hill and surrounded the base from the top and took their positions. Under the moonlight, the MAF rebels had put up tents. Some were guarding the area but most were sleeping. Kavita Sethi scanned the entire area through her night vision device. One of her teams was at the summit where the dam was built to create a reservoir for drinking water supply for the townspeople. The second team was stationed at the valley where the river Bhagat entered the plain area through a narrow channel flanked by big boulders on both sides. Her teams were ready for action.

'Now, you all will drown like rats,' she whispered in contempt.

She signalled. Deafening noises shattered the calm of the night and the air was filled with the smell of dynamite. The inhabitants of the camp came out and were horror-struck. The walls of the dam cracked and the water stored in the reservoir roared down the valley in an avalanche. At the exit point, huge boulders blocked the exit. They understood the gameplan of the attackers. Soon, the water would reach the bottom of the hill and after finding no exit route would eventually begin accumulating at their camp and drown them. They tried to move up the hill but the commandos started firing from the upper slopes. The RR clearly had the upper hand this time. The encounter continued till 6 o'clock the next morning, after which they retreated. In the morning, a large contingent of local police, accompanied by armed police battalions, reached the spot. The bodies of the terrorists had begun to surface and the count reached 50, along with a huge cache of arms and ammunition. The base camp of the MAF was destroyed.

The surviving Ultras took shelter in the forest.

34

15 March 2013, 11 A.M.

The events set in motion by Kavita and her team had increased the tension prevailing in the area. People couldn't stop talking about the attack. The Panchayat was called to discuss it.

'Sarpanch*ji*, the raid on Charulata's hideout has rattled us. She is not going to take this lightly. What shall we do?' one of the villagers asked the sarpanch, who was puffing on a hookah.

'We shall make arrangements for our security. The RBS can also take this opportunity to attack our villages and start a new war. Even Charulata can attack our villages. I order all the youth to form a *Suraksha Dal* to guard our village round the clock. Do not venture towards the river and confine yourself to your house after 6 p.m.,' the sarpanch declared.

A virtual curfew was imposed on Bhagatpur. Security was tightened at Ganesh Rai's bungalow and the STF was asked to be on guard for any possible attack on him. Similar measures were taken at Ajay Mishra's residence. The checkpost at Hanuman Ghati was withdrawn and the police force was advised to refrain from long-range patrolling.

At the NS2, Nisha and Gautam were discussing the turn of events.

'Gautam, see today's headlines,' Nisha shoved the newspaper towards him.

The newspaper report read—

> The MAF suffered a severe blow from the Razia Regiment. Twelve RR commandos raided the MAF base camp during the midnight. The area had been considered impenetrable hitherto. They have also recovered documents that reveal details of a plan devised for kidnapping Special Magistrate, Ajay Mishra. Two RR commandos died in the attack and Kavita Sethi was injured.

The newspaper also carried Kavita's picture, flashing a V-sign. She was blood-soaked and armed with an automatic rifle on her shoulders.

'This woman has grit. Yesterday, when we asked if she was contemplating something, she changed the topic. She did not want to tell us about this attack,' Gautam said.

'But now the MAF will try to do something big. Charulata has claimed that she will take revenge. How will she do that?'

'No idea,' said Gautam. 'Aren't you conducting any classes today?'

'Saroj has not come today either. Her cell phone is switched off. People have become more afraid after this ghastly incident. They will not send students to class.'

'After you become a full-time politician, what will Saroj do?'

'She will take over some of my NS2 responsibilities.'

'Do you really want to join politics?'

'Why is everybody asking me the same question again? In this country, politics is the most admired and most hated career option. This will take my struggle to a higher level and bring me closer to my goal of doing something constructive for society,' she said.

'I have never seen a genuine politician working towards the welfare of the common man,' said Gautam.

'This is the problem with the people of India. They are quick to blame the politicians and when it comes to ownership, they conveniently shy away.'

'Okay, okay. It is your choice, but, it is my personal opinion that nothing will come out of it. We should continue with NS2,' Gautam said.

'We? But you will leave one day.'

'Maybe, maybe not,' Gautam replied looking away.

Nisha sensed there was something going on in Gautam's mind. She was tempted to ask what it was, but got distracted by a police van that stopped in front of the office.

The SHO Kanahiya alighted from the vehicle and entered her chamber.

'What is it officer?' she asked.

'You must be aware that there was a serious attack on the MAF camp last night. We have recovered Saroj's dead body.'

All of them were stunned by the news.

'It cannot be. How can she be dead? Who killed her?'

'She was killed in the raid. She was with the MAF.'

'But that cannot be true. If she was one of them, why would she work with me?'

'As her cover. It is a common practice. She used your NS2 mission as her front and used it to propagate the MAF philosophy.'

'I also had a feeling that Saroj had some connection with Charulata,' Gautam added.

'I knew she had leanings with the MAF, but, I cannot believe she was actually one of them,' Nisha said.

'We raided her house and found a radio transmitter and a radio interceptor which she used to catch the frequencies of the RR and police radio broadcast. We also recovered volumes of communist literature in her house,' Kanahiya said.

'My God!'

Their attention turned towards the television where Charulata's interview was being telecast. She had her back towards the camera and her face was covered.

The reporter asked, 'The RR has inflicted a heavy blow to your forces. How would you react to this?'

'They will get our first reply soon. They will see what it means to attack us.'

'What are you planning?'

'Wait and watch.'

'The government has invited you to talks. Do you want to initiate a dialogue with the government?'

'We will talk, but, we have conditions. Withdraw the RR, halt the construction of the plant and release Gireesh Marandi. Only then will we agree to talk.'

'The government asked you to lay down arms. Do you propose to do that?'

'Never, we will lay down arms only when this place is on the path of true development. Till then, we will continue our struggle.'

'Are you certain this armed struggle will achieve anything? Don't you think Indian security forces will come down heavily on you one day?'

'We are not terrorists. We are reformers and we have people's support. The government cannot suppress the will of the masses.'

'Elections are approaching. What are your thoughts on that? Why don't you also run for office? If people support you, they will surely make you the leader. And, if you are indeed pro-development then why are you opposing the plant? It will provide power to the entire state.'

'People are not ready for elections yet. First, let the government provide proper compensation for the land they have forcibly snatched away for this construction. The government has to provide the basic necessities like schools, roads and electricity to our people so as they can live their life with dignity. Let there be development first. Till our demands are met, we will continue to obstruct the construction of the power plant and oppose the elections.'

Kanahiya took their leave once the programme concluded.

35

17 March 2013, 9 P.M.

Deep inside the forest, Charulata was pacing up and down at the makeshift camp her cadres had built after the attack on their camps at the Parshuram Valley. Chakradhar came running to her and halted—*'Lal Salaam.'*

'Why are you looking worried?' Charulata asked.

He handed her a piece of paper he was concealing in his clothes.

'This is my portrait. How did you get it?' Charulata jumped.

'One of the journalists who had come here was faxing it to a number in Delhi. The fax owner is our supporter. He smelled something amiss when he saw someone faxing this photo to Delhi and informed us immediately.'

'What did you tell him?'

'I told him we will investigate the matter and find out why that journalist was faxing it. The fax owner also overheard something—Informer is dead.'

'What the hell? Who are they? I thought you had investigated their credentials?'

'I had but it seemed they were genuine. I investigated the number to which it was faxed and—'

'And?'

'It was the Intelligence Bureau. The fax was sent to Joint Director Subhash Joshi.'

'What have we done? We showed everything to them? Who are they? IB men?'

'We sent their pictures to our lawyer in Delhi who is handling Vikas' case. They have identified them as Delhi Police ACP Gautam Dhaliwal and SI Mohan Singh.'

'Why have they come here? To spy on me?'

'Maybe, but since they communicated about the death of the informer, I presume they had come for the informer. Babu must be their informer. Remember, we had killed Sudhakar who had sent an informer here. We had thought that the informer was dead or could not infiltrate the camp. But now, it is certain it was Babu.'

'Keep an eye on them.'

'Shall we eliminate them?'

'No, not now. I shall know what their mission is. They did come here but they also saved lives of our cadres when they were ambushed by the RR while they were being escorted.'

'Commander, is it possible Nisha is involved?'

'I don't think so. Saroj knew everything about Nisha. If she would have been involved, Saroj would have known. Besides, we got the rooms of these journalists searched on Saroj's insistence, but found nothing. I think it is coincidence that Gautam and Nisha were college friends. Still, it is better to keep an eye on them.'

~

DCP Rajesh entered Subhash's room and found him in a pensive mood.

'What happened, sir? Why have you called me urgently?'

'Listen to this,' he said while pressing the button of a portable voice recorder.

'Comrade, the photo which you had sent here is of police officers. One of them is ACP Gautam Dhaliwal and the other is SI Mohan Singh.'

'What the hell? Who is he? Whom is he talking to?' Rajesh asked.

'We have kept anyone associated with Vikas and Aslam under strict surveillance. This is Vikas and Aslam's lawyer and presumably he is talking to the MAF. The cover of your officers is busted. Call them back urgently.'

'But sir, he is doing a good job there. Let him continue there at least till he provides concrete information about Charulata,' Rajesh pleaded.

Joshi ignored him and went out of the room.

Rajesh dialled Gautam's number.

'Gautam, I did not expect this from you. How was your cover blown?'

'I don't know what you are talking about.'

'You both have been identified by the MAF. Come back immediately. You have failed.'

'I have not failed. I got the information you wanted.'

'What?'

'No one had any information about Charulata. Now you know who she is, how the group operates. I also unearthed the informer, even though he was killed. It does not matter that my mission is no longer a secret.'

'It matters. Wind up your investigation and come back soon. The Home Ministry will look for other options in this case.'

'The fact is they have no alternative.'

The line went dead.

'What happened, sir?' Mohan asked.

'I am fed up. In the last five years I thought we were part of the best police force in the world. However, I came face-to-face with the ugly truth here. There is violence and corruption. For whom are we fighting? For Ganesh Rai, that wily politician; or Rohit, for whom money means everything? I do not want to go back.'

'But what happened, sir?'

'We have been identified by the MAF.'

'How?'

'I don't know the details. But we have been instructed to return.'

'Then, we must do so.'

'I will not go back. I will finish my job. You don't need to be a police officer to fight for your motherland. I am convinced that the MAF are not terrorists. They are born out of the failure of the administration. I will work for the people of Bhagatpur. I will work with Nisha and ensure the MAF has no reason to exist.'

'Sir, are you serious?'

'Yes, Mohan, I will resign and continue my work here. You prepare to go back.'

'Have you taken this decision in haste or is it because of Nisha?'

'I don't know why I am doing this but believe me, I feel relieved after this decision. I don't know whether I will be happy in the long run, but, at least I am happy now. I hope mother will understand. You go back.'

A knock at the door interrupted their conversation.

Gautam grabbed his service revolver and nudged Mohan to open the door. An enraged Nisha was standing outside.

'Nisha, what happened?' exclaimed Gautam.

'Saroj used me. She used Nai Soch-Nai Subah. It is enough. I am not going to be blind anymore. I will withdraw my compliant against Ganesh Rai. I will show the MAF that I am not going to be their puppet anymore.'

'But if you do that, he may be absolved of all charges,' Gautam responded.

'I will contest him in the election battlefield, not in the court.'

After a few moments of silence, Nisha spoke—'I am not feeling well. Can we go for a walk?'

'Now! Is it safe?'

'Of course. This place is not as dangerous as you make it out to be. Let us go to the village pond and clear our heads. Mohan*ji*, you also come,' she said.

They went to the pond near Ganesh Rai's palace. Gautam and Nisha walked near the shore while Mohan was a few steps behind. Not a soul was in sight.

They sat down.

'Nisha, I wish to say something to you,' Gautam spoke.

'What?' she looked at him expectantly.

'We are not journalists but police officers,' Gautam spoke with a straight face.

Nisha was stunned.

'What?'

'I am the ACP in Delhi Police and Mohan is my subordinate. It all began with Gireesh's arrest. Rohit laid a trap for Gireesh and that is how we arrested him. But, there was an informer in the MAF we had to locate and we were sent here. It helped that you were here. We traced the informer but he was killed.'

'Babu Lal was your informer?'

'Yes, we came here on a mission to finish the MAF. But, what I have seen here has moved me so much that I now believe there is far more to the reality we once perceived to be true.'

'So, you too have used me?'

'No, I have not used you. I wish to help you.'

'Thank you. I do not need any help.'

'But, I need your help. I joined the police force to serve the country, but after so many years of doing my duty, I have realised I am not happy. After meeting you here, I have found the true meaning of my life. I would like to work with you for Nai Soch-Nai Subah. I hope you will allow me.'

'I am so happy to have you near me. I am sorry for being rude,' she smiled.

Mohan cleared his throat to register his presence.

'Mohan. You leave tomorrow. I have already prepared my resignation. I will hand it over to you,' Gautam said.

'All right, sir. I am going to sleep now. Goodnight.'

Mohan left them alone.

Part III

The Seize

36

1 June 2013, 10 A.M.

The Jailor and Shukla*ji* were running towards Ganesh Rai's cell. He had every possible material comfort—an air conditioner, a refrigerator and a television—at his disposal. The STF members guarded the cell day in and day out.

'Shukla*ji*, I hope you have good news?' Ganesh reacted after his lawyer walked into his room.

'Yes sir. Nisha has refused to testify against you and the case has lost its strength. We have filed the bail petition. You could be released tomorrow,' replied the advocate.

'Why has she done that?'

'Maybe, she is frightened. Or maybe, she is doing this to mock Charulata, one of whose commandants turned out to be her friend, Saroj,' Shukla, the advocate said.

'We never thought that woman could have been working for the MAF. It means she was the one who killed Jagdish, whom I had sent to threaten Nisha.'

'Yes sir. Now that the MAF has weakened, it will be easy to fight Nisha.'

'Sir, I hope you would have liked being my guest?' the jailor asked.

'Tiwari*ji*, I liked the stay very much. Don't worry, I will speak to the chief minister about your promotion,' Ganesh replied.

The next day, as soon as the court ordered for Ganesh's release, his supporters burst into cheerful chants and surrounded the district jail shouting—'Ganesh *Bhaiya, zindabad*!'

Ganesh's cavalcade was to begin from the jail to Bhagatpur the next day. The same night, Samir updated Charulata about the latest developments.

'I knew Nisha would do something like this and withdraw her complaint. She is true to her principles. But unwittingly, she has done our job. Let them remove Ganesh Rai from the protective cover of the STF. We will close his chapter forever,' Charulata roared.

'One more thing. Mohan has left and Gautam has resigned,' Samir said.

'Keep an eye on Gautam. I am certain they must have been informed about our knowledge of their true identities. But, why has Gautam decided to stay back? I will have to know.'

'What about Mohan?'

'Let him go back. Whatever information they had, they have already passed on to their seniors. Now, Mohan will not be able to do anything against us. Concentrate on Ganesh Rai.'

~

Unaware of Charulata's game plan, Ganesh was being escorted by a police van and his followers. The convoy came out of the jail and took the path towards Bhagatpur, which included a stretch through forested areas. This makeshift road was infamous as 'killer road,' for it passed through the MAF territory. Many attacks on the police and RR battalions had taken place on this stretch. Somewhere, on a cliff overlooking that stretch, Charulata was waiting. The day of revenge had come.

Trees felled by MAF blocked the route for the convoy to move ahead. As soon the convoy slowed down, the MAF triggered an IED blast that destroyed the third vehicle of the convoy within seconds. In an attempt to flee, several vehicles collided with each other. Soon, the convoy came under fire from all directions. The police retaliated but could not keep up with the MAF cadres. One by one, they collapsed at the hail of bullets. Meanwhile, Ganesh's supporters reversed their vehicles and fled. The MAF men descended from the cliff to the site and began walking towards the police vehicle where Ganesh Rai was still sitting. They opened the doors and dragged him out.

'How are you, Ganesh Rai? I hope the government has looked after you well.' Charulata emerged from the bushes.

Ganesh Rai had a vermilion tika on his forehead. He kept his head low and remained silent.

'Why are you not speaking? I think you know these are your last few moments on earth. Did you think that you will keep killing our people and I will watch in silence? Today, with you, your misrule will also come to a bitter end. Not only have you killed innocent people, but, you have also maligned our name. Remember Sunil Kushwaha and Gopal Krishnan? You were the murderer, but, we were labelled guilty. Now the time has come to pay. These garlands will look nice on your dead body.'

She shot him at point blank range.

The district headquarters received the details of the encounter and rushed to the site. In Delhi, Rohit was shaken after reading about the latest developments in Bhagatpur. He stared at the newspaper on his desk.

> The violence in Bihar has taken a nasty turn after the MAF's killing of Ganesh Rai, the MLA from Bhagatpur. Since then, there have been massive demonstrations at Bhagatpur and Patna against the killings. In Patna, Rai's supporters gutted two police vans, forcing the police to resort to a lathi charge. The State Government has ordered a CID inquiry into his killing.
>
> Ganesh Rai was supposed to be the man behind the RakhtBeej Sena, an underground army which was started by his father and which has been locked in a battle with the MAF. After his death, the RBS is in disarray. He does not have any surviving family members; they had all been murdered by MAF founder, Gireesh Marandi. The RBS commander, Munna Yadav, is on the run. After this latest killing, the government seems more helpless than before. It is evident that the MAF has no fear of the police. Pressure is building up for an all-out war on the MAF. Even the construction of the power plant in Bhagatpur has been shrouded in doubt as the MAF has vowed to disrupt the activities.

Oh, God! Why do all my plans backfire? The SPCCL and the RBS are defunct now. They are not in a position to defend me anymore. My only hope is the Central Government. I have to meet the home minister, he thought.

The next day at North Block, a harried Rohit walked briskly through the corridors of *power*. He stopped at the home minister's chamber and gave the peon his visiting card. After a few minutes, some people emerged from the chamber and a bell rang from inside. The peon went inside, returned after a few minutes and asked Rohit to go in.

'What do you want?' asked the home minister.

'I need your support.'

'You remembered me after your protector has been eliminated. I know you are a businessman and will look after your interests only. So, we will talk pure business. How much can you provide to our Party funds?'

'Twenty crores,' he said.

'That is too little. You offered the MAF 10 and Ganesh Rai 20 per cent stake in your company. We will require 50 crores.'

'Fifty is too much.'

'Then, be prepared to wind up from Bhagatpur. We are going to award the contract to the next bidder in line.'

He thought for a while and said, 'All right, I agree. But, I have lost a lot of money and will adjust it somewhere in the construction of the plant. We will increase the construction cost and you will support us.'

'That is not a problem. Just take care of us and we will take care of you. Don't worry about the MAF. We are going to introduce a bill in the Parliament which will provide security forces more powers while dealing with the insurgency, like the AFSPA (Armed Forces Special Power Act). They will be free to take independent action.'

Rohit was relaxed after listening to these reassurances and thought that his woes were finally coming to an end. But his joy was short-lived.

A parcel was waiting for him at his table when he reached office. He tore open the parcel which had a CD and a note—'Watch this CD and if you don't want me to send it to the media or the police, then keep Rs 1 crore ready. I will call you soon.'

He placed the CD in his laptop. The visuals which unfolded before his eyes left him shocked.

37

10 July 2013

The monsoon was in full swing, supplying enough water to the river Bhagat. It turned into a monstrous channel of water, threatening to devour the banks. The PWD engineers had warned that they might be forced to open the sluice gates of the reservoir if the rain persisted. This hinted at a flood-like situation and the district administration issued an advisory to those residing along the banks of the river. The Bhagatpur residents had begun moving to the interior of the village.

In her office, Nisha was discussing the future of the NS2 with Gautam. In the background, the television flashed the news channel coverage of heavy rainfall throughout the country.

'The UNHRC (United Nations Human Rights Council) has decided to provide us funds if we expand our activities outside Bhagatpur,' Nisha said.

'I was also thinking on those terms. Once we get the funds, I will establish an office at Patna. Then, maybe, we can have a Delhi office too. If you become an MP, then it would be much easier to operate from Delhi,' Gautam replied.

'I think we should first concentrate on Bihar and then move to Delhi.'

During their conversation, Gautam got a call from Mohan.

'Hello Mohan. What are you doing?'

'Sir, I am investigating the Soumit murder case. We have kept Rohit Kumar under surveillance for a while now and yesterday we tracked something highly suspicious in one of his phone calls. He was talking to a woman about a CD. Then, he was called to a secluded place in Greater Noida and asked to deliver one crore in cash. Our team followed him but no one turned up to take the money.'

'Do you know what the contents of the CD are?'

'No idea sir.'

'Mohan, do you think it was the CD from the CCTV recording at Soumit's house? I had asked Aslam to investigate the maid then.'

'Aslam was himself a supporter of the MAF. He is behind bars now. I also had the same doubt which you are raising now, and I did check the whereabouts of the maid. But, she has simply vanished.'

'Okay. Let me know if you find anything else.'

'Sir, I came to know about us being identified by the MAF. I feel responsible because the fax owner gave us away. I am sorry for that.'

'No, I should have expected something like that to happen and been more vigilant.'

'You will always remain my boss, sir!' he said and disconnected the phone.

'What happened?' Nisha asked.

'While we were investigating Soumit's murder, we suspected someone made a CD of his death, but it could not be traced. Yesterday, Mohan intercepted a conversation on Rohit's phone about a CD, where the caller told him it would cost one crore if he wants it back. I suspect that is the same CD.'

'So, did he provide the money?'

'No one turned up to collect the cash!'

'Why?'

'Perhaps, the caller got a whiff of the police or—'

'Or what?'

'The caller is dead.'

'Who would have killed him?'

'I doubted the maid, Urmila, in Soumit's house. If it indeed was her who took the CD, the MAF would probably have killed her to take possession of it.'

'But why did it surface after so many days?'

'Urmila must have been waiting for the case to cool off to blackmail Rohit. But, it looks like she waited too long. The CD is a potential weapon to destroy Rohit and the MAF must have jumped at the chance to grab it.'

'I am sure Rohit will find a way out. He is too smart. Now, he has taken a turn towards our Party after Ganesh Rai's death.'

'But you were against him?'

'I am still against him but he has pledged funds to our Party, and, every Party needs funds during elections.'

'He has become a milch cow for all of you. First the MAF, then the State Government, and now your Party. But I want him finished.'

'I also want to nail him. As long as our people get justice.'

'Are you planning to raise this issue of compensation against land acquisition in the elections?'

'I wanted to but political complications have stopped me from taking such decisions.'

'What complications you are talking about? Earlier, you were fighting for the people and now you are not even able to raise such an important issue. What are your political complications?' he asked.

'The compensation problem has been settled by the High Court in favour of the government. The matter is now with the Supreme Court. What we have planned is that after we win, we will provide people the compensation through the chief minister's fund in the name of disaster relief. This will satisfy them and enhance the prestige of our Party.'

'Now that Ganesh Rai is gone, who will contest against you?'

'The CM himself. He has made it a prestige issue.'

'Then it is going to be a close finish. He is quite popular. Though his popularity is falling, he has maintained caste equations which will help him a lot.'

'You are right. Caste is still a big factor in the elections. But mark my words. One day, these people will vote for development. Bhagatpur has emerged as an important constituency and Nilesh Yadav doesn't want this to go to the Opposition Party.'

'I do not see the people here voting for development in the near future. There is no alternative to playing the caste card in the elections here.'

Suddenly, breaking news on television caught their attention and they turned their gaze towards the television screen.

'Business tycoon accused of murdering his deputy.'

The news anchor read out—'Today, we received a CD which shows visuals of business tycoon Rohit murdering his deputy.'

'We are now playing the CD.'

The scene which played out was—'Rohit?' Soumit exclaimed when he opened the door to his house.

'Yes, how are you?'

'I am fine. What a coincidence. Today, I was going through my collection of CDs and I found one of your interviews last year.'

'Forget about that. Did you know that Gireesh has been caught?'

'Yes. That is what you wanted, wasn't it? First, provide them money and then get their leader arrested. This requires a celebration.' Soumit walked towards the bar and took out a wine bottle.

'Where is your maid?'

'She has gone to the market. Why do you ask? Do you want anything?'

'No, no.' Rohit said, observing from the corner of his eye while his bodyguard George slipped something into Soumit's glass.

'Soumit, you should not have done that.'

'What? I did what you told me to do,' replied Soumit, surprised.

'You should have been more careful. The police are on your trail now.'

'Police?' he replied, 'How did they know about this?'

'They tracked your mobile number.'

'What will I do now?'

'Don't worry, I will fix it.'

'As always. Cheers.' Soumit raised his glass.

The Party went on for half-an-hour after which Soumit slumped on his seat. Rohit gestured at George. He strangulated Soumit before hanging his body from the ceiling fan. Then, they erased all the fingerprints and wiped the room clean. The video clip ended.

'What is this?' Nisha was stunned.

'So, the CD we were searching for reached the media. MAF used this opportunity to nail Rohit. This CD will surely create a political storm,' Gautam said.

Meanwhile, the Noida police recovered a body of a woman which was later identified as the missing maid from Rohit's home.

38

12 July 2013

The broadcast created a huge political storm and Nilesh Yadav was bombarded with questions. In his office, his PA, Amit Dutta ,was apprising him of the latest developments. 'The prime minister has formed a Group of Ministers (GoM) to look into the matter and put the construction of the power plant on hold. A CBI inquiry was ordered on the issue of the complicity of Silent Turtle with the MAF and the SPCCL. However, he put the ball in the State Government's court as the SPCCL belongs to Ganesh Rai from our Party. The police plan to arrest Rohit.'

'This is not good. Shall we scrap the power plant?' the worried PA asked.

'No, Mr Dutta. That will be a political disaster. We need the power plant to tide over the energy crisis and we will not get adequate land for the project anywhere else except Bhagatpur. We will have to win over the people. This has now become a prestige issue for me. Call Ajay Mishra to my office tomorrow.'

~

At the Patna secretariat, Ajay Mishra was waiting for the chief minister. His face looked swollen.

'You are not looking well, Mr Ajay,' said the CM's PA.

'Yes, I have high blood pressure which has affected my kidney,' he replied.

'Sorry to hear about your wife. She was a nice lady.'

Ajay was quiet. He asked, 'Why has he called me?'

'Only sir can tell.'

After an hour, the CM called Ajay to his office.

'How are you, Ajay?'

'Fine, sir,' he replied, meekly.

'I have important things to discuss.'

'Yes sir.'

'Look, the Bhagatpur situation is worsening with each passing day. Ganesh's murder has further weakened our Party there. But, Bhagatpur is an important constituency for me as it has become an issue of prestige for my Party. I have decided to contest from there. Because of the widespread resentment against our land acquisition policy, I have decided to scrap the post of special magistrate of Bhagatpur. Now, go and take charge as the District Magistrate of Jehenabad and oversee the activity at Bhagatpur from there. I have also decided to call Ravi Taneja from central deputation to be given the post of SP of Jehenabad.'

'Ravi Taneja! I have worked with him when we were posted in Gaya. He is very upright and brave officer. Besides, he has great regards for you.'

'That is why I have posted him there. I will create a post of ASP Operations there to fight the MAF, for which Abhijit Verma, a young IPS officer, will be designated. Work closely with Taneja. You two will have to ensure a few things. First, Nisha should not win the elections. Second, I am going to increase the compensation amount through the chief minister's Tribal Relief Fund and ensure that the people of Bhagatpur receive the money before the election. And third, ensure that the MAF does not indulge in any more violence till the election. Do not take any steps against them, but, do not allow them to take any steps either. I hope I am clear,' asserted the CM.

'Even if we enforce a unilateral ceasefire, will Charulata respond?' Ajay Mishra asked.

'I will try to talk to her,' Nilesh replied.

'She has refused to talk to the government.'

'I know the person she will be willing to talk to,' said the CM, smiling.

'Wait till the election. After that, I will finish Charulata. She will pay for killing my wife.'

'Good. Now, go and take charge from the present DM. Do not stress. The election is still a few months from now but you should begin your preparation. This Dusshera, I wish to address a rally at Bhagatpur. Get that arranged,' said the CM.

'Sir, what about the Razia Regiment?'

'It will die a natural death soon,' he said, smiling again.

Ajay left the office.

39

30 July 2013

In the dark, a shadow was moving towards the forest interior. Charulata was talking to her comrades when the guard on duty alerted them—'Someone is coming.'

'Take positions,' she ordered, ducking behind a rock.

'Stop, who are you?' Chakradhar warned the person who had ventured near their camp.

The shadow slowed down and put his hands up. As he emerged from the bushes, Chakradhar lowered the gun and whispered, 'Swami*ji*?'

Charulata emerged from behind the rocks, went up to Narendra Nath and touched his feet.

'How are you?'

'I am fine, Swami*ji*. You could have called me. Anything urgent?'

'Yes, an important matter. I have to discuss something with you, in private.'

'Okay,' she said and looked towards Chakradhar. He nodded and waved at all the cadres to move out.

'Tell me Swami*ji*, what is the issue?'

'The CM has asked me to offer you something.'

'I do not want anything he offers.'

'Be pragmatic. The way the situation is unfolding is not good for you.'

'What does he want? That we surrender?'

'He does not want you to surrender, but demands a guarantee from you that the upcoming polls in Bhagatpur will not be disrupted.'

'Why should we do that?'

'In return, he will halt all police operations against you and ask the police force to destroy the RBS. He will covertly help Sulochna's efforts to wind up the RR, abolish the post of special magistrate and also move Subhash Joshi from the IB to his home cadre, Maharashtra. The compensation amount will be increased too.'

'Why this sudden generosity?'

'He wants to win from here.'

'What about Nisha?'

'Let them fight it out in the political arena. You become neutral.'

'Nisha is your *niece*. Do you also want her to lose?'

'I just want peace in this region. Whoever wins is immaterial to me. You are as lovable to me as is Nisha. We all want development of this region. Isn't it? At present I think this is the right solution. Let the people of Bhagatpur decide whom they want in the election.'

Charulata stood up from her seat and started pacing up and down with her hands clasped behind her back. After some time, she sat down again.

'What shall I tell him?' Narendra Nath asked.

'Ask him to announce all that he said in his upcoming rally. We will not make any formal announcement but we will not disrupt the election either. We will not support any Party. Let them fight. But if the police arrest or kill any of our members, we will not take it lying down. This arrangement will work till the elections. After that, we will review the case again.'

'Take care. I will leave.'

~

On the eve of Vijaya Dashmi, the people of Bhagatpur gathered at the field outside the community hospital to witness the burning of Ravana's effigy. Chief Minister Nilesh Yadav used this occasion for his rally and spoke directly to the people. Earlier that day, a lot of enthusiasm was generated when his helicopter landed at the makeshift helipad at Vikramgarh Fort. From there, the CM was escorted under heavy security to the community field. He began his speech, thus.'Brothers and sisters of Bhagatpur, I have come here not as the chief minister of the state, but, as a friend. I realise we have committed grave mistakes in the past and I have come here to express my regret and grief. I know you are unhappy with the compensation sum. But, what could I have done? This was deemed *just* by our honourable courts. I have something to share that will cheer you up. I have set up the Chief Minister's Tribal Development Fund to help you resettle. You will receive the money from this fund within one month; and we have also decided to provide you lands on the other side of the hill for you to start a new life. In the new compensation scheme, we have included the landless labourers who did not provide the land for the power plant, but, whose livelihoods were equally affected. All of them will also receive their share of fair compensation.'

A huge round of applause broke the monotony of his speech.

He continued, 'Last week, there was an attack by the central forces in the valley. This was done without informing our police. Many people lost their lives. I want to ask the Central Government, who gave them the mandate to kill our people? The ones they call terrorists are not terrorists but our youth, our friends, who are fighting for the cause. The Central Government, instead of hearing them has launched into blatant killing. Enough is enough. Now, they should realise that we will not bear the high-handedness of the central forces.'

Again, the public applauded.

'I have heard many complaints regarding the callous behaviour of the officials here. I have abolished the post of special magistrate. Now, the administration will be looked after by the district magistrate of Jehenabad. The Opposition thinks I am afraid of a CBI inquiry against Ganesh Rai and his misdeeds. But, let me assure you that I hail the CBI inquiry in the case. Let the truth come out. However, I want to know the Central Government's motive behind their interference in the workings of the state. Two officers of Delhi Police had been sent without a reason. In a federal set-up, the centre should enquire the local police before sending in their officers. But, they have scant regard. The Central Government has become arrogant. It is time to throw them out.

'To assure you of my intentions, I have decided to contest the coming election myself. Let us show that under the garb of running an NGO, Nisha and her Party want to be the unopposed rulers. They claim I am responsible for the rising prices. They have forgotten that it is their government at the centre which is overseeing the food and supplies. Besides, I do not want to comment on the credentials of the home minister, who himself, is being interrogated by the CBI regarding the CWG scam.'

A huge applause followed.

'Believe me, I only think about the welfare of the state. You have trusted me for the last 10 years. Vote for us this time too. I will not let you down. *Jai* Bihar, *Jai* Bharat.'

'CM sahib, *zindabad*. CM sahib, *amar rahe*,' the crowd roared.

The rally was a huge success. Home Minister Prabhat Advani was astonished at the State Government's gameplan. He was already a troubled soul, thanks to the CWG scam. He decided to keep mum till he got a clean chit.

40

5 November 2013

An inquiry commission was instituted to probe into the links between Silent Turtle and the MAF. The three-member inquiry commission comprising ex-Supreme Court judges met at the Silent Turtle office in Noida, which had been sealed. Rohit felt like a prisoner at the place where he once used to lord over as the king supreme. He was being grilled by the inquiry commission.

Member 1 spoke—'Mr Rohit, this inquiry commission has been instituted to probe allegations against you. The major allegation is that you have colluded with the enemy of the state to further your business interests. Do you want to hear the charges?'

He nodded.

'You provided money to a terrorist organisation in the hope that they will provide you protection.'

'Yes, I did provide protection money. But, this points to the failure of administration. The fact is that like most Indians, I have lost faith in our police force, so I was compelled to turn to rogue parties for protection.'

Member 2 asked—'Mr Rohit, you cannot protect your sins by accusing the police. How can you say you have no faith in the police force of this country? You are well educated, a successful businessman with access to the best judicial mind available in the country. Also, on what basis can you say that you were threatened? You have never approached the police for protection.'

'What was the use of going to the police? They themselves blackmailed me.'

Member 3 said—'This cannot be substantiated by any evidence. But, we do have evidence that you had given money to the MAF. This makes you guilty of sedition and acting against the interests of the nation. You have also adopted unfair business practices and this may debar you from conducting business anywhere in India.'

The commission inquiry lingered on for a month but could not implicate Rohit. A police case was filed against him for Soumit's murder, but, even then, he was granted anticipatory bail.

~

It was the first day of the *Chhath* festival and the chief minister of Bihar was preparing to go with his wife to the Ganga ghat. As Nilesh Yadav was getting ready, his PA Amit Dutta came running towards him.

'What happened?' the CM asked.

'Some Bihari emigrants were thrashed in Mumbai while celebrating *Chhath*. Two of them have died and four are critical.'

The CM thought for a moment and then smiled. *'Chhath maiya* has provided us another chance to salvage our image. I will proceed to Mumbai.'

The political flares soon began to fly. The Ruling Party in Maharashtra, in the name of promoting regional identity of Marathis, had come out in support of thrashing Bihari migrants. They have decided to oppose the Bihar chief minister's visit. The Maharashtra CM Ranjit Chavan was in dilemma. He was warned by the Intelligence that if Nilesh Yadav came to Mumbai, there would be violence. He flew to Delhi and called the Bihar CM there.

'Please do not come to Mumbai. Your life will be in danger,' Chavan told him.

'Why am I being stopped?' he asked.

'See, you are correct. But, understand the situation. You can condemn the killing by staging a small rally at Azad Maidan. We will secure it. But don't tour the city,' advised Chavan.

He thought for a while and then said. 'I will not tour the city. After the rally, I will say that my health is not cooperating. But, you have to do something for me.'

'What?'

'One of the Maharashtra cadre police officers, Subhash, is on deputation in IB, Delhi. Call him back.'

'But why?'

'He is meddling too much in our affairs. I don't want him to be on any active police duty,' he demanded.

'Okay, what will you have now? Vodka or rum?'

'Vodka should be fine.'

~

By the end of the year, the Election Commission had declared by-elections at Bhagatpur. Nisha became involved in her political campaigns while Gautam took control of NS2. One morning, they were discussing the latest turn of events.

'What has happened to the MAF? They are lying low and the police are also not using this opportunity to press them,' said Gautam.

'No one wants to finish the MAF. Subhash Joshi had been called back due to the mounting pressure from the Maharashtra government. Now, no one is looking after the MAF case in the IB. Kavita has also been forced to keep a low profile. But the way the situation is taking its course is unnerving me. The chief minister did what we were planning by providing compensation from the chief minister's fund. He has put his weight in the election. But, he still wants to keep the MAF alive. Seeing that the RR is getting stronger, he has addressed the MAF cadres as friends in his rally. We are back to square one,' Nisha said.

'Yes. Again, no one wants to use force. The opportunity created by the Razia Regiment assault on the MAF has gone waste. But, I think the MAF might be planning to do something bigger to register its presence,' Gautam said.

'But, why would it take the risk of doing something when everything is going in its favour? The government is wary of using force. Ganesh Rai has died. Ajay has been made the district collector, but, he no longer wields the same power as he once did as the special magistrate. Why would it do something which will bring them negative publicity and tempt the government to act strong?'

'You have forgotten one critical thing from where this whole thing started.'

'What is that?'

'Gireesh Marandi. Even if the government doesn't use force, they would never release him unless it is forced to do so.'

'You mean to say they would take hostages?'

'Yes. Only then would they be able to force the government to release him. '

'And what will Rohit do?'

'It will be difficult to nail him. The CD cannot be taken as evidence as it was blurred and the sound was not clear. Rohit can easily claim it was doctored. The power plant construction will continue. In fact, I have heard he is planning to shift to Bhagatpur to oversee the construction himself. He has assembled a personal guard of around 50 heavily-armed people to protect him and his site. The CM's decision to provide enhanced compensation has already blunted MAF-engineered attacks in the area. Any attack on him and the MAF will be considered malicious.'

'What will come out of it?'

'Something extremely dangerous.'

41

5 January 2014

At the RR camp, Kavita was in a contemplative mood when Shweta walked up to her.

'You called me, madam?' Shweta asked.

'Yes, Shweta. I have an urgent thing to discuss. Call our entire battalion to the training ground.'

'What is it, madam?'

'We have received a court notice.'

'What is it about?'

'I will tell everyone together.'

When the battalion assembled at the training ground, she waved a piece of paper at them, 'This is a letter from the Supreme Court, asking us about the details of the Operation we undertook in the valley few days back. Sulochna has filed a PIL against us in the Supreme Court. In the PIL, they have argued that the encounter was fake; the rebels had surrendered and we murdered them in cold blood. They have also said that we damaged the town's drinking water supply and acted recklessly without informing the local administration. They have also pressed for a CBI inquiry in this.'

'How can she file a PIL like that? Whatever we have done was part of *Operation India One,*' said Shweta.

'She is protected by political backing. It is an open secret that we are considered the most distrusted lot by the State Government. They are raking up the issue of us not liaising with the local police. Moreover, *Operation India One* is an undeclared operation.'

'What does the Home Ministry say?'

'They say our case is weak. The Supreme Court may ask the Home Ministry to disband us. Now, we are in the same position as we were during the days of the PRM. We may have to wind up unless—'

'Unless what?'

'Unless, we do something to justify our presence here.'

'Madam, why don't we plan another operation to flush them out of the forest? After the previous attack, they have suffered miserably.'

'The home minister has asked us to keep a low profile. But, you go ahead and plan for another operation. Maybe, we will get the chance if conditions become favourable. But, I know that despite them being short of ammunition they have grown stronger.'

'How?'

'During the raid in the valley, we had seized some papers there. There were details of a plan to kidnap Ajay, but, there was another plan which I did not make public.'

'What?'

'They had contacted a terrorist organisation in Kashmir and sent some members there to learn.'

'Learn what?'

'The art of suicide bombing.'

'They are planning something dangerous?'

'Only time will tell.'

Kavita went inside her office and sat with a gloom. *When will God give me another chance to close Charulata's chapter once and for all?* she thought.

~

At the Jehenabad DM's office, the police were having a tough time controlling the queue. The villagers of Bhagatpur and nearby villages had gathered there to receive the compensation announced by the CM.

Ajay Mishra had announced the first batch of beneficiaries of the new scheme. He disbursed the compensation to about 100 among the 1,000 villagers entitled for the enhanced compensation.

'It is still a long way to go, but this is a good start,' he thought.

'Rohit has come to meet you,' his peon announced.

'Send him in.'

Rohit entered his chamber.

'See, the public is with us,' he told Ajay.

'They are just a few who have turned up for the money. Many are still not happy.'

'They will, once this project gets over. The construction is moving at a very fast pace and the chimney and the control room have been completed in a record time of two months. We have already assembled the boiler. Now, we are not facing much trouble. But, we had pushed for enhancing the security to the CISF (Central Industrial Security Force). Do you have any news on that, yet?'

'The Home Ministry has not cleared the file, but, they will do it soon. You are doing a wonderful job. Now, keep going like this and who knows, our CM could announce the completion of the plant just before elections next year.'

'Sir, we still need one year for the successful generation of commercial power.'

'I was only talking about the announcement of its opening. Also, please remember not to do away with any safety precautions just to complete the plant.'

'We are taking adequate precautions.'

'Okay, you can go now. I am tired and will head home now,' he said, preparing to leave.

Rohit left after a warm handshake.

42

15 January 2014

Nisha was summoned to appear at the Delhi headquarters of INP to deliberate on election issues.

During the meeting, the home minister gave Nisha a magazine which had a feature on the MAF.

'Have you seen it?'

Nisha shook her head to reply in the negative and began to read the story.

The Lost Opportunity

On January 10, the Patna High Court's fast-track bench convicted Gireesh Marandi of mass murder. He is guilty of planning the Rajdhani Express bomb blast and raising an armed struggle against the Central Government. He has been sentenced to death, against which he has filed an appeal to the Supreme Court. He is currently lodged in a high-security cell in Tihar Jail, Delhi. The MAF, meanwhile, is seething with anger. There were loud demonstrations on the streets of Patna to protest the conviction. The demonstrators demand a complete shutdown at Bhagatpur. The chief minister has urged the people to maintain peace and harmony while the Bihar assembly passed a resolution to put a hold on Gireesh's execution. The chief minister visited Delhi to discuss this issue with the prime minister, who assured him that the law would take its own course and the outcome of the Supreme Court verdict should be respected. Charulata has issued a threat warning.

The report went on to enumerate the success as well as the uncertain future of the Razia Regiment. It concluded that the government has lost its opportunity to suppress the MAF.

Nisha told her Party colleagues, 'The situation in Bhagatpur has turned explosive. You have to do something. The MAF will not let Gireesh Marandi go to the gallows like this.'

'I know. They will definitely act now. The State Government's manoeuvre of addressing them as 'misguided youth' will miss its target. Even if the State Government does not take a stringent step against them, the MAF will take unilateral action to release Gireesh,' Prabhat spoke.

'But, we should do something to prevent this.'

'What can we do? I have decided to take a back seat and observe how the case unfolds in the court of the State Government. Let them decide what to do. On my part, I have cleared the proposal to depute CISF for the security of the power plant. They will be posted in about a month,' explained the home minister.

'I think the State Government is also reeling under pressure. They have deputed Ravi Taneja as SSP of

Jehenabad. He is known as a no-nonsense police officer of the state. Till now he was on central deputation, but, suddenly he has been called back. His stint at National Security Guards (NSG) has hardened him more. Maybe, the chief minister is also worried about Gireesh's conviction.'

'There is one more reason why Taneja has been brought in,' explained the home minister.

'What?'

'Taneja and Ajay are known sympathisers of the BYP. They will do anything that suits Nilesh. They will do anything to stop you from winning there. They will also not allow the RR to take any action.'

'I never thought of this. But, whatever is the politics of the region, I have full faith in our democracy and I believe that one day the truth shall prevail—*Satyamave Jayate*.'

'Yes, we have a great democracy. While we were crafting our final strategy for the polls, the judiciary has independently changed the story plot. And we can do nothing but align ourselves with it.'

'Okay.'

'Now, back to our poll strategy. The Election Commission will announce the poll dates soon. Have you finalised the publicity strategy?' the home minister quizzed.

'Yes, yesterday I met the CEO of A2Z Ltd, an advertising company. They have done a great job.'

'The advertisement part is all right but I need some new issues to be on the agenda this election. Do you have anything in mind?'

'Sir, I wish to declare Bhagatpur a SEZ.'

'SEZ? That is a dead idea. Besides, we do not want to go into another land acquisition hurdle.'

'Sir, listen to me first. I'm not talking about a Special Economic Zone. I mean a Special Education Zone.'

'What is that?'

'See, most youth in our state are forced to go out of the state for higher education. Even if they excel academically, they are subjected to hardship and humiliation by people from other states. If we convert this area into a Special Education Zone, where we establish institutions for higher studies, it will be supported by the villagers much like the bygone era of the Nalanda and Vikramshila. This could help give a boost to the economy too.'

'All right, we will take this up in the polls. Let us see how people respond. This is a new idea which needs to be explored.'

43

19 January 2014, 10 A.M.

At the MAF camp in Bhagatpur, Charulata was visibly distressed while her comrades sat helpless in front of her. The sound of jackals rummaging for food could be heard far in the distance, accentuating the eerie atmosphere.

'Commander, what are you thinking?' asked Samir.

'Samir, how much ammunition have we got?'

'Of the 50 AK-47s at our disposal, we have ammunition only for 20. We have 10 hand grenades, two rockets and a few bullets for pistols. If anybody attacks us now we will have to surrender,' he replied.

'Don't utter negative words,' Chakradhar chided him

'He is telling the truth. We are helpless,' Charulata said.

'Commander, something has to be done. Our cadres are nervous,' Chakradhar said.

'Yes. We have to ensure the situation doesn't go out of our hands. If the CISF takes over the security of the plant, we will have to fight two central forces. Ravi Taneja has improved the fighting capability of the state forces. This is not good for us. Our support base, the tribesmen, are moving out from here after receiving hefty compensation. Apart from all this, we have the shortage of ammunition to deal with,' Charulata said.

'We should destroy the power plant before the CISF arrives,' Chakradhar advised her.

'But, that will go against our image. Everyone will label us as an enemy of the people and we will lose the support of civil society campaigning on our behalf.'

'But, how long will we wait? The Supreme Court will also authenticate the High Court's judgement as the government is fielding a canny lawyer, Siddhartha Bhardwaj, against our leader. Nothing can be done after that. How far will Sulochna and Narendra Nath help us? The only thing they will do is apply for presidential clemency which is difficult because the Central Government is already against us.'

'That is what is worrying me.'

Someone suddenly came rushing towards them from behind the bushes. '*Lal Salaam*, I have news which can help us out of this situation.'

'What is it?' asked Charulata with eagerness.

'Today, Rohit was at the power plant to inaugurate the control room building. But, a major accident led to the collapse of one of the site buildings under construction. Local labourers have been killed in the incident. The situation has turned volatile. Villagers have started agitating against the company and Rohit and his engineers are trapped inside.'

'How did the accident happen?' Charulata asked.

'Few days back, I was casually chatting with one of the employees at Silent Turtle. He said ever since the cost of construction increased, the quality of the work has suffered.

If things continue the way they are, an accident at the site is inevitable,' Chakradhar said.

Charulata let out a sigh of relief.

'The time has come for direct action. We will strike now. The villagers think Silent Turtle is responsible for the accident. This is what we needed—a spark to ignite the deep-seated hatred in the heart of villagers against the Silent Turtle.'

'But we are not prepared, nor are we equipped with enough ammunition,' reminded Samir.

'There is no time for preparation. We have two hours before our strike and we cannot afford to miss this opportunity. We will attack now and take the engineers of the company as hostages. Besides, Rohit too is present at the site. Rohit as a hostage will be more useful than ordinary engineers.'

'What is the need to attack the site? We can always bring the hostages here or take Rohit as a hostage,' replied Samir.

'No, we will attack at the heart. If we succeed, it will bolster our image in the region and our dream of creating the Red Corridor will get a boost.'

'What if we fail? We will be finished. We are not well-equipped to fight the security forces. I am sure they will come on us with all their might,' Samir was apprehensive.

'We do not have ammunition, but, we still have the guns. The police do not have an accurate knowledge of how much ammunition we have. We need to use it to our benefit. Chakradhar, you lay the mines on the road through which the police force is expected to come. This will delay their entry in Bhagatpur. Till their arrival, we will consolidate our positions at the site. Do not engage with them, since, it will waste our ammunitions. Just delay their entry and return to the site. Till then, I will take control,' she instructed the other comrades.

'But—' Samir tried to intervene.

'Enough, when the commander says we must attack, then we will attack,' Chakradhar counter-intervened.

Charulata rose her hands up in the air. 'Long live the revolution. We will not stop till we get our leader released.'

'Long live the revolution!' Samir also raised his hand. But deep in his mind he was not convinced about the purpose and the timing of the attack.

The others also stood up and joined the chorus.

~

The villagers had placed the corpses of those who had died in the accident at the plant and had encircled the whole site. They were armed with bows and arrows and spears. The guards had closed the gate from inside, but, this did not deter the people from agitating. In the midst of this, a truck arrived, stopped near the gate and opened its doors to reveal an army of masked soldiers. As they began firing shots in the air, the villagers were taken aback. As silence fell, the group leader climbed onto the bonnet of the truck and announced—'The time for revolution has come. This power plant has robbed us of our land, our people. We will show them that we will not just sit back and watch. I will go inside and fight for you. I request your help in fighting against the government.'

The leader took out her mask, lifted her gun in the air and roared, 'I am Charulata.'

Her kohled eyes were red and looked ferocious. She had a vermillion tika on her forehead. A red cloth covered her forehead and her hair was neatly tied at the back.

'Our saviour has come,' said the village *pradhan,* with tears in his eyes.

'Why should we fear when Goddess Durga has come to us?' announced the temple priest.

The crowd was exhilarated. It began chanting, 'Charulata, Charulata, Charulata!'

'Beat the drums. Call all the villagers from the nearby villages.' She turned towards the gate where, upon seeing her, the guards ran away. She entered the site along with some of her people.

'Sweep the entire area. Take anyone you find as hostage and bring them to the control room. That is where I am going,' she ordered.

Just then, the sound of a volley of bullets being fired shocked everyone. Charulata looked around to find Rohit's bodyguards attacking them. 'Rohit? He dares to fight me?'

'This is my site. No one can enter without my permission,' Rohit yelled from the control room.

'Okay. Let us see who owns this site,' she yelled back and started shooting at him and his men.

An intense gun battle ensued between the MAF and Rohit's men. Charulata took cover behind the fire water tank and aimed at Rohit with her sniper gun. She pulled the trigger, but before she could do anything, one of Rohit's men came in front and took the bullet.

'No George, no,' shouted Rohit when he saw his trusted aide falling in front of him.

Charulata proceeded to take over the control room, where her men had dragged the 19 engineers they found hiding around the site.

'Commander, look who we found,' Samir entered the control room with one hostage.

'Rohit? So you could not escape?' she exclaimed.

'You are doing a terrible mistake. There's no way you can escape alive. The security forces will storm this place and kill you all,' Rohit was still defiant.

'Let me kill him. He is behind this mess.' Chakradhar moved forward with his gun.

'No, take him hostage. It will help in our negotiation,' said Charulata.

'Chakradhar, where is your team? Have they placed mines on the approach path of the police?' Charulata asked.

'Yes, they have mined the stretch near the forest and will be joining us soon.'

'Okay, Samir, ask your men to secure this building. When Chakradhar's men arrive, send them to secure all the other buildings at this site including the boiler.'

As the men moved out of the control room to their respective positions she moved towards the engineers who had been taken hostages.

'Do not fear. We have no enmity towards you. You will be safe here. Just cooperate with us,' Charulata soothed the engineers who were trembling in fear.

~

SSP Ravi Taneja was sitting with Ajay in his office at Jehenabad when his cell phone rang. 'Please save us, sir. They have taken the site under control and will kill us,' a girl's voice pleaded on the other end.

'Who are you? Who will kill you?'

'I am Shiwani, an engineer with Silent Turtle. The MAF has attacked the Bhagatpur plant site and has taken many of us hostage. I am hiding in an empty panel at the switchyard control room. Please do something.'

'Don't panic, remain where you are. Put your phone on silent. We are reaching.'

'What happened, Taneja?'

'The MAF has attacked the power plant!'

'What? Dial Rohit's number,' he said.

Rohit's phone was switched off. Next, Ajay called Rohit's deputy, Rajiv Kumar, who was in charge of the BMTPP site. He filled them in on what had taken place, and also disclosed the fact that he had fled from the site after the incident. He told them that Rohit and a few engineers were inside the plant.

'Sir, we will have to move to Bhagatpur immediately. No peace meeting this time. Only action,' said Taneja.

'Yes, Taneja. You are fully entitled to take any action. But this has to be stopped.'

Taneja immediately summoned the entire police force of the district and began the journey with them towards Bhagatpur. Within an hour, the convoy was passing through the narrow forest lanes leading to the district. Suddenly, Taneja noticed an excavated stretch on the road in front of him. He immediately asked the convoy to stop.

'Everybody, take position,' he ordered while disembarking from his vehicle. 'Check the stretch with mine detectors.'

The constables found mines in the area with the help of detectors.

'We will have to take an alternate route. They have placed mines in this area. Two of our men will stand here to guide passers-by to avoid the mines on this route. The media would also be swarming the place soon,' he ordered.

They were delayed by an hour to reach Bhagatpur.

'Sir, are you listening to the beating of drums? What is this?' Taneja asked as they reached Bhagatpur.

'It is a call to all the villagers of other villages to join them. I think they are in a mood to fight,' Ajay replied.

The villagers had dug trenches and were ready with bows and arrows on the other side.

Taneja announced—'This is a warning to all the people gathered here. We have imposed Section 144 in the area. Let us march towards the site. We will not allow this lawlessness. They have taken hostages. Kindly move towards the villages.'

The villagers remained where they were and shouted, 'Police *prashasan murdabad*, Charulata, *zindabad*.'

'We will begin a lathi charge if you don't budge,' threatened Taneja, but to no avail.

'Battalion, get ready,' Taneja shouted.

The police force jumped from their vehicles and formed a barricade. With their bulletproof jackets and helmets on, they carried lathis and shields made of cane. When they charged, the villagers threw stones at them and the battle began. Soon, the police were able to disperse the villagers. They finally made it to the site, only to find a large number of villagers blocking their way to the power plant. Taneja wanted to free the engineers, held captive at the site, as his first move. He began forcing his way through the crowd towards the power plant. But, the villagers began hurling stones and arrows at them. This time their number was larger and the arrows were poisoned.

'Sir, we have to fire,' he asked Ajay.

'Go ahead,' Ajay replied.

The police force took position and started firing. The villagers began to disperse. Suddenly, a gunshot injured Ajay's legs.

'The DM is shot, the DM is shot,' shouted the villagers.

Ajay fell on the ground as the guards rushed and lifted him up. Taneja took out a pair of binoculars and looked in the direction of the gunshot. He saw someone taking aim at him. He immediately ducked behind a vehicle. The bullets struck the windshield.

Only an expert marksman can fire with such accuracy from this distance! It means Charulata is inside the site with hostages. I will have to get in by all means, he thought.

'Take Ajay sir to the hospital,' he ordered the guards who were carrying the district magistrate.

On his way, Ajay told Taneja, 'Kill that bitch, Charulata.'

'We will. Go and treat yourself. I will handle all.' He called his guards and said, 'I am going inside the site. Cover me.' He reached the gate and hid near the guard's outpost.

A bomb exploded near the guard's post and Taneja's bodyguards came running towards him as firing began in all directions. While the police force took position in the bushes near the gate, three truckloads of rebels in war fatigues carrying automatic rifles whizzed past them and headed for the control room.

The locals surrounded the power plant, digging ditches all around and tearing up the approach road. The MAF forces fanned out inside the plant and secured the highest places at the site.

Taneja understood that they had been outnumbered and ordered his forces to retreat. The police force took positions behind their vehicles which were now being slowly reversed. The police force retreated while the firing continued from the control room. As soon as they secured themselves out of the firing range, the police force boarded their vehicles and drove towards the hospital.

Taneja reached the hospital and apprised Ajay of the situation. Ajay was out of danger as the bullet had just brushed past his legs inflicting some minor injury.

'What to do now?' Ajay asked.

'I have called the Bihar battalion from its camp at Gaya. Its sergeant, Rammohan, has left the camp with reinforcement of 100 men. I have also summoned ambulances and fire brigades from the district headquarters. ASP operations head Abhijeet will also join soon. When reinforcements reach here, we shall move towards Bhagatpur again.'

'What about the RR?'

'We should call them even though I don't want Kavita involved,' replied Taneja.

'Inform the CM,' instructed Ajay.

Meanwhile Kavita Sethi received a call directly from the home minster. She picked up the phone to hear a short message—'Kavita, be prepared. The MAF has attacked the power plant and you will be required for the rescue operation. This is the time for you.'

She rushed to her office and pushed the emergency siren button. The battalion was informed immediately. She contacted Taneja who reluctantly asked her to join him at the hospital.

~

Nisha was in a meeting with Party representatives in Delhi when she received a call from Gautam.

'Nisha, where are you? When are you coming back?'

'Tomorrow. What happened?'

'Rush back immediately. The MAF has attacked the power plant and taken hostages including Rohit.'

'Oh my God, I will leave right now. Are you okay?'

'I am, but the situation here is not. The police forces have been driven out of the town. They have taken shelter in the hospital. I think they are preparing to mount a counter raid on the MAF. There will be more bloodshed, I presume.'

'No, I will not allow any bloodshed there. Bhagatpur will again become a godforsaken place if we allow such violence. I will come soon and try reaching a negotiation between the MAF and the police. Gautam, can you do something?'

'I have a plan but I need your permission.'

'You don't need permission from me. I am willing to do anything to restore peace and tranquillity in Bhagatpur.'

'Okay, meet me tomorrow at NS2 office.'

'What are you going to do? Take care of yourself.'

'Trust me.'

~

Journalists began pouring in. After they crossed the bridge at Tailorgunj and took the road towards Bhagatpur, the policemen stationed there guided them to take alternate routes. Media persons were not attacked when they entered the village and were allowed to go near the plant site uptill the area where the villagers had dug the trenches.

One of the villagers walked towards the media waving a CD in his hand. He went near the reporters and asked them to hand over the CD to the administration. The CD contained recordings of the demands of the MAF.

The war had begun.

Part IV
The Rescue

44

20 January 2014, 5 A.M.

The Bihar battalion, led by sergeant Rammohan, reached the hospital building where Kavita and Abhijeet Verma joined them. It looked more like an army cantonment than a hospital with the police occupying every nook and corner. The field outside the hospital was filled with police vehicles, ambulances and fire brigades. As Rammohan and Kavita were briefing Ajay in his ward, he received a phone call from Nilesh Yadav.

'Will you please wait outside,' Ajay requested the people standing in his room.

All of them went out as he received the call.

'Ajay, how are you?'

'I am fine, sir. I am sorry we could not prevent the attack.'

'You remain at the hospital. Let Taneja take charge. He should make a team with the Bihar battalion and the RR, and move towards Bhagatpur. However, the RR should be involved as little as possible. I hope you understand.'

'Yes, sir.'

Outside, Taneja was briefing Kavita and Abhijeet about the situation in Bhagatpur when he saw a car entering the hospital compound. The policemen at the gate signalled at the occupant to leave but they could not stop him.

'Gautam, what are you doing here? Where is Nisha?' Kavita recognised Gautam as he approached them.

'Nisha will join us today. But I...'

'You are the one who had come here to spy on the MAF and have now resigned from the police force to join Nisha?' Taneja intervened.

'Yes sir, Gautam Dhaliwal, 2004 batch IPS. But now I am working with Nisha,' Gautam replied with an incomplete salute.

'It is strange that Nisha's father resigned to start the NGO and now you have taken it upon yourself to further the cause of that NGO. Time does not allow me to get into the nitty-gritty of what led you to resign and what led you to come to this place as a spy.' Taneja replied sternly.

'I came here as part of *Operation India One*,' Gautam replied unabashedly.

'What do you know about *Operation India One*?' Kavita intervened.

'Everything. I was sent to restart the stalled progress in *Operation India One*.'

'If you were part of *Operation India One* then why didn't you tell me?' Kavita asked.

'That was part of the mission—to remain secretive. I am sure you do not know much about the mole in MAF.'

'Yes, after Sudhakar's death, I have no knowledge. You know him?'

'Yes, I did find him but he was killed before...'

'Wait, what is this *Operation India One*?' Taneja interrupted bewildered by their conversation.

'It is a long story. *Operation India One* was a mission to finish the MAF. Kavita and I are part of this mission. And I have come here to complete the unfinished agenda of the mission,' Gautam said.

'Frankly, I do not need your help here. We are preparing to raid the power plant site.'

'That is what I came here for. The attack will only result in bloodshed. I am the only person here who has seen and talked to Charulata and her commanders. I can help.'

Taneja thought for a while and then said, 'What help?'

'At the outset, this place is far away from the site. To launch a counter-attack we would need a safe and secure area near the site. The NS2 office may serve the purpose. Also, we should wait for Nisha as she is popular here and can be a catalyst in easing the brewing tension between opposing camps.'

'Your first proposal seems a fine idea. However, do you think talking to the villagers or initiating a dialogue with the MAF could resolve anything?'

'Definitely. I have stayed at the MAF camp, and had the opportunity to interact with many of the MAF cadres. Not all of them are as ideologically inclined as Charulata. I think you know about her two commanders. Chakradhar is an old friend of Gireesh and hence more loyal, but Samir has joined the group recently. He is only concerned with money.'

'Yes, I have heard about this group's notorious activities, but what is the point here?'

'The point is you are concentrating only on Charulata. We have to widen our horizon and examine the possibility of manipulating members like Samir and others to win the war against the MAF. This is the objective of *Operation India One*,' Gautam argued.

One of the constables approached Taneja and said, 'DM sir is calling you inside.'

'Let's go inside. Gautam you can accompany us,' Taneja replied.

Ajay briefed Taneja about his conversation with the CM and asked him to proceed towards Bhagatpur.

'You are the one who had come for the hearing as a journalist?' Ajay asked Gautam.

'You have a sharp memory, sir,' Gautam replied smiling.

'All of you proceed to the NS2 office and start deliberating the plan of action,' Ajay commanded.

~

At the Patna airport, when Nisha's plane landed, she got a call from the CM as well.

'Ms Nisha, I hope you will cooperate with the government and use your influence in the area to put an end to this crisis.'

'Yes, sir. Don't worry. Our political differences will not interfere.'

Nisha hopped into a taxi and proceeded to Bhagatpur. She took the road through the fields and entered Bhagatpur from the back of the tower clock and moved towards NS2.

Meanwhile, till Tower Chowk, Taneja and his team met with little resistance, but, beyond that the villagers had blocked the road.

He asked his forces to erect a barricade there, so as to stop anyone coming from the direction of the power plant.

Taneja along with Kavita and Rammohan reached the NS2 office around 8 a.m. The RR commandos surrounded the entire office building. Gautam took them inside one of the classrooms. While they were deliberating on the next course of action, Nisha joined in.

~

While they were trying to come to a consensus about Charulata's demands; one of the RR commandos knocked the door.

'Sir, one of the media persons has brought a video of the demands made by Charulata,' the commando uttered and handed a pen drive to Taneja.

Taneja played the video on Nisha's laptop. The video showed the control room with hostages huddled behind panels looking at the camera with blank faces. The camera focused on Charulata's. She said, 'We have no enmity with these people, but, we want the government to understand that we will not surrender to the might of their oppressive forces. We have five demands—

1. Our leader, Gireesh Marandi and our friend, Vikas Marandi, shall be released.
2. The government shall shelve its plan to construct the plant and return the land to our people.
3. The families of those killed in the accident shall be provided a relief of Rs 5 lakhs each by the State Government.
4. The RR battalion shall be moved out from here.

5. The government shall drop all charges against the MAF cadres.

If our demands are not met within 48 hours, we will start killing the engineers here one by one. Any police action by the government will have disastrous results.'

After Taneja informed the CM of the situation, he was instructed to use minimum force.

'The chief minister has categorically denied accepting any of these demands,' Taneja told the others gathered at the NS2 office.

'But, what do you intend to do in 48 hours?' Nisha asked.

'We have only one option—storming the plant. But, it requires a lot of planning. The plant is 5 km from here and all ways leading to the plant are blocked. See the place around us. It looks like a ghost town because everyone is around the plant. Any action can result in heavy causalities,' Taneja replied.

'We will have to talk to Charulata first. It is our fault. We knew this would happen, but, nobody dared take any pre-emptive action. In the game of centre and state jurisdiction, we forgot that the plant construction is a national issue and needs to be tackled deftly,' Nisha said.

'This is not the time to deliberate on what we did not do. Who will talk to them?' Taneja asked.

'I will talk. I hope Charulata will not have an objection to me talking to her,' said Nisha.

'I think she is right. Charulata will listen to her,' said Gautam.

'But, you are a candidate of the Opposition Party. Will you negotiate on behalf of the government?' Taneja asked.

'She has a soft corner for me and I hope she will listen to me. I am an Indian first, and then a politician. If you do not have any objection I wish to use the media to convey to Charulata that I will be talking to her.'

As soon as she went out, reporters surrounded her.

'Madam, how are the authorities going to take care of the situation?' was the usual question.

'We have received the tape containing their demands and we are keeping all our options open.'

'Does that mean the government will release Gireesh Marandi?'

'I wish to talk to Charulata. Only after that, will we be in a position to comment. Please give this message to Charulata.'

Her message was aired live by the media. In the control room, Charulata could hear it on her radio set.

'I knew you would come.'

Within minutes, Taneja got a call from Charulata. 'Hello, Taneja. I heard that Nisha wants to talk to me. Please pass the phone to her.'

Nisha took over. 'I want to go inside the plant to talk to you about your demands.'

'You are always welcome, but, come alone and unarmed.'

'I will.'

She put down the phone. 'I am going inside,' announced Nisha.

'Why are you doing that? I am ready to face her with my troops. We will finish her this time,' said Kavita.

'You don't know Charulata. She is very dangerous. Let me talk first.'

'Okay, Ms Nisha, go ahead. My vehicle will drop you there,' said Taneja.

45

20 January, 10 A.M.

Nisha was driven past the crowds at Gate no. 1 of the plant. Thousands of villagers were protesting on the streets, shouting slogans against the government. It seemed that they were in mood of another revolution, as propagated by the legendary tribal leader—Birsa Munda. The situation was tense and needed only a spark to ignite in flames. Nisha could sense that Charulata's vision of a revolution had almost materialised. The bodies of the dead labourers were still at the chowk outside the plant. At first, the villagers tried to stop the vehicle, but, seeing Nisha inside, allowed her to proceed. As soon as she stepped outside, villagers surrounded her.

'Master*niji*, look what the government has done. They have killed our people. Look at the families of the victims. How will they survive?' they cried, pointing to the corpses lying on the chowk.

'Look, I understand it is a big tragedy, but, it was an accident.'

'Madam, you are also speaking the language of the government.'

'I have not come here as a politician but a friend. I am going inside to talk to Charulata. We have to find a solution. Nothing will come out of the bloodbath. Let me go inside and we will think about it.'

'There is nothing to talk about. This power plant has robbed us of our land and now our people. We do not want this plant. Charulata is right.'

She walked past the crowd towards the gate, which was protected by 10 masked guards in military uniforms, carrying automatic rifles. Four of them were women. Two of the women guards stepped towards her and checked her thoroughly and then asked her to follow them. The television crews were stationed a few metres outside the gate.

At the NS2 office, all of them were watching the news. 'As you just saw, Nisha Kushwaha, who has been chosen as the official negotiator of the government, has entered the plant premises. Curiously, Nisha is the candidate of the Opposition Party, but, is negotiating for the State Government. The MAF have taken the entire plant in their control. We once again inform you that the accident, which sparked these events off, occurred when the building of the compressor house under construction collapsed, killing 10 workers. Speculation is rife that this occurred due to the negligence of Silent Turtle which is constructing the power plant. People here have been fed up with the violence associated with the plant and now want its complete withdrawal. But, the government has pumped in exorbitant sums of money that they do not want it shelved. The State Government had taken loans from the Central Government which in turn convinced the World Bank to fund this project. The World Bank has sought a report from the Central Government on the issue and has threatened to cancel the loan if the situation fails to return to normalcy. The State Government has, on its part, refused to take the assistance of the army or the NSG (National Security Guards). Let us hear what the chief minister has to say about this incident.'

The chief minister was on a visit to Darbhanga for an inaugural ceremony regarding new facilities in the Sanskrit College there. As soon as his chopper landed at the Darbhanga air base, he was surrounded by reporters.

'Sir, how are you going to handle the situation? You have refused to take the help of the Central Government,' asked a reporter.

'We have sent Nisha to talk to them. We do not want any violence.'

'Will there be a commando operation?'

'We will not use commandos against our own people. We will not use any force. They will soon free the hostages.'

'Will you free Gireesh Marandi?'

'No comments.'

He waved his fingers towards his guards, who politely began pushing the journalists out of his way.

'This was the chief minister of Bihar who is confident that he will not use force. Let us hear what the families of the hostages have to say.'

The scene shifted to New Delhi, where the NGO Mahila Shakti had organised a candle march at India Gate to protest police action in Bhagatpur. 'How do you feel?' One of the anchors put the microphone towards one of the relatives of the hostages.

'What do you mean by asking us that? We want our children back at any cost,' said an agitated parent.

'Will you put pressure on the government to get Gireesh Marandi released from jail?'

'If the terrorists are adamant about that, then we would definitely ask the government to free him. We want our children back.'

'The Bhagatpur hostage crisis has shaken the entire nation. On one hand, the family members are pleading for the release of their loved ones, and Bihar's CM is certain about taking control of the situation. The home minister has condemned the incident, but, refused to intervene unless the State Government demands it. A team of NSG guards has been deputed for any emergency-like situation. Meanwhile, the top management of the Silent Turtle are unavailable for comments. The owner of Silent Turtle, Rohit has himself been taken a hostage by the MAF. Back to Bhagatpur.'

'What will be the next plan of action, sir?' Gautam asked Taneja, looking away from the television screen.

'We have strict instructions to use force as the last resort.'

'Will they release Gireesh?'

'The possibility is dim. Let us hope Nisha finds a solution.'

'Attacking the plant is the only available solution,' Kavita debated.

'Even if we have to use force, your cooperation is not required here. Anyway, this is not the work of a woman,' Taneja replied.

'Charulata is also a woman and Nisha, on whom you are pinning your hopes, is a woman too. And do you think your force can fight the MAF? You need to be a guerrilla to fight a guerrilla. They are all armed with AK-47s and your force is equipped with .303 rifles and no bulletproof vests. We are equipped with state of the art weaponry and our commandos are well-trained for this kind of combat,' refuted a visibly miffed Kavita.

'I think she is right. The state police won't be able to fight the terrorists,' Gautam supported her.

'That, we will see. First, let us see what Nisha does,' said Taneja.

46

20 January 2014, 11 A.M.

At the plant site, Nisha followed the guard, who led her through the rubble of the compressor house to the unloading bay, from where they took the stairs to the control room. She looked all around the site while she walked through. She could see the MAF men entrenched at every corner of the site. They were at every elevation of the boiler and near all the major equipments of the plant. Ten men were patrolling the ground in front of the control room. She entered the control room where men were standing with automatic rifles in their hands. The hostages, all young engineers comprising two women among them, were huddled in a corner behind the control desk. Rohit was sitting silently in one corner, crestfallen.

Charulata was in front of a Large Video Screen (LVS) mounted above the control desk, where pictures from the CCTVs around the plant could be seen. The radio was airing reports of the protests raised by the hostages' families in New Delhi and newsreaders were speculating the government's course of action. They were inviting viewers to engage in a discussion on the issue.

Charulata greeted Nisha when she entered the control room. 'Welcome, Nisha. We are meeting after a long time,' she said.

'Why have you done this? I had dreams for all of you that one day you will all be educated and free of the tyrannical rules of people like Ganesh Rai.'

'We are free from that tyranny. I killed Ganesh. I shot him here between the eyes,' Charulata responded while pointing to her forehead between her eyes.

'I thought you were with me when we talked about the importance of development. But, you have resorted to extreme violence.'

'I was with you because I believed in you and I still do. But, we want a complete revolution, an absolute revamp of society.'

'And, this is your way of revolution, to torture innocent people.'

'Nisha, this is not personal. We are at war and unfortunately on opposite sides. Now, tell me what message have you brought,' said Charulata, pointing to an empty chair in front of her.

'First of all, free the women among your hostages,' she said.

'Why are you asking me to do this? Do you think women are the weaker sex? Your demand is refused. Next.'

'Ask the men outside to go back to the village. The government has agreed to give Rs 2 lakhs as compensation to the families of the deceased. They are asking for Rs 5 lakhs which is too much.'

'These people who are agitating outside are my shield against any government action. Do you think I am so naïve that I will ask them to go back?'

'Oh! You are using the people as a protective shield. If that is the case, then, why do you proclaim yourself as a champion of the poor?' asked Nisha, sarcastically.

'You are very clever Nisha. You use my own words against me, but, this time I am not prepared to listen to you. Now, put forward your next proposal.'

'Don't press for the withdrawal of the plant. There is too much at stake for both the Central and State governments and besides, the government has already provided compensation. The electricity generated will be useful for the people.'

'Nisha, you were against the power plant in the beginning. What makes you change your mind?' Charulata asked.

'I am not against the power plant. I only wanted a justified compensation for the displaced. The government is fulfilling its promise by transferring the contract to a government company. Very soon Silent Turtle will be thrown out of the contract and the work will be awarded to BHEL which is a government company. The government also has enhanced the compensation amount,' Nisha replied.

'Look, Nisha, I am not against development. I am willing to relinquish this demand only if the government promises to look into the grievances of the people and also drop all charges against the MAF soldiers.'

'They will do that.'

'Then, we are prepared to drop this demand. Tell me your next proposal.'

'Don't press for the release of Gireesh and Vikas. They have been convicted by the court and we can fight for them in the Supreme Court. I will get a good lawyer for them to file a review petition.'

'On this point, I shall allow no argument. Our resolve is final.'

'The government is ready to provide you big money for releasing the hostages.'

'Nisha, you still do not understand me. Money means nothing to us. Gireesh has started a revolution and we want him to lead us in this war against the oppression of the government and the rich. We want our leader out at any cost.'

'I again request you to leave all this. Ultimately, your people will suffer.'

'Our people have suffered since eternity. Now, the time has come for their deliverance. We are ready and we do not fear death. What decision have you taken about the withdrawal of the RR?'

'RR is a paramilitary force. The Home Ministry is the competent authority to take the decision.'

'I don't know who the competent authority is, but, I want this woman Kavita out of here.'

'Why do you hate Kavita? She is doing her duty.'

'We will never forget what she did when she was incharge of the PRM.'

'If PRM methods were brutal, MAF is equally brutal. I have not forgotten you have killed my father too.'

'Why would I kill your father? It is true that he was instigating the villagers not to help the MAF. We had threatened him, but, we never wanted to kill him. Everybody thinks we have murdered him. We tried to find out who did it, but, could not. Our guess was Ganesh who did it because your father had slapped a police case on him. I never kill innocent people,' Charulata said.

'Even if you didn't kill my father, you did kill the DM of Jehenabad a few years back. He was an honest officer trying to help the villagers by halting illegal mining,' Nisha replied.

'Why do you believe every version the government feeds you? Have you seen the post-mortem report of the officer? He was poisoned before being burnt in the grenade attack in which he was burned. He was poisoned by Ganesh Rai because he had discovered his illegal activities. After being poisoned, Ganesh Rai's men deliberately threw a grenade on his vehicle. It was shown that the MAF had killed him. It created a hue-and-cry and the Central Government formed the RR to fight against us. But, it only helped Ganesh Rai.'

'What about the Silent Turtle engineers and Rajdhani train passengers, and the RR soldiers on the bus?'

'We did not intend to harm the Rajdhani passengers as the bomb we had planted was timed to blast after the train had passed. But the driver applied the brakes early, thereby slowing the pace and the bomb exploded upon the arrival of the train. Also, the RPF began firing at us and this resulted in casualties. As for the Silent Turtle and the RR, they were our enemies.'

'The engineers were only doing their duty.'

'I realised about our mistakes later, but, we have to stick by our principles.'

'If you have realised your mistake, then, why these hostages?'

'Do you think Rohit is innocent? No, he is not, along with the people working for him. In any case, we will not kill them, not even Rohit, provided the government listens to us. Now, you may go and convey our message to the government. It has already been six hours and 42 hours are left for the deadline. Otherwise, we begin killing the hostages,' Charulata came back to herself.

Nisha left the room and went downstairs. She made a mental note of the number of rebels she saw around her.

47

20 January 2014, 2 P.M.

At the NS2 office, Gautam was growing nervous as there was no news from Nisha. At 2 p.m., images of Nisha walking wearily to her parked vehicle were shown. As soon as the vehicle reached the gate, reporters blocked her way and bombarded her with questions.

'Madam, how was the talk?'

'I will first brief the SP and then talk to you all,' she replied and continued on her way to the office.

'How many terrorists were there?' Taneja asked Nisha once she reached.

'There were almost 50 of them all around the site. Charulata and her commandants, including Samir, are in the control room. The rest of them are scattered all around.'

'Did she agree on any of our proposals?'

'Only the issue of the withdrawal of the power plant. She agreed to that only if the chief minister announces a committee to look into the grievances of the people here and drop all charges against the MAF. She was adamant about the release of Gireesh and Vikas.'

Taneja phoned the chief minister and briefed him accordingly. He nodded while listening to him and explained his conversation to the others later.

'The CM has asked us to announce the grant of Rs 5 lakhs to all victims of the accident and asked us to lure them away from the site to buy more time. We have to think of the possibility of a covert operation.'

While addressing the media, Taneja announced CM's willingness to accept Charulata's demands of providing the compensation and appealed to her for more time to accept the other demands. Charulata got the message and extended the deadline by 12 hours more.

While the group was deliberating on the future course of action, Nisha stood by the window of the room, and gazed outside.

'God knows what will happen. Do you think she will surrender? Then everything will go back to normal,' Gautam said.

'She was in no mood to surrender.'

'What are you doing there? Come here, we do not have much time,' Taneja called them.

'It will all be okay. Come,' Gautam touched Nisha's shoulder and they moved towards Taneja.

They deliberated for some time on the issue and then chalked out a plan. Nisha was to go among the villagers and present the victims' family members cheques of Rs 5 lakhs each and ask them to cremate the bodies. Once the villagers decide to move away from the site, the roads would be cordoned off by the police who would further encircle the plant and attempt to initiate a dialogue with the rebels again.

This time, they would try to convince them to surrender. This tactic might reduce their strength considerably.

As per the plan, Nisha reached the crowd of villagers outside the plant site with the cheques Ajay had handed her—10 cheques of Rs 5 lakhs each. She addressed them in their native language.

'I have come here to give you a message from the chief minister. He has agreed to your demands of compensation of Rs 5 lakhs to the families of the deceased, and I have brought with me cheques of the same amount for the families of all the 10 labourers killed in the accident. Now, I urge you to accept the money and move the bodies towards the cremation ground near the river. I request all of you to move from here.'

'No, we will not move from here. First, let the chief minister announce the withdrawal of the plant and full compensation to the villagers,' one of the villagers shouted.

'The chief minister has already announced the formation of a committee to look into all the issues you have a problem with. I am one of the members of the committee and will see that justice is delivered. I hope you trust me.'

'We trust you, but, what is the decision they have taken concerning the other demands?'

'The Central Government is mulling over releasing Gireesh and this will satisfy Charulata. I ensure that no harm will be done to her.'

The crowd cheered and began making preparations for the cremation of the dead. The smoke that billowed from the funeral pyres about an hour later created an envelope of dark smoke screening the moonlight like a lunar eclipse. Till the cremation ceremonies were performed, the police force stealthily surrounded the plant. But, they committed one mistake. The media beamed all their activities live and Charulata heard it on her radio set while sitting in the control room.

At the NS2 office, Nisha received a call from Charulata.

'What games you are playing? If you ever storm the plant, the result will be disastrous.'

'This is for the security of the common people. Why should they be involved in all this? I have talked to the chief minister and he has assured that he is looking into the matter of Gireesh's release. However, that involves concurrence from the centre as his case is under the jurisdiction of the Supreme Court. This will take some time. I request you to give us some more time.'

'No more time. Eighteen hours have passed. You have another 42 hours. Do what you can, but remember, I will do what I have said.'

'She is adamant. We do not have much time,' Nisha said as the phone line went dead.

At the control room, Charulata was deliberating on her future strategies. Samir was watching her and after some time, said—'Commander, don't you think that it is dangerous to be here for a long time? They have circled us and can attack anytime. During the night hours, there is heavy fog here and they can use it to their advantage.'

'Are you afraid? Do you say we shall run away after coming so far?'

'Not like that. But, we can move out to someplace safer. What is the use of holding out here? We can take the hostages to the Parshuram Hills, and then we find shelter there.'

'How will we move out from here? They have fortified the area, and we cannot move in small vehicles.'

'I have a plan. See, there is a railway track built up to the unloading bay. Goods trains regularly come to that spot to unload heavy items. We will demand a train that can drop us to the Bhagatpur yard near the Panchayat Bhavan. From there, we will cross the river and walk to our camps.'

'You are right. We can do that. We are not equipped to combat an attack here. We will be safe in our camps. Our aim to take hostages and warn the government has succeeded, and now we can operate from our camps. Once Gireesh is released, we will find out a way for getting more weapons and ammunition. Now that Ganesh Rai is dead and the RR is on its way out, we will emerge as the most powerful group here.'

'Why don't we demand money from the government?' Samir asked.

'No, asking for money is against our ideology. It makes us feel like petty criminals. Once Gireesh reaches here, we will find some way out of this mess,' she replied.

48

21 January 2014

At 2 a.m., Taneja and his team were frantically trying to devise a strategy when Nisha received a phone call from Charulata.

'Nisha, we want a train to be arranged at the unloading bay at the site. We wish to move away from the site. Arrange the train until morning and give us a safe passage to Bhagatpur yard.'

Nisha communicated the new demand to Taneja.

'What? They are demanding a train to escape from there? Are they out of their mind?' Taneja exclaimed.

'No, she is very clever. She has understood that sooner or later we will storm the plant and so she wants to go to a safer place. Bhagatpur yard is near the river and from there they can easily move into the forests and the Parshuram Hills, and there they would be pretty safe,' Kavita explained.

'This is our last chance. If they are able to return to their camps in the forest, it will be difficult for us to flush them out,' Taneja said.

'Does that mean you will storm the plant before she embarks on the train?' Nisha asked, alarmed.

'Yes, precisely, let us draw out a plan.'

'But, why don't we launch the attack in the night? The dense fog would guarantee us cover.'

'We do not have night vision devices, and if the fog can shield our moves, it can very well guard them too. One mistake on our part could cost us.'

'Why don't you ask the RR soldiers to attack the plant? They have sophisticated weapons and skills,' Nisha asked.

'No, we will go alone.'

Nisha could not understand the reason behind the several attempts to minimise the involvement of the RR. She took Gautam aside and asked, 'Has he gone mad? Why doesn't he take her help?'

Gautam explained, 'He has clear instructions from the government not to involve them as the CM wants to show that the RR is nothing but an unnecessary hindrance to the internal affairs of the state. The personal rivalry of the two big leaders will definitely hamper the rescue operations. But beyond all this, they are forgetting that it is no longer a state issue but a national issue, and that it shall be dealt with strongly. The present situation demands us to help Taneja in whatever way we can.'

'Okay, come.'

A goods train used for ferrying coal was arranged from the Gaya station and hurriedly dispatched towards Bhagatpur; although the wagons were coal-laden. A rescue plan was formulated; according to which a team of 50 police officers would be on the train supposed to be sent to the unloading bay.

Upon reaching the unloading bay, some rebels would come to inspect the train. Snipers would be positioned to eliminate them and the police force would storm the plant. First, they would target the control room and gradually take over the entire plant. Rammohan would be stationed near Gate no. 3, and in case of any eventuality, he would barge into plant from the same gate. Later, Taneja would initiate another round of attack from Gate no. 1 and progress towards the control room. Once the hostages are secured; the remaining terrorists would be apprehended.

Kavita had vehemently opposed the operation plan. 'Why don't you understand? You are jeopardising the lives of the hostages.'

'Kavita, our plan is perfect and this is our last chance,' Taneja said.

'But, there are many flaws.'

'Can you list out the flaws?' he scorned at her.

'How many snipers are you using?'

'Ten.'

'It is a basic tenet of sniping operations that at least two snipers for each known target are essential. Here, the number of targets is not known. In theory, you are prepared for only five targets. Even if Nisha's assessment about 50 terrorists on the site is correct, at least 10 of them will definitely come to inspect the train. If the opportunity of the first strike is missed; they would get alert and may start shooting the hostages as a counter-attack. Moreover, the sniper guns are outdated versions of Heckler and Koch which may not prove effective in this operation. These guns have a barrel length of 510 mm which reduces the shooting distance to about 600 m. The nearest high rise near the plant is located at about 800 m. It would be a tall order to shoot with accuracy from that range. Your snipers are not an experienced lot. Also for shooting at such a range the snipers shall have a clear view of their targets. The train which will ferry your commandos will cover the entire unloading bay, up to the Gate no. 3, from where the train will enter. This will act as a shield for the terrorists to dodge the snipers' view. In effect, the snipers could buy a few minutes to execute their plans. Even if the snipers manage to unsettle them through an initial shock, your force is ill-equipped to get on with the situation at hand. They are armed with guns which are not compatible for close combat. We have been supplied and practiced with the Tavor class rifles—the elitist rifle used by Israeli forces. We are trained to operate those. We can fight them,' Kavita explained.

'Well done, Kavita. You think you know too much? Where did your expertise go when Gireesh fled from your custody?'

'Don't dig into the past. He did not flee, but, our convoy was ambushed by the MAF. We put up a brave fight, but, unfortunately we were overpowered and they took him away,' Kavita roared.

'Ultimately, you were a failure.'

'Let us bring this matter to rest. There is no use fighting over on how and why we missed our target in the past. The fact is, we are against one of the most dreaded commanders of the Naxalite movement—Charulata. She can fight against a whole battalion all by herself, without an aide,' Gautam intervened.

'Okay, but I am the mission in-charge here. Let Ms Kavita refrain from dictating terms on me. I know how to fight them. Once my men penetrate the site, I will handle the rest. Today I will show this *Robin Hood* Charulata who Taneja is,' Taneja roared.

Dismissing Kavita's observations, Taneja gave a go-ahead to the plan. The train was arranged as decided. The 50 well-armed police personnel boarded the train from the Bhagatpur station at around 6 a.m.

ASP operations—Abhijit Verma was leading the group.

'Sir, have you seen Charulata?' one of the constables asked.

'No.'

'Sir, I have heard that she uses both her hands while shooting and can alone kill a dozen?'

'Once, a cobra had almost smothered a toddy-tapper that rendered him motionless. All the villagers and police had surrendered in their attempts to save the person. Charulata descended from somewhere and she killed the snake in one shot. The person was rescued,' narrated another constable.

Everyone gasped upon listening to this miraculous tale of bravery and courage.

'What rubbish? She is not a demigod. We too are equally trained in this type of warfare.'

'Our weapons are unmatched,' added another constable.

The battalion was nervous and Abhijit tried his best to pump up energy into his force's depleting levels of morale.

'I will not die this useless death. I have two little children,' one of the constables said and jumped down from the train. Some other constables also followed him. The ones who remained with Abhijit hardly seemed to be confident of their victory.

'What shall I do? Shall I inform the boss? But, the boss has warned us not to use radio communication as the frequencies are not secure and this could put the lives of the hostages at risk. I should probably stop the train,' Abhijit said and moved towards the driver's engine.

He was one compartment away from the engine when the train came to a halt. He looked outside and realised they had already reached their destination.

'Oh my God, we have reached the site,' he murmured and turned towards his men who were following him.

'I understand that we have been outnumbered, but trust me this plan will work. Once the snipers neutralise the terrorists, we will storm the site. The other group led by the boss will attack from the other side. I will fight till my death. If anyone decides to withdraw then I advise them to remain in hiding. The rest—be prepared to fight for the motherland.'

~

The guards positioned at Gate no. 3 took a first glance at the train and asked the driver to go up to the unloading bay. However, the train driver committed one mistake. He surpassed the marked distance that he was instructed to stop at and brought the train 50 m ahead. This shielded the view of the staircase from where the terrorists were supposed to land. The snipers deputed at the buildings were getting nervous. Taneja was oblivious to the fact that a substantive part of his force had deserted the train without informing him. Finally, the terrorists came down to inspect the train. Samir was the team leader. The snipers waited with bated breath. When Samir started moving towards the train, the first sniper fired. The bullet missed the target and slid past his shoulders. The terrorists retaliated and fired in the direction of the shot. The scene was aired live on television.

Abhijit and his men emerged from the train but to his horror, Taneja realised the number of the charging force was abysmal. He concluded that some of his men had betrayed him at the eleventh hour. However, he resolved not to look back. He ordered the group stationed at Gate no. 3 to immediately mount charge. They threw a grenade towards the gate and moved forward, and took positions behind the train and the gunfire ensued. The number of shots fired at them belied the claim that there were 50 of them.

'It seems there are more than a 100 inside,' Nisha exclaimed.

'Yes, your estimate was wrong, Nisha.'

'At the time I went to meet Charulata it seemed they were not more than 50.'

'These groups are smart. They never reveal their full strength to the negotiators. These are the basics to begin with. I have no idea how you decided to go ahead with this operation,' Kavita exasperated in utter desperation and buried her head in her hands.

Taneja was perplexed. His calculations and estimations about charging through Gate no. 1 had gone for a toss. Witnessing the battle live on television, he doubted whether he should himself rush to the site.

Inadvertently, the newsfeeds helped the operatives keep a close eye on the police force and the positions that they were guarding. The police force could be an easy target. CCTV cameras revealed their movements within the site in greater detail. They successfully assessed and decoded the positions of the snipers and fired an RPG (Rocket Propelled Grenade) towards the building after much scrutiny. Two snipers were killed on the spot and the rest hurried their way back.

Soon Abhijeet's men surrendered to the raining bullets. Abhijeet too was severely injured.

'Commander, they have deceived us. We need to answer back,' Chakradhar shouted while firings continued without a break outside the control room.

Charulata was silent.

'Commander, order. We need to shoot at least one of them,' Samir also pitched in as a bullet whizzed past him and hit one of the annunciators at the control desk. The broken glass splattered all around.

Charulata browsed through the list of hostages she had compiled. Then, she looked at their faces.

'If we have to kill one, then, let us kill the person responsible for this fiasco,' she said and turned towards Rohit.

Chakradhar gave a nod to a man standing behind him. He moved towards Rohit, grabbed him by his arms and dragged him towards the window. Rohit remained silent, tears rolled down his eyes. The MAF man pointed the gun to his head and asked, 'Commander?'

'Your time has come, Rohit. Goodbye, for your journey to hell,' she said and turned her back towards him and whispered, 'Yes.'

A gunshot followed, there was a loud thud, and then silence descended.

The gunfire between the two groups was at its peak, when suddenly, something was flung outside the control room. The television cameras zoomed in on the thing and to everybody's horror, Rohit's lifeless body lay on the ground. Taneja took cognizance of the fallacy of the operation and ordered his men to stop firing at once.

Nisha received a call from Charulata.

'Nisha, you have deceived us. If the police refuse to leave the compound, we will not shy away from killing more hostages. Even the train driver is our hostage now.'

Nisha put the phone down and looked at Taneja whose face had shrunk like a defeated man. He ordered the police force to retreat from the site. ASP Abhijit was sent to the hospital and the police officers who deserted the train were suspended.

A press conference was arranged in Delhi. The home minister was at the receiving end of fielding tough questions from the reporters.

'Sir, could you offer an explanation about Rohit's death? Is this not the failure of the police?'

'This operation was not initiated by us. The State Government gave it a go-ahead,' he replied.

'But, the onus of securing the citizens' lives rests on you,' interjected another reporter.

'Yes, I am responsible. We have decided to ask the Razia Regiment to take charge. We have also sent a special team of NSG commandos to Patna. We have a cabinet meeting this evening. We should be able to reach a decision on the

MAF and their demands,' the guilt-ridden home minster explained. Elsewhere, protests against the government's failure intensified. Media covered these protests and shared reports on the plight of the victims' families.

At the Dharbhanga circuit house, the CM was watching the news. He asked his PA, 'Call Taneja and tell him to let Kavita take over. This issue has gone out of our hands.'

49

21 January 2014, 10 A.M.

At NS2, the atmosphere was tense. No one had slept a wink. Taneja was in shock and was not able to come to terms with his mission's disastrous failure. Charulata called Taneja in the morning at 10 a.m.

'What have you thought of our demands?'

'Listen, we wish to send Nisha to talk to you one more time.'

'I will not talk to Nisha.'

'I assure you, nothing untoward will happen this time. Allow her to come in.'

'No, I don't want to talk to her. Find another negotiator.'

She wants another negotiator. It is time I call Narendra Nath. I know she will talk to him. I will also get an opportunity to talk to him, Gautam thought.

'Ask her if Narendra Nath will do?' he told Taneja to ask Charulata.

'We wish to send Narendra Nath in. Is it okay with you?' he asked.

Charulata thought for a moment and said, 'Okay.'

'I will visit his camp,' Nisha said. As she came out, she briefed the media about the new negotiator and went to Narendra Nath's camp.

Swami Narendra Nath was in his meditating chamber. Attired in saffron, his face glowed while he chanted, 'Om.' He opened his eyes as Nisha touched his feet.

'Nisha, after such a long time! What is the matter?'

'We need your help in the hostage crisis.'

'Oh! So, you have come to seek help, and not to meet me.'

'I have been very busy.'

'Yes, you are going to be a politician. How will you get time to meet your poor uncle? Anyway, what is the problem?'

'Charulata has taken hostages at the power plant site. We wish you to negotiate on behalf of the government,' Nisha pleaded.

'I will help. Come.'

Their vehicle reached the site and Nath stepped in. Escorted by guards, he went inside the control room. Charulata was determined not to concede to any demands made by the government, but, she respected the Swami and listened to him.

'How are you, Swami*ji*?' she asked.

'I am fine, but what is this? Is this how you fight for the rights?'

'I am sorry, but they have forced us to do this.'

'So now, what do you want?'

'You know what I want.'

'Yes, I know. Gireesh will come to you But, I advise you to forget all other demands. Concentrate on one. '

'But Vikas is also my trusted lieutenant. Besides, if I change my plan at this stage, people will lose faith in me.'

'Don't think about the lieutenants, concentrate only on the leader. Don't bother about the people. They will understand once you make them understand. They love you.'

'Okay.'

'I will see that the government agrees to release Gireesh. I request you to revoke all other demands and give them more time to complete all the relevant formalities.'

After the failure of the rescue operation, Gireesh's release was the only logical thing to do, reasoned, Narendra Nath. He thought he would talk about this to the government later.

Charulata analysed the proposal at hand and agreed, 'Okay, we will give them 24 hours more. We will require some food items and medical kits. Ask them to leave those essentials near Gate no. 1. Also, warn them not to attempt any more attacks on us. After they release Gireesh, I shall free all these hostages. As a gesture of goodwill, I am releasing two women hostages and the train driver.'

Narendra Nath agreed. As he came out with the three released hostages, the media surrounded him.

'How did you manage to get them out?'

'I cannot tell you anything now. I have only done my duty. The rest is up to the government,' he commented as he sat inside his vehicle.

After he drove off, the media swarm descended on the freed prisoners.' How were you treated? Did they misbehave with you?'

'No, they did not do anything. All the hostages are fine,' one girl remarked.

As the vehicle moved away, Taneja, who was watching the news averred, 'This man has something in him. They always listen to him.'

After Narendra Nath reached NS2, he asked Nisha, 'What are you planning to do now? I have promised Charulata that Gireesh will be released.'

'Swami*ji*, how can you make such a promise when the government has not yet decided?' asked Taneja.

'Do you have any choice?'

'But, if they can forgo all the other demands, why not this one too?' Gautam asked.

'I did not press for it,' Narendra Nath said.

'But why?'

'Because I knew she would never agree.'

'How can you be so sure?'

'I know one secret that you all are unaware of. Charulata is Gireesh's wife.'

'What?' everybody cried in unison.

'She had married Gireesh last year. She will not let him go to the gallows. So, I had to promise her. What do you say, Nisha?'

'You seem to know so much about this group. How do they respect you so much?' Gautam asked.

'Respect has to be earned.'

'And, you have earned their respect by helping them. Or is it because Gireesh is the son of your friend James?'

'No. I would have earned the same respect had Gireesh been someone else. In fact, Charulata does not belong to this place and she still respects me.'

'You seem to be a traitor,' Taneja intervened.

'You can say whatever you wish because you are far removed from the story of Bhagatpur.'

'We know the story, but, that does not mean you support people who take up arms,' Gautam said.

'You also support them; that is why you have left your job to be here.'

'But, I do not believe in the armed struggle.'

'That is your belief, but, you do believe that something is not right here.'

Nisha, who was listening to all this, went to Narendra Nath, looked in his eyes and asked, 'How was my father killed? I think you know.'

Narendra Nath looked up and replied, 'Nisha, he was a great man. He came here with a mission—to do what he could not achieve in his youth. When we returned, the situation in Bhagatpur had dramatically changed. James was killed and Gireesh had become a rebel. Saroj's father Shyam Lal was actively supporting him. This did not go down well with Sunil, your father. He confronted Shyam Lal.'

'What have you done to our children? You have given guns in their hands. Why, Shyam? What was the need to take up weapons? What was the need for the Eklavya Sena and the MAF?'

'After so many years you suddenly remember to come to this place with your non-violent teachings? Where were you when James was burned? Where were you when our women were raped? We have taken up guns to protect ourselves. Gireesh has done what any self-respecting son would have done for his father. He will take revenge not only for his father but for the sons of this village,' Shyam Lal replied.

'No, I don't believe in all this. I have worked in the police force and I have respect for the law. I believe in education. I will show that you are wrong.'

'I will be happy to be proved wrong.'

'You have turned our children into dacoits.'

'It is the government who is the dacoit, looting our property. We are the defenders.'

'It is futile to argue with you.'

Narendra Nath continued, 'After the government announced the land acquisition policy, Shyam Lal's land was the first to be occupied. He decided to protest and asked Sunil for help but Sunil agreed on the condition that the protest should be non-violent. They sat on a *dharna*, and were attacked by the police. Shyam Lal was killed and the bloodbath increased. Sunil sat on a fast unto death to persuade the MAF cadres to give up arms. This put pressure on Gireesh and they asked me to persuade Sunil to call of the fast, but Sunil refused to listen. Gireesh then issued a threat to Sunil. They planned to attack the fast site, terrify the villagers and force Sunil to withdraw.'

'What did they do then?' Nisha asked.

'Before they could do anything, another incident occurred in this village.'

'What?'

'On April 12, one of the villagers, Kalu Chacha, if you remember his name, went for his daily prayer. He was thrashed by Ganesh's goons for entering the temple; a price he had to pay for being a Dalit. He died in hospital, but, the police refused to register the case. Sunil took it as his own cause and protested in front of the police station, forcing the police to lodge a complaint. A warrant was issued to arrest Ganesh. To instil pride in the villagers, Sunil decided to celebrate Ambedkar's birthday that year, and planned to unveil Ambedkar's statue which had been installed by the government at the Panchayat Bhavan. However, pressure from upper-caste communities had prevented its inauguration. Ganesh , the leader of the upper-caste groups in the village, always felt that Ambedkar was an icon of the Dalits and therefore, could not allow the inauguration of his statue. Ganesh used the opportunity to punish him and put the blame on the MAF. His henchmen, disguised as villagers fired when Sunil unveiled the statue. Incidentally, Jagdish, the leader of the group which attacked your father, was the one who threatened you when you had recently filed a PIL against Ganesh. He was killed by Saroj and his corpse was left hanging from the banyan tree.'

'Saroj killed that guy?'

'Yes, she could not bear him threatening you.'

Nisha could not hear anymore and ran to the balcony.

Gautam consoled her. 'Come inside, the press is clicking your pictures,' he said while putting his hand on her shoulders.

'To hell with the press. Here, they have assembled to witness the end of the MAF which had saved my life so many times.'

'Don't be emotional. Charulata may be your saviour, but, she is also an enemy of the state.'

'I don't care about her enmity towards the state. I don't want to be responsible for her death. I quit.'

'You can't. Despite being courageous and righteous; she is against the well-being of our motherland.

Listen to your conscience. One day, you listened to the call of duty and came here. The time has come again.'

'I am tired of sacrifices, Gautam. Take me away. I want to quit.'

'I will not let you quit even if you want to. I have left everything and joined you in your mission. Your defeat is not only my defeat but also the defeat of the nation. This is the battle for the truth and truth always wins. *Satyamave Jayate*. Come inside,' he said, holding her hand and pulling her in.

'Now, will you keep my word? Will you release Gireesh?' Narendra Nath asked again.

'He is an enemy of the country,' Taneja joined.

'Who are you to say this? For me, they are not criminals. They are fighting for their rights. How can you think that what you are doing is good and what they are doing is a crime? No one is God. You are fighting for the country. Which country? The country where the poor have to fight for their rights?'

'We will think about it, Swam*iji*. You may go now and let us do our work,' Taneja said waving his hand towards the main gate signalling him to leave the NS2 office.

'You can't talk to my uncle like this,' Nisha intervened.

'At least I am not arresting him for now. We have to concentrate on ending the MAF menace. We cannot waste our time listening to his moral sermons. Once we complete this mission, we will see what to do with him. '

'But, now who will talk to the MAF? They will not talk to me or anyone else,' Nisha voiced her concern.

'Nisha, do you still think we have time to talk?'

Nisha slumped helplessly on her chair, while Kavita looked out of the window.

50

21 January 2014, 6 P.M.

Shweta went near the window where she saw Kavita in a contemplative mood and put a hand on her shoulder.

'Madam, the home minister is calling,' she said while handing her the phone.

'Kavita, we are under a lot of pressure here,' said Prabhat.

'The cabinet has taken a decision to release Gireesh. I will be taking him to Bhagatpur tomorrow. You have time till then. Do anything you can, but, don't let any of the hostages be killed.'

Kavita looked tense after the conversation ended. Taneja asked, 'What is the matter?'

'They have taken the decision to release Gireesh. Tomorrow, the home minister himself will escort Gireesh here. We have 24 hours to do whatever we can. But, any mistake on our part can cause severe damage. An NSG team has been dispatched to Patna. In case of any eventuality they will take over,' Kavita announced.

Another thought struck her, she had to prevent the media beaming live pictures of the operation. She went out to speak to them. 'As you are aware, our previous operation failed miserably. Please understand that live streaming of these events is helping the MAF gauge our moves. We have planned another operation and we request you to keep silent,' she spoke.

'Why do you blame the media for the fiasco? It was a failure on the part of the police,' one of the mediapersons answered.

'I am requesting you to help us.'

'We too have risked our lives in this event. We want the viewers to see the truth.'

'They have hostages out there whose lives depend on our actions. One has been killed. We have lost five of our men. The honour of our country is at stake. How can you be so insensitive?' Nisha pitched in.

The media understood the gravity of the situation and promised to extend their support to the police.

Inside the building, Kavita was addressing the group gathered there.

'The situation here is very serious. The eyes of the nation are on us. Any more mistakes and we would jeopardise the lives of more hostages. We have to plan carefully. We cannot charge from the ground. They are all situated at higher positions. We have to get to the site's topmost point, the boiler drum, and from there move downwards. We have to find an alternate way to get inside.'

'How will you do that?' Taneja said.

'I want assistance from the site's engineers. Maybe, they can suggest something useful. Where is the person in charge of the BMTPP?' she asked.

'He is under custody,' Taneja asked.

'Custody? Why?'

'What do you mean, why? This accident was due to his negligence. He will be held responsible for this.'

'This is not the time. We need his help.'

'He is in Jehenabad. It will take time to get him here.'

'We do not have time. Call him.'

Taneja called his office and got Rajiv Kumar on the line.

'Listen, Mr Rajiv, your negligence has landed us in a big soup. But, I am providing you another chance. Help us here and we may forgo the case against you.'

'I will be happy to help sir,' a meek reply came from the other side.

'We want full details of the site, to the last nail.'

'It is difficult to provide that without diagrams. There is one engineer who can help you out. His name is Ashish, from the design department of the Silent Turtle. Look for him. He knows the plot like the back of his hand.'

'Where is he?'

'He has escaped from the site after the MAF attack. He was terrified when he called me after exiting the site. I advised him to hide in the field hostel hoping that it will not be attacked. I would have informed the police to take him out, later.'

'In the field hostel? There are people holed up there and you are speaking to us now?'

'What to do, sir? Your men took me in custody and confiscated my mobile phone. Nobody listened to me.'

Taneja put the phone down and announced to the group. 'We have to look for one engineer, Ashish, hiding in the hostel.'

'Field hostel. That is one kilometre east of the site. We did not know there are people hiding there. There may be other engineers,' Kavita exclaimed.

'Nobody knows that. Otherwise, they would have attacked the hostel also. We have to storm the building and take them here.'

'Why do you always talk of storming? We have to do that discreetly. Remember, that building is near the area you had put the snipers. That place may well be under Charulata's scanner. We will do it discreetly. Shweta will bring them back here,' Kavita said.

'Yes, madam,' Shweta came forward.

'Shweta, listen, there is a drain that flows from here all the way to the site. I know it will be a dirty job. But, go inside and through its route reach the storage yard behind the field hostel. There, under the cover of the store items, find your way to the field hostel building and bring back any survivors hiding in there by following the same route. Be quick. We do not have much time.'

Shweta went away to the back of the building with two of her commandos. Stealthily, they reached the building which was shrouded in darkness. They jumped into the compound, scaled the wall, broke the window of the balcony and entered the building. Inside, there was complete darkness. They began their search. On entering Room 104, they discovered one person cowering in the corner. Seeing people with guns, he raised his hands in fear.

'Don't kill me, please.'

'We have come to rescue you. We are the police,' Shweta soothed him.

He put his hands down and went towards them, still shivering. 'Anybody else in here?'

'One more. He is hiding in the bathroom.'

As the guard recovered the other person, Shweta handed them two special suits.

'You have to put it on to avoid the filthy water. Tell me one thing, how have you landed here? Why did nobody know about you?' she asked as they moved towards the drainage.

'Last night, our team had a meeting. Shiwani was adamant on stopping the work as she was confident that the pillar design of the compressor house was faulty and that it could collapse anytime soon. Rajiv Kumar did not pay heed to her logic and she was asked to look into the construction of the switchyard control building, instead. I was asked to survey the layout of the boiler. Rohit Kumar had come for the inauguration of the control room. Rajiv Kumar was with him. As the incident happened, I immediately climbed down the boiler below, threw my helmet and moved towards the gate, but till then, the agitation had started and I could hear gunshots. I jumped in the drain. Seeing me, Raghav, who was at the CHP (Coal Handling Plant) also jumped and we entered here. We switched off all the lights and hid. We informed Rajiv Kumar on the phone, but I think in the melee, nobody got time to think of us. I don't know where the rest of us are.'

'It is very sad. They have killed Rohit Kumar. About 20 engineers are held hostage inside the plant. I have come to take you so that you can help in rescuing them.'

'What can I do?'

'We need information about the site.'

Soon after, they reached NS2.

Ashish was offered some tea and Kavita introduced herself, 'Hi, I am Kavita. I am going into the site to release your friends. Tell us whatever you can.'

Ashish nodded and explained the layout to them. 'The site has three gates. Gate no. 1 is the main entrance through which one can go straight to the control room. Gate no. 2 is at the eastern corner which is far away from the control room. Gate no. 3 is near the boiler. The boiler is an open structure, and so, terrorists stationed there have a clear view of the entire site. From the control room, only Gate no. 1 is under the visible range. The power plant has almost 50 CCTV cameras placed at strategic locations and these images can be monitored from the control room.'

'The terrorists have taken position at each and every corner of the plant. However, the boiler is the tallest structure, which means we have to first mount an attack on the terrorists holed up on the boiler. Only when they are neutralised can we charge from Gate no. 1,' she said.

'The boiler has a furnace and is enclosed with water tubes which run all around the furnace.'

'Is there a way to reach the boiler without getting on the ground?' she asked him.

'One way is to go through the water canal from the Panchayat Bhavan to the water treatment plant inside the site. Once you reach there you can make your way up to the boiler. Another way is to use the coal handling plant and use the conveyer belt to enter the mill section and then make a way up to the boiler. I can show you some ducts which will lead to the boiler once you are inside the site,' he said, pointing to the plan laid out in front of him.

'You are right, but, in all these ways we have to be on the ground for a few metres and that will ruin our chances. I want a stealth passage right to the boiler,' she said.

Ashish thought for a moment.

'The chimney is the tallest structure of the site. This structure flushes out the waste gas from the boiler to the atmosphere. It is about 250 m high. The fog reduces the visibility to a few metres these days. If you can enter the chimney of the plant from the top, the persons standing below or even at the boiler top may not be able to notice you. Inside the chimney, there is a staircase which can guide you down. At the height of 6 m, there is a big fan called ID (Induced Draft) fan which sucks the waste gas from the furnace region of the boiler and throws it in the chimney. A duct is connected from this fan to the boiler furnace. There are many gates and dampers in between, but all of them have been kept open now. You can use the duct to go straight to the furnace region, which is the centre of the boiler. No one can see it from outside. Inside the furnace, there is a sky climber which can take you to the top of the boiler. At the top, you will find a manhole at about 60 m height. There, you will find a 10 ft. high monkey ladder which will take you to the iron platform of that elevation. That manhole was open for maintenance and I think it might be open till now.'

'This option suits us well. Tell us about the control room building.'

'The control room is situated at the height of 17 m near the turbine. There are two staircases which lead to the control room. One staircase is from the front which can be approached from Gate no. 1; the second, near the boiler, is at the right side which can be reached from the side of Gate no. 3. Below the control room, there is one floor at 8 m. Above the main control room, there are two floors. The AC control room and the UPS (Uninterrupted Power Supply) room are above the main control room. Above them, at 32 m, there is another floor which is known as the *deaerator floor*. The control-room building is connected with the boiler at two points—one at the same level that is at 17 m and the other at 32 m. The AC duct from the AC control room goes to the false ceiling of the main control room.'

'The AC duct? Yes, the AC ducts. If we can enter the duct, we can reach right above the control room. This is our chance,' Kavita jumped on hearing this.

She thought of the plan for a while and then discussed it with the entire group. She took the crossection layout of the power plant diagram and pinned it to the drawing board in front of the people assembled there and explained to them her plan while marking the locations on the diagram.

'I, along with some RR commandos, will be in a helicopter at the dead of the night. The dense fog will act as a protective shield. The helicopter will drop the rope down the chimney, paving the way for us to go inside. We will reach the boiler furnace following the route prescribed by Ashish. Once inside, we will move up the boiler using the sky climber and come out from the manhole. We will use the sniper rifles to kill any terrorists at that elevation. After neutralising the rebels positioned there, we will take our positions to eliminate the remaining rebels stationed at the heights. After dealing with them, the battalion at Gate no. 3, headed by Taneja, will move stealthily and get cover behind the train and wait for the signal to attack. We will come down through the boiler and enter the control room structure using the *deaerator floor* and get to the AC control room. We will

Bhagatpur Plant Site

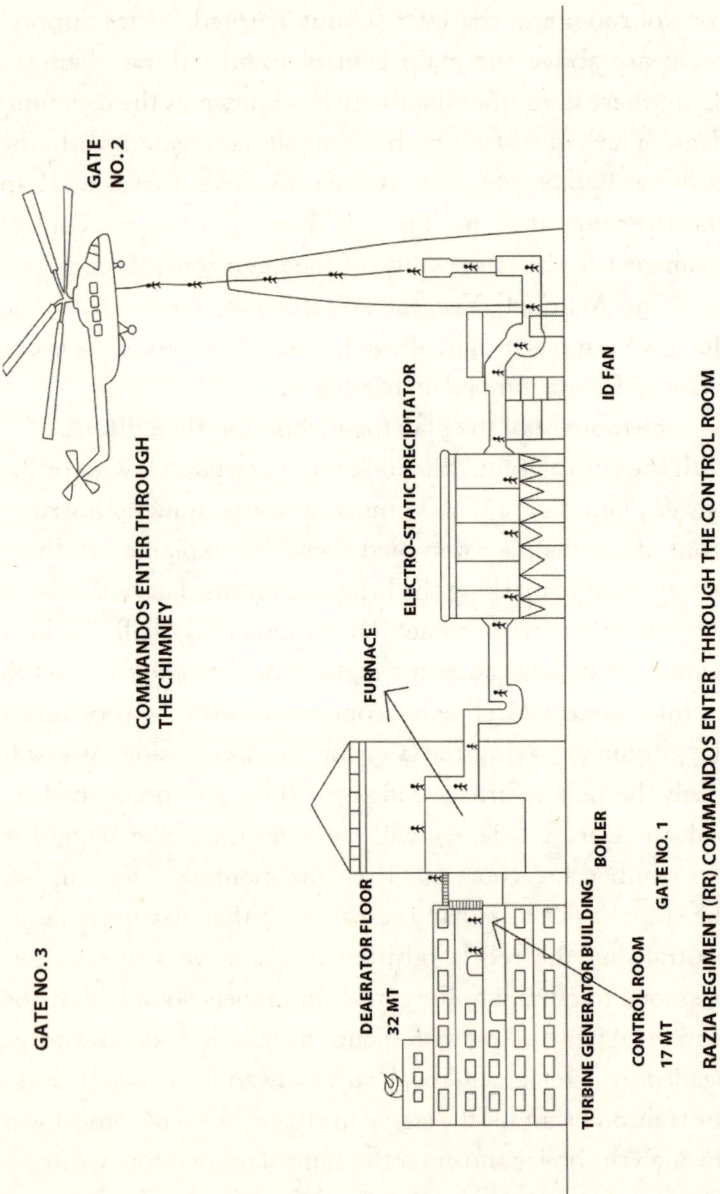

enter the AC duct which will take us to the top of the control room. When we reach there, the group at Gate no. 2, under Shweta's leadership, will begin firing to distract the rebels.'

'How will I know you have reached the destination? If we use a wireless set, they can easily intercept the signal,' asked Shweta.

'I will carry a transmitter. You can monitor my position on a handheld device which will indicate the position as a dot,' Kavita said.

'Will that work, considering the fog?' Nisha asked.

'That will work anywhere, except underwater.'

Kavita went on, 'As soon as the rebels rush towards Gate no. 2, we will first secure the hostages and gain control of the remaining rebels. At Gate no. 1, sergeant Rammohan will command his battalion along with the fire brigade and ambulances. As the groups at Gate no. 2 and those behind the train take charge, the forces at Gate no. 1 will weaken. This will give Rammohan a chance to force his way towards the control room from Gate no. 1. Some snipers will be stationed at the destroyed building top and will offer cover to the troops entering from Gate no. 3. Once all of them take their positions, the helicopter will drop more commandos on the roof of the control room. They would charge together and attack the terrorists. Ashish will provide the exact location of the CCTV cameras. They have to be avoided,' she said.

Ashish deftly marked the locations of the cameras on the plot plan.

'Charulata will be flanked by her two trusted guards, Chakradhar and Samir. Chakradhar as we know is a fierce supporter of Gireesh and Charulata. Samir, though

Charulata's trusted aide, has an ambition of his own. Perhaps he is the only weak link we have to use to our advantage. He is the only one who has a mixed response to the idealistic principles of the Naxalite movement. The others will fight with Charulata till their last breath.'

She continued. 'Tomorrow, we will fight our last battle against those who think that the power of the weapon is supreme. Tonight is the night for all of us. Come; let us pledge to succeed. Let us prepare to either emerge victorious or die for our nation. *Jai Bharat.*'

The commandos raised their hands and their voices echoed, '*Jai Bharat.*'

Nisha looked at the commandos. All of them were in their 20s with innocent faces and eyes gleaming with pride. She recalled the faces of the terrorists who were holed up inside the site. They were also in their teens and she had sensed a similar resolve on their faces too. It was ironical that all these brave men and women of the same country were pitted against each other because the idea of the motherland was different for both the groups. Both claimed to fight for the motherland. It was immaterial who would win, the country would suffer at the *success* of either of the parties.

Nisha wanted to be a part of this operation.

'We also want to go with you,' she said, looking at Gautam.

'No. I cannot take civilians with me. You be with Taneja, and enter only when the mission is over. Keep these guns for your safety. They are loaded. See, here is the safety lever. Just move it this way and it is ready for use,' Kavita trained Nisha.

'I don't wish to use it,' Nisha said, while taking the pistol from her.

Kavita called the chief minister who was camping at Dharbhanga.

'Sir, we will need your helicopter!'

'What are you planning to do?'

'Till now, you did not have faith in me or my commando force. I urge you to believe me tonight. I do not have time to explain.'

'Okay.'

Kavita telephoned the home minister, 'Sir, spread the news that you will reach Bhagatpur tonight and hand over Gireesh tomorrow morning. Just spread the news. I have a plan.'

'Okay, but be careful. I do not want any bloodshed.'

'Be assured. *Operation India One* will succeed this time, *Jai Bharat*.'

'It is showdown time. This will be a decisive battle, not between the good and evil, but, between the ideals, thinking and the methods of two groups who have opposing perceptions about our history, and contrasting views about our future,' Nisha ruminated.

51

21 January 2014, 11 P.M.

'Commander, come and look. They have deployed flares at Vikramgarh Fort,' the guard at the top of the boiler said on the wireless.

Charulata hurried towards the boiler top and looked through the binoculars. Nothing could be clearly seen in the dark, only Vikramgarh Fort, was lit to guard the helicopter. She could hear the helicopter engine hovering above.

'They are preparing for a helicopter landing. It means they have brought Gireesh!' she exclaimed.

The cadres cheered on hearing this. She phoned Taneja, 'I hope you are not doing anything foolish. I heard a helicopter.'

'That was Gireesh and the home minister. They have arrived at the fort. He will be released tomorrow morning and you will be given safe passage,' Taneja replied.

Charulata went into the control room and checked her radio.

'Breaking news—The Bhagatpur hostage crisis is going to end soon. The government has decided to release Gireesh.

The home minister has left with him towards Bhagatpur and will be arriving any moment. Sources say Gireesh will be released in the morning.'

There was a joyous mood in the control room. The rebels were dancing and the hostages also allowed themselves to feel a small measure of relief. Charulata was oblivious to all the happy scenes. Her intuition said, *something was wrong*.

'Commander!' Samir shouted.

'Samir, send your men and search each and every inch of the site,' she ordered.

'Yes commander.'

Samir sent his men. They looked all around but could find nothing. Charulata, meanwhile, was pacing up down the control room with her hands firmly clasped together at her back.

~

A vehicle with its lights off was plying silently towards Vikramgarh Fort. Kavita and her 10 commandos were armed to the teeth with Tavor rifles, bulletproof vests, Glock17 pistols, hand grenades, night vision devices and daggers. They alighted from the vehicle and rushed towards the police station where a makeshift helipad was constructed.

The helicopter had landed a few minutes ago.

'Welcome aboard. I am flight lieutenant Vikram Singh. Best of luck for your mission,' the pilot announced.

'Thanks, how is the visibility?'

'Very poor, but I will drop you there,' he assured.

'We cannot use radio frequencies because they can be easily intercepted. We will use signs. While disembarking through ropes remember—*one tug* means pull right, *two tugs* mean pull left and *three tugs* mean down. Continuous tugs would indicate we have reached the platform at the chimney top,' Kavita tutored the commandos and the pilot.

Fortunately, that night seemed to be covered with the densest fog of the season. Despite low visibility they positioned themselves above the chimney and after a few manoeuvres; Kavita was able to locate the platform. One by one, the commandos jumped carefully on the platform at the chimney top, and the helicopter was sent back. It returned to the Vikramgarh Fort to ferry 10 more commandos to the site.

At the upper platform of the chimney, Kavita commanded the battalion to their way down.

'It is too dark and at too much height, beware,' she warned. Kavita and her group descended down the stairs and reached the height of the ID fan. Two of the men there grew suspicious and approached the duct entrance. As soon as they reached, two commandos pounced, dragged them inside the chimney and killed them.

Slowly, the team then neared the ID fan duct which would lead them to another structure—ESP (for purifying waste gas). Shweta was monitoring the dot on her handheld screen.

'She has entered the site,' she announced jubilantly.

In the control room, Charulata was growing nervous.

'Commander, there is blood near the big fan close to the chimney,' Charulata heard on her wireless.

'Search there.'

Fifteen Ultras searched but found nothing. They pierced the ducts nearby with bullets but could discover nothing. On probing further, however, they spotted two bodies.

'Two bodies near the chimney,' they informed Charulata.

Their frequency was also intercepted by Shweta. *They have discovered the bodies. Act fast, madam,* she prayed.

Kavita and her team were crawling their way towards the furnace. Once inside, Kavita looked up.

'We have entered the den of the tiger. The fight will assume dangerous proportions from this point. Be prepared to die. Are you ready?' Kavita asked her team.

They stretched their hands outwards in unison.

'The sky climber will not work in this blackout. We will have to use that ladder. We have to climb to that place,' she said, while pointing at a small hole from where a dim ray of light from the fire, which the rebels had lit for light and warmth, could be seen. Kavita climbed up first and peeped through the manhole.

Two terrorists.

She signalled *two* with her fingers to her group.

Two commandos moved out stealthily and killed the terrorists, throwing the body inside the furnace. They took their positions at the top of the boiler and killed the guards at Gate no. 3. Thanks to the fog, nothing could be sensed by the rebel groups. The group waiting at the gate entered the compound and hid inside. The snipers took aim at the watchtowers near the gates and helped provide cover to the group at Gate no. 3.

The faint sound due to the movement of the troops near the train startled Charulata's men. They got suspicious and marched towards the train to confirm their doubts.

Kavita and her group were progressing well, killing the Ultras at each elevation. The silencers attached to their guns emitted minimum sound. There were no CCTV cameras till they descended to 32 m. At the entrance to the control room building they found one camera. Kavita moved under the camera and pulled out its power cord. Chakradhar Munda, patrolling at that elevation, spotted her.

'You have come to get the commander? First fight me,' Chakradhar charged at them.

'As you wish,' Kavita yelled and fired.

Chakradhar aimed at Kavita, but one of her commandos came in front and got killed. Kavita fired a burst of bullets from her Tavor rifle. Chakradhar dropped dead in an instant, along with some other rebels.

The gunshots startled the group in the control room and Samir went to check what was happening. Charulata tried examining the footage of that elevation but the camera was not working. Kavita and her group had almost reached the AC control room and entered the duct.

Charulata was growing restless. When Samir came back to report, she asked, 'Is anything suspicious up there?'

'I think we have visitors inside the plant. Chakradhar and his men are dead. The men at the boiler are also not responding. I found the body of one RR soldier up there.'

'Chakradhar!' Charulata exclaimed as tears rolled down her eyes. The MAF rebels were stunned to see her weep.

'Commander!' Samir touched her shoulder.

She wiped her tears and roared, 'Kavita, you are up to your old tricks again. You will have to pay.'

She turned towards Samir. 'Go down and guard the entrance and ensure nobody comes from below. I will be in front of the control room. Send 10 men upstairs to look for them. Two men will guard the hostages and if any unusual events take place, shoot them. Ask the men at the gates to be vigilant.'

She left the control room.

52

22 January 2014, 4 A.M.

At Gate no. 2, Shweta and her team were hiding behind the bushes, monitoring the moving dot.

'The plan is working,' she announced.

'She has reached the control room ceiling. Now, time for the next POA.'

She ordered her group to fire recklessly in all directions.

This confused Charulata's men as they could not judge the real direction of the firing. They followed suit. Taking this as their cue, the group waiting at the train also started firing.

Kavita crawled to an opening at the false ceiling of the control room and peeped down. She found two men guarding the hostages. She took out a bullet from her gun and threw it in the opposite direction of the men. One of them went to look for the source of the sound. As he turned his back, Kavita launched a surprise attack and slashed one man's neck. The hostages were amazed but Kavita put a finger on her lips signalling them to keep quiet. As her victim fell on the ground, Kavita jumped on him and made a tight grip on both the legs to prevent any sound. As the movement subsided, she stood up and hid behind the control panel. When the other man returned, she pounced on him from the back of the control desk panel and killed him too. She rushed the hostages to the panel room at the back. The rows of panels erected at the back panel room gave her cover. All her commandos descended from the ceiling and waited behind the panels.

Charulata soon sensed the firing was a trap and ordered her men to stop. She told them to move into the control room. But just as they neared, Kavita fired at them. Two men fell down while the remaining took positions.

'Kavita! She is in the control room. How did she get there?' Charulata was furious.

She ordered her men to take positions behind the turbine and fire. She understood Kavita was in a better position as she was shielded by the panels. Charulata took out a grenade and threw it at the control room. A loud explosion ensued, killing three commandos who were at the forefront while the room was up in flames. Kavita and her group moved to the back of the room along with the hostages who were visibly shaken to witness this mindless carnage. The Large Video Screen (LVS) set was destroyed, denying Kavita the advantage of watching the CCTV recordings.

'Rammohan, send in the fire brigade. The control room is on fire,' Kavita ordered on her wireless.

As Rammohan tried to enter through Gate no. 1, he had to overcome heavy resistance from the Opposition as it was directly in line of sight from the control room. The MAF rebels had blocked the way by placing huge cable drums on the road leading to the control room.

'It is difficult to send fire tenders now. I am charging in on foot. Once I clear the way, the tenders will move in,' he communicated through the wireless as he, along with his group, crawled through Gate no. 1 towards the control room. His group suffered the maximum causality and 10 soldiers died on their way to the cable drums. Still, he could not move towards the control room, and, took positions behind the drums.

'Shweta, move your forces towards the back of the control room. We will try to take the hostages down from the back,' Kavita spoke on her wireless.

As instructed, Shweta and her men headed towards the back of the control room. Killing eight rebels who were guarding that area, she positioned herself behind the control room. Taneja, meanwhile, tried to move towards the stairs, but there Samir and his group were waiting for him.

Charulata's castle had crumbled, but nothing could deter her. Meanwhile, the team waiting at the helicopter at the Vikramgarh Fort, also took off.

'Samir, stop anyone coming from the stairs. My men will guard this side. I am going to blow up the control room,' Charulata ordered as she moved towards the makeshift hut on the turbine floor that doubled up as storage for their arsenal.

She kicked open the door of the hut, pulled out the RPG from there, went near the microphone of the PA system of the plant and shouted, 'You have done a good job, Kavita, by penetrating my defence, but now you have reached a dead end. I am going to blow up the control room using this RPG and you, along with the hostages, will die a terrible death. Then your friends out there, Taneja and Nisha, will have to answer questions about your foolish operation.'

Her voice reverberated in all directions of the site.

Kavita also crawled to the nearest microphone and shouted, 'You are going crazy, Charulata. If you blast the control room with RPG, the whole building will collapse and you too shall die.'

'I do not fear death. You people will soon know what happens when you meddle with the MAF.'

Beads of sweat were visible on Taneja's forehead. 'Nisha, do you think Charulata will carry out her threat?'

'She will. I know her. Order the men to stop firing at once.'

'All units hold fire. I repeat, all units hold fire,' Taneja ordered using his wireless set.

The firing came to an abrupt halt.

'Think fast,' Nisha asked Taneja.

'There is no use of a ceasefire now. I am going to blast the building,' Charulata yelled.

'Commander, just hold it. It will also kill us,' Samir tried to soothe her.

'I knew Samir would not show his willingness and enthusiasm to fight like the rest of Charulata's men,' Taneja thought and tried to seize the opportunity to break the unity of Charulata's team members.

'Samir, I know you will not get out of this place. We promise to let you off with minimum punishment. Chakradhar Munda has already died fighting. I know you do not want to die. Surrender now,' Taneja offered the bait.

Samir stood motionless for a moment, perplexed by the chain of events. Convinced there was no way out he put his weapons down.

Charulata was taken aback and grew enraged on this act of betrayal by her trusted men. She took out a pistol and shouted again. 'Samir, you traitor, you do not deserve to live.'

'Commander, I have saved your life many times.'

'You are not fit for the revolution. It was my mistake to let you into this organisation. The time has come to rectify the same.'

Samir understood she meant business. Without any warning, he fired at Charulata.

Charulata proved to be quicker as she dived towards her left while taking aim at him with her gun and fired. Samir got hit by a hail of bullets and his body slumped down to the ground.

Samir's group, on seeing their leader dead, dropped their weapons and stood at the corner of the floor with their hands up in the air. The surrender of Samir's group weakened Charulata's condition but she was relentless. Kavita, meanwhile, broke the window glass of the control room, while Shweta reached the back of the control room. With the help of the winch machine, used to ferry construction materials to the top of the control room, Shweta began ushering the hostages out from the building. Fire tenders had arrived but could not go near the control room because the MAF rebels had opened fire. The fire was steadily engulfing the equipments in the control room.

Nisha crawled to the nearest microphone and tried one last time to reason with Charulata. 'Charulata, don't be foolish. You won't get out from here alive. It is better to surrender.'

'I will make sure you people do not go out of this place alive either,' she responded.

'We will give you a safe passage out of this place. Put down the RPG.'

'What are you saying?' Taneja whispered.

'She is right. While she keeps her busy talking, we should use that time to do something,' Gautam whispered back.

'I don't believe you anymore. I am not going to drop this,' Charulata shot back.

Gautam looked around in search of something and he fixed his gaze on a crane standing near the control room.

'Give me a sniper gun,' he asked Taneja.

'What are you going to do?'

'I am going to climb over that boom of the crane. I hope the height of the boom is more than 16 m so that I am able to reach the level at which Charulata is fighting. I will try to take her out. Trust me; I can aim well.'

Taneja gave him a sniper rifle, a Dragunov, and he moved stealthily towards the crane. To avoid being discovered by the MAF men, he entered through a cable trench which was shielded by huge cable drums. Meanwhile, Nisha was trying to buy time. Kavita was busy getting all the hostages out. Rammohan was waiting at his position.

Crawling through the trench, Gautam reached the crane and climbed on the boom. Soon, he reached the end of the boom, but, from there he could only see Charulata's hands.

'Damn, lucky you, if only I could have aimed at your head instead! This will have to do,' he said, and aimed for her hands.

The shot pierced through her hands and the RPG that she was holding went flying away from her. She stood bereft of her only trump card. She shifted her gaze towards the crane; and without bothering to ascertain the identity of her adversary, took out a grenade and threw it in that direction. Gautam saw that and jumped down on a heap of cable shreds. The crane was blown into pieces. The boom crashed on the control room building, damaging it severely. Charulata went inside her arsenal room and looked for more grenades.

'Commander, we are out of stock,' one of her assistants apprised her of the situation.

Since he was standing near the microphone his voice was heard all over.

'What the hell?' Charulata shouted while destroying the PA system with the butt of her gun.

'They have exhausted their grenades!' Taneja was overjoyed.

'All units mount a charge simultaneously,' he ordered.

Charulata came under heavy fire from all directions. She could hear the helicopter hovering above the control room. Commandos were disembarking.

'It is futile to fight them now. We shall abandon this building and move towards the villages. We will run towards the switchyard, and then using the cover of the equipment there, we would move towards Gate no. 2, and then try to move out of the plant,' Charulata explained her plan to the remaining men.

As soon as they moved towards the stairs, Kavita emerged from the control room and fired at her with her pistol. The shot injured Charulata's left arm and in return, she fired a volley of shots from her AK-47. Kavita fell down, writhing in pain.

'Do you feel the pain of death? Remember the innocent men who were killed when you and your PRM men raided our villages?' Charulata came near Kavita and glared at her contemptuously.

'Your unwarranted rage has blinded you. You have become oblivious to the destruction,' Kavita replied, stealthily sliding her transmitter into Charulata's boots.

Charulata took Kavita's Glock pistol and shot her.

'Die—' she yelled.

'Commander, we shall get out of here. You jump down from there. I will stop them,' one of her guards said.

Charulata with her trusted soldiers jumped down the building through the point where the boom of the crane had damaged the walls and created a hole in the roof. She then fled towards the switch yard. Charulata's men engaged the RR soldiers who were still holding at the control room.

The commandos who had dropped on the roof of the control building rushed and gunned down the MAF men. Meanwhile, the police force led by Taneja succeeded in forcing its way through the stairs up to the control room.

Rammohan also managed to clear the way. The fire tenders and ambulances waiting outside Gate no. 1 reached the ground below the control room.

The fire tenders did their job well. The rescued hostages were driven to the hospital for medical assistance. Rammohan ordered his forces to sweep the entire site to find the remaining hostages and rebels. The girl hiding at the switchyard control room was also rescued.

Nisha and Gautam rushed to the control room where Kavita lay.

Nisha held Kavita in her arms.

'Take her to the ambulance,' Gautam asked the constables.

'How did this happen?' Nisha asked.

'I did my duty. My transmitter is with Charulata. Go, get her. *Operation India One* should succeed,' Kavita uttered her last words as the constables lifted her.

The control room was under the supervision of the police and RR soldiers. The building was severely damaged. Bullet marks could be seen on all its walls. Two more police vehicles entered the site. Taneja saw Ajay emerging from one of them. Ajay limped his way to the staircase. He asked Taneja, 'Where is Charulata?'

'We are looking for her,' he replied.

'I saw her moving towards Gate no. 2, but, once I confronted her, she turned towards that structure,' Sergeant Rammohan said while pointing towards a building near Gate no. 2.

'What is that building?' Taneja asked one of the engineers.

'That is the water treatment plant,' he replied.

Shweta checked her transponder and detected signals from Kavita's transmitter.

'Taneja, go get her. She shall not go out from here alive,' Ajay shouted.

'Rammohan and Shweta, take your forces and search that building,' Taneja ordered.

Nisha also accompanied them as they moved towards the building. Her heart was racing. The RR soldiers and police could not locate her. The signal from the transmitter also went dead.

Nisha, then, noticed traces of blood near the water reservoir. She asked the engineer, 'where do you get water in this reservoir from?'

'A canal links it to the pumping station near the Panchayat Bhavan. The pumping station gets water from the main reservoir of the dam,' he answered.

That will work anywhere, except underwater.

'Good lord! Charulata is underwater, that is why the transmitter is not working. She is an expert swimmer. She can easily work her way up to the Panchayat Bhavan using this canal. Beyond the Panchayat Bhavan are the villages. Once she manages to enter the village, she can easily escape to her camp near the hills,' she exclaimed and ran towards Gate no. 2.

Gautam and Taneja saw her running towards Gate no. 2.

'Where is she going?' Gautam asked the engineer.

'I think towards the Panchayat Bhavan,' the engineer replied.

'This means Charulata has escaped through this water channel. What an extraordinary woman, she has two bullets in her and still she is unstoppable,' Gautam uttered.

'No wonder, they call her Robin Hood!' Taneja exclaimed.

Both of them immediately rushed outside Gate no. 2 and ran towards the Panchayat Bhavan.

53

22 January 2014, 1 P.M.

As Nisha reached the BR Ambedkar statue near Panchayat Bhavan, Charulata rose like a phoenix from the water and headed to the fields. Nisha blocked her way.

Charulata was severely injured and she was bleeding profusely. Drops of water dripping from her body had turned red in colour after getting mixed with blood.

'Nisha, get out of my way or I will forget our relationship,' she said, pointing her gun at her.

Nisha also took out the pistol and aimed at her.

'You will fire? Whatever happened to your pledge of non-violence and Gandhi's teachings?' Charulata made a sarcastic remark.

'This is against your method of violence. Gandhi also taught not to give in to the evil forces.'

'You think I am evil. I am against the tyranny of the government. I am also fighting for the motherland.'

'No, you are fighting against the motherland. Gireesh has been convicted by the courts. This is not a way to get him released.'

'He is our leader. I will do anything to free him. I don't believe in the courts of India. The law is skewed against the common people.'

'You are pursuing a personal vendetta. Gireesh is your husband and you want him to be released at any cost. My father was also killed here, and he was murdered exactly at this spot while garlanding the statue during the inauguration. I did not choose the path to violence. You cannot justify your act.'

'As long as the present judicial and political systems continue to work against the interests of the poor people, Gireesh and Charulata will take many births. Only a revolution can be the agent of permanent change.'

'For all those who dare to wage a war against the country, a Nisha will stand as a shield. Surrender now and I promise that you shall be let off lightly.'

'Charulata will die fighting, but she will never surrender to the police. I am not in the mood of further negotiations.'

Nisha put pressure on the trigger.

The atmosphere reverberated with the sounds of the gunshots.

'No—,' Nisha cried and ran towards Charulata, oblivious of the fact that the shot from Charulata's gun had pierced through her shoulder.

Blood was gushing out of Charulata's abdomen. The gun dropped, fell from her hand, and she collapsed. Gautam emerged from behind her, holding his gun through which the fatal shot was fired.

'Gautam, why did you fire? She could have surrendered,' Nisha was fuming.

'She would never have surrendered. She would have killed you! She had already fired a shot at you.'

Nisha took Charulata in her arms. Her body was soaked in blood.

'Why did you have to do this?' Nisha asked, crying.

'Nisha, don't forget your promise. Our people need you. I was also fighting for them but my method was different. I will die and I have no qualms for what I did. I would never have killed you because I admire you. I am aware you are also fighting for the common people. Preserve your sincerity once you join politics. Refrain from turning a politician. Stick to the Gandhian principles you have always adhered to,' Charulata choked as she spoke.

'I promise to be the pillar of strength for all the people. This is my mission. However, I would have been happier to have you by my side.'

'You are fortunate; Gautam is with you. God bless you both. Long live the revolution.'

She raised her arms in the air and took her last breath in Nisha's arms.

Nisha was inconsolable.

Nisha felt a hand on her shoulder. She looked up to find Gautam next to her. She got up and hugged him.

'Gautam, are you all right?' Nisha asked Gautam, who was also badly injured.

'I am fine. How is your shoulder?' he asked.

'The bullet just whizzed past. It was deliberate on Charulata's part to target my shoulder; she is an expert marksman; she never misses her aim.'

'I know. Even though you belonged to two opposing camps, the mutual admiration that you shared for each other is unmistakable,' Gautam said while hugging Nisha.

'I never wanted her to die,' Nisha's voice broke as she struggled to wipe her tears.

'I hope the MAF chapter is closed forever,' Taneja exclaimed. Soon, the entire area was cordoned off by the security forces.

The news of Charulata's death reached Vikramgarh Fort. The home minister's chopper had landed a few minutes back. The minister and Gireesh were in the SHO room.

'Charulata is killed. The mission is successful,' the SHO of the police station entered the room and appraised the home minster of the situation.

'No, it is not possible,' cried Gireesh.

Almost as a reflex, he snatched a gun from the guard standing near him and tried to flee. One of the guards shot him in the leg. He fell to the ground. Upon regaining consciousness, he found Nisha looking at him. Gautam and Taneja were standing nearby.

'I am sorry Gireesh,' Nisha spoke.

Gireesh looked at Nisha and then uttered, 'You will pay.'

Gautam could sense the fire of revenge burning in his eyes.

As all of them moved out of Gireesh's ward, a news report on the television caught their attention.

> This afternoon, Shweta Bhatnagar, the RR's assistant commandant, unfurled the tricolour at the control room building and declared *Operation India One* a successful mission. Fifty terrorists, including their legendary

commander Charulata, were killed in the attack and 25 others surrendered. But, the police suspect that around 10 terrorists fled to the forest. They may have crossed over to Jharkhand. A huge cache of arms has been recovered. Gireesh Marandi, who was being escorted to Bhagatpur for release, has been rearrested. His attempt to escape failed and he is now in the hospital. Twenty security personnel, including RR chief Kavita, died in the operation. Sergeant Rammohan of Bihar Military Police and 10 other security personnel have been injured.

NS2's managing director, Nisha, and her friend, former ACP Gautam Dhaliwal, braved all odds during the attack and have been reported out of danger.

The security forces destroyed the MAF camps on the Parshuram hill, and the nearby forests. The home minister and the chief minister congratulated the security forces on their success.

During a press meet, the home minister shared the history of *Operation India One* and how it had started a few years back to fight the MAF. However, the operation failed to make much progress and the mission had to be abandoned midway. Gireesh's recent arrest ignited the spark. The operation resumed and turned into a full-blown assault after the MAF attacked the power plant. The chief minister expressed satisfaction that all hostages were safe. Only one hostage—Rohit Kumar, the owner of Silent Turtle, was killed by Charulata at the site.

Meanwhile, the Central Government has decided to form a committee to look into the matter of the power plant construction. Sources say that the contract for construction of the power plant will be awarded to a government company.

Epilogue

1 March 2014

An eagerly impatient crowd had gathered outside the electoral control room. The election results would be announced soon.

At about 3 p.m., Ajay Mishra, also the returning officer of the poll, came out and announced, 'The INP candidate, Nisha has won the election by a margin of 10,000 votes.'

The crowd burst into jubilation on hearing the news.

'Congrats, madam,' Taneja wished her.

She went to Gautam and hugged him.

'We have won,' Gautam said, overjoyed.

Prabhat called Nisha, 'Nisha, congratulations.'

'Yes, it indeed is spectacular. After *Operation India One*, I thought my support base would dwindle and people would hold me responsible for being instrumental in killing Charulata—their legend. But, after a sustained election campaign, people were convinced about our objectives and showed confidence in us. Also, the officers—Ajay and Taneja—gave us their full support. They ensured the elections were conducted in a fair manner.'

'Yes, the Election Commission monitored the poll with a strong vigil. It was free and fair. I can feel the change of heart in the officers known to you.'

'The people of Bihar are slowly opening up to the idea of progress and development. They are trying to have faith in the system. I am certain about a watershed victory like this in the coming general elections as well.'

'How is Gautam? How is the NS2 mission going?'

'He is fine and looking after the NS2 affairs very efficiently,' she said while looking and smiling at Gautam.

'How is the situation in Bhagatpur now? I hope it is more peaceful than before.'

'Yes, the plant construction is in full swing. The compensation issue will be settled soon once the committee starts addressing the grievances. I believe they have given a detailed report to the government about the compensation amount and other relief schemes and plans. The CM has promised to expedite its implementation. The power plant which, till last year, seemed to be a mistake has now the potential to be turned into a symbol of pride for the state.

'However, the police there have arrested some youths who wanted to celebrate today as martyr's day in the memory of slain MAF cadres. They wish to revive the MAF. In fact, they have renamed the organisation as PSRG (People's Socialist Revolution Group).'

'The police need to keep an eye on such sprouting operatives. No organisation like the MAF or RBS should be allowed to form again. The government should keep a check on the appropriate implementation of all the developmental schemes in that area,' the home minister replied.

'Sir, what about Gireesh Marandi?'

'The Supreme Court has affirmed Gireesh's death sentence. He has filed a mercy petition before the President. His execution will be a political decision, which the government will take once the political climate changes for the better. By the way, how is your uncle Narendra Nath?'

'He is still angry with me. But, I hope he will make an effort to understand that *Operation India One* was a necessary mission for the country.'

'Definitely, time will heal all wounds.'

'What happened to the RR? I have heard they are shifting base to Delhi?' Nisha enquired.

'Yes, they are moving to Delhi. Kavita Sethi has won laurels for the regiment. We have nominated her for the Ashok Chakra Award. The RR has become one of India's best commando forces.'

'I am delighted to hear that. Has Shweta taken charge of RR?'

'Yes, she is leading the RR team. Subhash has asked me to convey his regards to you.'

'Please allow me to take your leave now. The Party workers are calling us for a photo shoot.'

'Sure Nisha, come to Delhi soon. We will discuss the future strategy of our Party for the Lok Sabha election.'

As she disconnected the call, Gautam came near her and said, 'I am leaving for Delhi tomorrow.'

'Why now?'

'Mother wanted to meet me. I forgot to tell you; she was asking about you.'

'What about me?'

'Why don't you also come to Delhi and meet her?'

'Yes. The Lok Sabha elections have been announced. I will go there to discuss our poll strategy with...'

'Polls, Party, police, bloodshed... Don't you think you deserve some time off from all this?' he asked, looking at her.

'Yes, you are correct. Next week, I promise to join you and your mother in Delhi. No Party, no politics and no NS2,' she smilingly replied.

'Madam, the Party workers are waiting,' someone interrupted her.

'Okay, I have to go now,' she said to Gautam, while walking towards her supporters.

Gautam kept his gaze fixed on her for a moment, and went near his car. The air was filled with the chants of celebratory slogans—

Nisha madam, zindabad.

Gautam caught a glimpse of Nisha in the rear-view mirror; he could see that she was surrounded by an army of supporters. Gautam caught Nisha looking at him while he drove away from the crowd.

Acknowledgements

I would like to thank:

The department head of my previous company, for investing his precious time to read my manuscript and sharing valuable comments and words of encouragement;

All my friends, especially Biswajeet and Sachin, for their constructive feedback and suggestions;

Satish, for designing the maps used in the book;

Kanishka Gupta, my literary agent, for sharing insights to improve the story;

Ajay Mago and Dipa Chaudhuri of Om Books International, who found this story fit to be told;

The editorial team of Om Books International, for editing and improving the story, and turning my dream into a reality;

My wife, for her undying patience during the time I spent working on my laptop, my constant companion;

Colleagues, seniors and juniors at workplace, for their presence, continued support and encouragement;

My parents and my family members, who constantly encouraged me to work hard;

God, who transformed a reluctant engineer and an accidental bureaucrat to a passionate writer;

Above all, my readers, who though had many choices, chose to read my story.

Bibliography

Behind Naxal Lines

www.youtube.com/watch?v=S5TdQjqdH4E

Barbarism, the New Naxal Signature

www.youtube.com/watch?v=XEfjZVDUJgE

Embedded with the Commandos of Operation Green Hunt

www.youtube.com/watch?v=h1GTbmbQc5g

Caught in the Crossfire

www.youtube.com/watch?v=BJdCBndkoSg

India's Red Tide

www.youtube.com/watch?v=OvUVzvt_jtg

At the Heart of it with Shoma Chaudhury (May 29 2010)

www.youtube.com/watch?v=bqjcQnFveew

India's Silent War against the Naxalites: Al Jazeera

www.youtube.com/watch?v=CyL7IzI6pEM

Is Maoist Violence Being Tackled Correctly: Politically Incorrect

www.ndtv.com/video/player/politically-incorrect/is-maoist-violence-being-tackled-correctly/207054

Why Operation Green Hunt Will Fail

http://akashbanerjee.com/2009/10/20/why-operation-green-hunt-will-fail/

Walking With the Comrades by Arundhati Roy

http://www.outlookindia.com/article.aspx?264738-1

Naxals are Heartless, Cruel: Chidambaram

http://ibnlive.in.com/news/naxals-are-heartless-cruel-chidambaram/115655-37-64.html

2013 Naxal Attack on Darbha Valley

http://en.wikipedia.org/wiki/2013_Naxal_attack_in_Darbha_valley

Bihar Too Soft on Naxal

http://articles.economictimes.indiatimes.com/2013-10-31/news/43561583_1_bihar-police-north-bihar-maoist

We Must Root Out Naxal Menace, Build on Our Successes: Manmohan Singh

http://www.dnaindia.com/india/report-we-must-root-out-naxal-menace-build-on-our-successes-manmohan-singh-1923622

Maoist Ideologues Keeping Naxal Movement Alive: MHA

http://www.thehindu.com/news/national/maoist-ideologues-keeping-naxal-movement-alive-mha/article5354632.ece